THE CUCKOO'S CHILD

THE CUCKOO'S CHILD

Marjorie Eccles

severn
House

This first world edition published 2011
in Great Britain and the USA by
SEVERN HOUSE PUBLISHERS LTD of
9–15 High Street, Sutton, Surrey, England, SM1 1DF.
Trade paperback edition first published
in Great Britain and the USA 2011 by
SEVERN HOUSE PUBLISHERS LTD.

British Library Cataloguing in Publication Data

Eccles, Marjorie.
  The cuckoo's child.
  1. Industrialists – England – West Yorkshire – Fiction.
  2. Woollen and worsted manufacture – England – West
  Yorkshire – Fiction. 3. Fires – Casualties – Fiction.
  4. Family secrets – Fiction. 5. Police – England – West
  Yorkshire – Fiction. 6. West Yorkshire (England) – Social
  conditions – 20th century – Fiction. 7. Detective and
  mystery stories.
  I. Title
  823.9'14–dc22

ISBN-13: 978-0-7278-8032-1 (cased)
ISBN-13: 978-1-84751-345-8 (trade paper)

All Severn House titles are printed on acid-free paper.

Severn House Publishers support The Forest Stewardship Council [FSC],
the leading international forest certification organisation. All our titles that
are printed on Greenpeace-approved FSC-certified paper carry the FSC logo.

MIX
Paper from
responsible sources
FSC
www.fsc.org   FSC® C018575

Typeset by Palimpsest Book Production Ltd.,
Falkirk, Stirlingshire, Scotland.
Printed and bound in Great Britain by the
MPG Books Group, Bodmin, Cornwall.

Prologue

1887

When Benjamin Kindersley left his home on Castleshaw Moor on the bleak Pennine heights between Manchester and Huddersfield, the day after his nineteenth birthday, he took with him the only clothes he possessed, plus a pound of ripe cheese, five pieces of oaten havercake from the creel above the kitchen fire where they'd been drying, the last spice loaf left from Christmas, a pork pie and two stone bottles of Prue's home-brewed ale. And his books.

'All t'same, he'll get neither far nor fat on that,' Mary fretted, thinking of how much six-foot-two Ben could eat at a sitting. If he gets far at all, she thought, peering anxiously through the kitchen window at the darkening winter sky.

'He must ha' gone for a soldier!' Lisbeth, who was only thirteen, was desolate, but she pictured how grand her big brother would look in uniform, even handsomer than the recruiting sergeant in the market last month. Though if he *had* gone to fight for the Queen there wouldn't have been any need to take his own victuals, the army would surely feed him – and why had he taken the velveteen waist-coat Heloise had stitched for him, that he'd scorned ever to wear?

'To sell, of course,' said Prue, sharp as usual. 'What d'you think he's going to live on, fresh air?'

He would have nothing else to sell. He'd never sacrifice his few precious books, packed in with the food in the best carpet-bag slung over Grandpa Kindersleys' walking stick.

But it wasn't until they all met in the kitchen for a breakfast which none of them, except Prue, had much appetite for, that they discovered he had taken Lucie Picard, too.

'He's sure to come back,' Mary said softly, though Ben's brief note had sounded very final:

To my dear family. I am going away, I am no good at being a farmer, and I do not want to be. Do not try to find me, remember me in your prayers and I will write when I am settled somewhere, though that is not my intention just yet.

'There now, don't you go crying your eyes out, Lisbeth, love, he'll be back.'

'Appen he will,' said Prue, putting the note into her apron pocket with finality. 'But you know our Ben. When he says summat he generally means it.'

'Aye, and 'appen he'll find hissen not welcome, if he ever durst show his face at North Brow again,' said Pa, and walked out of the kitchen, leaving the rest of his bacon on his plate and Ben's three sisters looking at one another. His face had sort of folded in on itself, the way it had when their mother died, and then, later, Heloise. He had never mentioned either of them since.

Though Mary had tried to speak confidently, in her heart she agreed with Prue. Ben had learnt to think before he spoke, since most of what he did say was likely to get Pa's back up. Like his book-reading did, and the scribbling he was for ever at. Joe Kindersley didn't believe farmers had any need to read, and as for writing, well, there'd been Kindersleys at North Brow since the seventeenth century, and not one of them had ever felt the need to put pen to paper, apart from the odd letter.

But what had Ben been thinking of, taking Lucie Picard?

Part One

London
Twenty-Two Years Later

One

It was a room of no distinction, plain and shabby, with drab-olive paintwork and the walls washed in a faded parchment colour, but it had a friendly warmth: a bright fire glowed in the grate, there were books all around. Best of all, it was blessedly quiet, the only private space in an overcrowded house that more often than not was shrill with women's voices and noisy with children's shouts and laughter, and the crying of babies. Laura never ceased to be amazed how, amongst all that, in addition to the raucous noises from the street outside, this little room could be so peaceful. Especially now, when the green rep curtains were drawn, a single lamp burned, the firelight winked on the leather spines of the books, and there was the warm nutty smell of toasting muffins.

There wasn't the money to spare for luxury. The Settlement here in Stepney was run on a shoestring by an ecumenical group of committed Christians, with a doctor willing to be called upon in emergencies, of which there were not a few. But most of all, it depended upon the quiet influence of Ruth Paston.

Ruth was middle-aged, unremarkable and dowdy, and yet underneath it all she had such a sense of quiet strength, purpose and warmth. No wonder the women who found themselves washed up here were so ready to turn to her. Supported by her Quaker beliefs, Ruth never showed outrage or astonishment and could be relied upon to give a balanced and clear-eyed opinion. She rarely said outright what she thought ought to be done, but after a chat with her, one usually left with a feeling of some satisfactory decision having been reached. However, it wasn't advice Laura sought tonight. A modern young woman at the beginning of the twentieth century, she had already made up her own mind: one of the quick, and occasionally mistaken, decisions that characterized her impulsive nature.

She knelt on the hearthrug, holding the long-handled toasting fork to the fire while Ruth made the tea, and then, after the muffins had been disposed of and they were both provided with a second cup, she sat back and came straight out with it: 'Ruth – I'm so sorry, but I'm afraid I'm going to be leaving you in the lurch. I shall be going away in a week or two.'

A small silence fell until Ruth laid a quiet hand on Laura's arm, the hand that had stilled many a weeping woman, and often those who were too angry or too drunk to know what they were saying or doing. 'I shall be sorry, too, you've been worth your weight in gold, but I hardly expected you to be here forever, child. And as for leaving us in the lurch, that's nonsense. Help always comes from somewhere. Tell me . . .'

'I don't expect to be away for long. May I come back afterwards?'

'Of course you may, that goes without saying.' For a while Ruth said nothing. 'But only as a friend. You've been here long enough, and I hope it's given you something you needed. You have your life before you – and who knows where it will lead?'

What she was too tactful to say, Laura felt, was that although Laura had energy and willingness to spare, she did not possess the dedicated motivation the other helpers had, especially Ruth herself: that strong, calm commitment she had through her faith as a Friend, which kept her going, tirelessly, selflessly, year after year, in what was all too often a thankless task. And it was true, Laura admitted humbly, she could never aspire to that. She often felt torn in two, consumed by guilt at the contrast between the Spartan surroundings here and the luxurious comfort of her own home, while knowing she could not forsake that part of her life forever.

Yet over the last months, she had given of her best. Who could do less? It was in a sense repayment. The Settlement had been something of a lifeline for her after leaving college, when she had found herself feeling uncharacteristically lost, unable to make up her mind what to do. Her friends at the Royal Holloway had already made plans for their future. Most of them were taking up teaching, two already having gained positions in prestigious girls' schools. But Laura had no burning desire to be a teacher. The truth was that she had no burning desire to tie herself down to anything yet. She had chosen to go to college mainly as a gesture of independence.

And what had independence done for her? For several weeks after saying goodbye to the friends she had made, she had trailed along in her aunt's wake, doing all the things expected of her, inwardly despising their triviality. It was only by chance that she had heard of the work being done here in the East End with destitute women, and had immediately volunteered her services. To her amazement, her offer had been gratefully received. They were always glad of an extra pair of hands at the Stepney house, a temporary shelter for women who found themselves homeless for whatever reason: wives and their children knocked about by drunken husbands until even the streets were preferable to the marital home; young women pregnant and without a husband; rough, incorrigible women who had been in prison. Women for whom the only alternatives were the workhouse, prostitution, or the river. As long as they kept themselves and their children clean and sober, did not fight with each other and took their share of the cleaning and cooking, no one was turned away. Relieved that they were not forced to read the Bible or get down on their knees and pray unless they wished, they by and large followed the unspoken rules and respected those who ran the shelter.

Laura's privileged upbringing had not prepared her for work that was so physically back-breaking, and sometimes heart-breaking. She had often, at first, been shocked by the women's language, and their unruly behaviour, but she had grown used to it. Her eyes had been opened for the first time to appalling situations she had never dreamed could exist, the grinding poverty of the people she had worked amongst, the conditions in which they were forced to live. All the same, she had always known that her time in Stepney must sooner or later come to an end.

'You see, it's like this,' she began, pushing back her hair, that bothersome light brown mop, whose pins *would* slip out, no matter what, while Ruth listened with her usual attentiveness. 'I'm afraid my aunt and uncle won't understand – well, Aunt Lillian anyway,' she finished ruefully. 'But I mean to go on with it.' Laura's chin, a rather sharp, determined little chin, went up. 'I don't see what all the fuss is about. I'm not committing myself permanently. It's only a temporary thing.'

'Well. You must do as you think fit. But be sure of your reasons for doing it, first,' Ruth replied, after the careful consideration she gave to everything. 'Do think carefully about why you're doing this . . . are you sure you're not reading into it more than Mr Carfax intended?'

No, not Philip, thought Laura, reflecting on this now two-week-old conversation as, having said her final goodbyes to Ruth and the rest, she began her last journey across London to the solid comfort of home in Chetwyn Square, leaving behind for good the dingy poverty and squalor, the teeming life and general rowdiness of the east London streets and the Settlement house. She was never allowed to make her way home unattended after darkness fell, and tonight that duty had been allotted to a cocky, sharp-witted urchin called Artie Spink. He was only eleven years old but a survivor of life in the gutters of Stepney, and smart enough to keep her safely out of the way of street fights, drunks, pickpockets or any other danger that might arise. He kept close to her through the noisy crowds along the Commercial Road, until he could expertly whistle up the first motor cab which came along. Laura reached into her pocket and pressed a florin into his grubby palm. 'I'm going to miss you, Artie. Good luck, and mind you keep away from the truant school.'

'Ta, miss, good luck to you an' all.' Nonchalantly pocketing the two-shilling piece, unheard of riches, he gave her his cheeky, unstoppable grin, stepped back hastily to avoid the kiss that might be coming, waved to her and was off.

Laura let the cab take her within a mile or two of home. 'Stop here, cabbie, please. I'll walk the rest of the way.'

'You sure, miss?' He looked at her doubtfully but she smiled and handed him a generous tip as she stepped out on to the pavement. 'Well, then, mind how you go,' he called after her.

'I will.'

No, she could not believe Philip Carfax's intentions had been open to misinterpretation, she decided, recalling Ruth's words as she walked through the gaslit streets. Not Philip. He was habitually cautious and thought before he spoke, not only because of his training as a partner in his father's solicitor's firm, but by inclination also; a trait Laura endeavoured to copy, though never with much success. What he'd said had been clear enough. This opportunity he'd presented her with was nothing more than what it seemed, just a short period of work in the north of England, which he had picked on as something that might be helpful to her; a thoughtful gesture typical of Philip. That did not preclude his having considered all the possibilities, and any likely pitfalls, before he put the suggestion to her. Always thorough, Philip would surely have done that – he always had her best interests at heart, never mind that he was sometimes perplexed in the matter of what they were. Which possibility, she reflected with a little laugh, probably applied to most men at the moment with regard to women.

All the same, when the idea had first been broached, over an agreeable dinner at a restaurant whose prices she suspected were at the limit of what he could afford, amid the well-dressed crowd, the soft carpets and the muted hum of conversation and laughter, when she was feeling at her best, wearing a new beaded frock in crushed strawberry charmeuse, with shoes dyed to match, and her hair fixed up securely for once into a becoming style by Cox, her aunt's maid, he had fidgeted for some time before saying tentatively, 'I want to ask you something, Laura.'

She put down her starched napkin. 'Please, Philip—'

'No, it's not that. I promised I wouldn't ask you again, didn't I? And I won't – or not for another six months anyway,' he answered, still good-humoured, though more than a hint of irony had crept into his tone. He hesitated, then said, 'I've come across something that might interest you. Some work.'

At first she hadn't thought much of the idea. It appeared that some rich manufacturer somewhere in the north apparently had a library full of books which he wanted cataloguing. It was a job any reasonably competent person could have undertaken without stretching themselves, providing one had the qualifications – which she had not. Why then had Philip thought of her? She searched his face for clues, but nothing there gave her an answer.

'This may be what you need at the moment – a bit of perspective, don't you think? Time to see your way forward. Away from . . . everything.' He lifted her hand, then gently laid it down. It did not match the rest of her appearance; the nails were cut short, the cuticles jagged, it was rough and reddened, and rested incongruously against the white damask tablecloth, the glittering glass and elegant silverware. However unintentional, his gesture had been only too eloquent of how everyone regarded her work at the Settlement. In silence she finished her sole and he drank his soup.

Was this what this business was all about − a stratagem to get her away from what they all − Philip, her aunt and uncle − really regarded as that hopelessly altruistic project of Ruth Paston's, something they applauded in principle but deplored in practice? She thought Philip would not be so devious, but she could not be sure. Open as he was, he was still a lawyer, a breed not unknown for its wiliness.

The only person who seemed to approve of what she'd been doing since she left college, in fact, was Eva, Philip's younger sister, but her opinions didn't count for much since she was, as their father constantly complained, being a bit of a handful at the moment. Stirred by an awakening social conscience, wrapped up as she had become in what he considered this foredoomed campaign for female emancipation, she had taken to lecturing everyone at every verse end, Philip grumbled.

'Well, think about it,' he said to Laura eventually, regarding with resignation this charming, animated, sometimes head-strong girl whom he had known all his life and who had for so long occupied most of his thoughts, 'but not too long. I suspect the offer won't remain open indefinitely. And when you come back, you may well see the future a little differently.'

'Oh, Philip! I shan't change my mind, you know . . . I do love you − as a dear friend,' she added hastily, seeing his expression change, 'but we should soon drive each other mad if we were married, can't you see that? Look how we used to fight when we were children.'

'So did you and Eva, but look at you now. The best of friends.'

'That's altogether different.'

'And besides,' he added with a wry smile, 'I fight scarcely anyone now.'

She looked at him sadly, watching him stirring his coffee into swirls. Could he not see that it would never do? Philip, so pleasant and kind, so sensible − and so conventional, from his smoothly parted, butter-coloured hair and high collar to his polished boots. He would always follow the correct road; he was born to do so. Whereas she . . . she might well have a stormy path in front of her, but at least she might have *lived* on the way.

He said seriously, 'Laura, I think you should take this opportunity.'

There was something he wasn't telling her, which was not like him. Philip and secrets didn't go together.

'And what if the opportunity isn't one this Mr Ainsley Beaumont would wish to take up? He may not think I'm suitable – for one thing, I'm not qualified. Not to mention the fact that he hasn't even seen me.'

'Apparently it's nothing very specialized, and he doesn't need to see you, he says. Not if you are someone recommended by us. We've acted for him for years, he trusts us implicitly and he'll go by what we say.'

Despite the nonchalance he tried to assume, the 'we' as he said it sounded a trifle self-conscious. With the Arroway part of Carfax, Arroway and Carfax having long since occupied a place beneath a marble slab in the churchyard, and the senior Carfax, Philip's father, being seriously afflicted at the moment with gout which had resulted in having himself driven down to Bath for a month's Spa-Cure, Philip was finding himself solely responsible for making the firm's decisions for the first time.

'Think about it, Laura. But don't rely entirely on me; I suggest you ask your uncle's advice.'

'I don't think I need to do that,' she returned, somewhat sharply, but then she smiled. 'I've rather learnt to like making my own decisions, you know.'

And instantly her mind was made up. Sorting out books hardly sounded as exciting a prospect as she might have wished, but perhaps Philip was right, and something peaceful like that was what she needed, a period in which to take stock after the rough and tumble of life in the Stepney house.

Two

Laura had come into the childless lives of Lillian and George Imrie at the age of eighteen months, after both her parents had been killed in a railway accident, when an express train in which they had been travelling had collided with a stationary one, a disaster in which fourteen people in all were killed. She dutifully kept a photograph of them on the mantelpiece in her bedroom, one given to the Imries by an old cousin, the only relative the dead couple had had between them, a woman who was herself now deceased.

They disappointed Laura. An uncompromising pair, both looked as though they might never have been young. It seemed impossible to believe that the stony woman looking out of the frame had produced any child, much less *her*, Laura, and although she had to admit that must be where her sharp chin had come from, she did not care to think of anyone who could wear a hat like that being her mother. That was a thought she was a little ashamed of, however – it sounded too like one of Lillian's sillier sentiments. And yet . . .

Lillian was easy-going and affectionate, not troubled too much by uncertainties such as wondering what she might have become had her life been otherwise. Married as she was to a good man whom she loved and respected, she could not conceive of any woman wishing any other existence. Her time was fully occupied with an endless social round and, since George was a senior partner in Imrie's bank and a wealthy man, indulging her passion for spending his money. She had a beautiful skin, a wasp waist and a fine bosom, and spent many hours being measured and fitted for clothes which would enhance all three.

What Laura proposed to do was totally beyond her comprehension, 'Yorkshire!' she cried, as if it were the last place on earth fit for human habitation. 'Dear child, you can't *think* what it's like up there!'

'Goodness, I'm not committing myself to being there for

life, Aunt, or even for very long. For the next few weeks, or for however long it might be, I'll just follow my nose and take whatever comes, and hopefully enjoy the experience.'

'Then I hope you are prepared to enjoy being frozen to death. When I was up there that time with your uncle for the grouse I cannot tell you how simply *glacial* it was.'

This occasion was one which was not often referred to by Lillian. Since neither she nor her husband normally moved in circles where Saturday-to-Monday grouse-shooting parties were usual, she had expected it to be a grand social occasion, one where she would make new and interesting friends. She had not bargained for the miserable, cold and wet affair it had turned out to be; much of the time spent standing behind the men on the soaking heather, applauding them as they shot as many birds as they could from the sky, while at other times the women in the party showed such excessive politeness to her she was made very much aware that she was not of their exclusive world. George had been under no illusions as to the reason for the invitation, which he knew was solely motivated by the impecuniousness of their host and his own ability to alleviate that circumstance, and it was no surprise to him that the weekend had not come up to Lillian's expectations. But he was sorry for her and future invitations were not accepted.

Laura laughed now at her aunt's renewed efforts to dissuade her from the horrid prospect she envisaged. 'I shall scarcely be out on the moors all day, I shall be working for most of the time in a comfortable library.'

'Cataloguing books, yes! Is this all your education has been for?' cried Lillian, doing an about-face. She had known no good could come of it, though she had known Laura too well to do more than tokenly object: opposition was only too likely to strengthen her resolve. In private, she had confidently asserted to her husband, 'She'll never stick it for more than a month or two at most, mark my words, George.'

George had by no means been so sure. Women were very different now from what they had been in Lillian's younger days, and in general he supported the idea that they should be well informed and educated if they so wished, though he had his doubts when it came to some of these fearsomely clever New Women, riding bicycles in bloomers and demanding the vote. But he believed that the very fact that Laura had set her mind on this course would make her see it through.

'I did think that when you left that college,' Lillian continued with a sigh, 'I might have more of your company. But I suppose you'll do as you wish, as usual.'

'Oh, really, I don't know what all the fuss is about.' Laura was beginning to feel exasperated. 'I shall be here, back home, long before the end of summer.'

'We would never have been allowed to do this sort of thing when I was a girl. Going to goodness knows where, doing heaven knows what. You'll be joining Eva Carfax and *those women* next.'

'I've no intention of joining Eva,' Laura replied shortly. Philip's sister was her oldest and dearest friend, and they had few secrets from each other. At the moment, however, Laura was finding Eva, with her frustrated ambitions to become a journalist and her new-found enthusiasm for the Women's Movement, a little too intense. The Women's Social and Political Union which she had joined came up 'at every verse end' as Philip said, and Laura was in truth as glad of the respite from her as her brother was, since she had been ordered to accompany their widowed father on his recuperative trip to Bath. 'Oh, do buck up, Aunt! I shall be home again directly, and meanwhile I shall do perfectly well, trust me.' She fastened those clear, candid hazel eyes of hers on her aunt's face and smiled. Lillian did not feel reassured.

Laura was fiddling while Rome burned. She was already twenty-one and it was high time she got rid of all this nonsense about being independent and doing good works, and got herself launched into society – by which Lillian meant finding a husband. Not Philip Carfax, however. Philip did not enter into the equation. He was likeable enough, but not one to fasten one's hopes on. Besides, Laura would run rings round the poor boy.

'Well, at least all this will stop you going down to that terrible place in Stepney—' she began, incautiously voicing her thoughts.

'Please. Don't.'

The dangerous spark in Laura's eyes should have been

warning enough. 'Dearest child, it's all very well for your friend Ruth to waste her life making cabbage soup and scrubbing floors for these women, she has her religion – and I'm sure these Quakers are wonderful from what one hears, but all the same . . .'

'Aunt Lillian, the women scrub the floors themselves!' Laura took a deep breath and held on to her temper. 'And if only you could see what a difference living in that house does for them, even for a short time, you would not say any effort was wasted. Maybe you should come down one day and see for yourself before you make judgements.'

'Yes, well, there's no need for that, I'm sure,' Lillian said, barely repressing a shudder. 'Oh, by the way, there's a box of clothes in my dressing room. Cox has been sorting through my wardrobe, it's nearly Easter and I shall be needing my new spring fashions . . .' She caught a glimpse of Laura's expression in the mirror, coloured slightly and had the grace to look ashamed. 'Well. Well, of course, they can be sold, I suppose.'

'Yes, of course they can, Aunt, and thank you. The money will be appreciated,' Laura said, getting up to kiss her. Lillian was really very good and kind, and it wasn't her fault that it had not even entered her head that thin silk gowns, dainty cambric underwear and delicate shoes were unsuitable wear for penniless women for whom a warm skirt and a pair of resoled boots was the highest luxury they could hope for.

Unusually, Lillian joined her husband for the substantial breakfast he took to fortify himself before setting out for business, albeit in her wrapper and with her hair still in its night-time plait. The serious business of bathing, dressing, being laced into her stays, having her hair done and generally being prepared for the busy day ahead needed time and concentration.

She eschewed the porridge, nibbled on a piece of toast and sipped her tea while she screwed up her courage to mention yet again the matter that was constantly on her mind.

'I do wish Philip Carfax hadn't put this idea into Laura's head,' she began.

George set his coffee cup down and reached for more toast.

'Philip Carfax is a fine young man,' he replied, without taking his eyes off *The Times*.

'Well, yes, there is no question of that. Though one does wonder, sometimes, if there is enough – if he isn't a little too – well, *sedate*. For Laura, I mean.'

'You know what they say about judging a book by its cover.' George turned over the front page of the newspaper with a crackle, propped it against the coffee pot and addressed himself to his second egg. Lillian sighed.

'George, you are not listening.'

'Oh, yes, I am.' It was an art he had long since perfected, allowing Lillian to rabbit on while he pursued his own thoughts. 'You want me to put my foot down and tell Laura she mustn't embark upon this mad escapade. Well, Lillian, I'm not going to do any such thing.'

George Sandford Imrie was a successful and distinguished banker. The most important things in his life were his business, his passion for Japanese art and the well-being of his wife and the child whom he had almost forgotten wasn't his own daughter. Laura, from the moment he first lifted her wriggling little body into his arms and she had pulled his moustache, stuck her finger in his ear and then planted a wet kiss on his mouth, had been the apple of his eye. He was not a man, however, for making a show of his affections. He thought that was evident enough in the provisions he made for domestic comfort, for the general welfare of his wife and Laura and the freedom he allowed them with money – so long as they did not exceed in extravagance. In return he expected, and usually got, an ordered life and a household that ran smoothly. He did not like being assailed at breakfast with something which had already been chewed over until there was nothing left of it.

'My dear Lillian,' he said at last, folding the newspaper and pushing back his chair. 'Laura is twenty-one. She is basically a sensible young woman, if a little too impulsive, but if she's going to make mistakes, there is nothing you, or I, or anyone else can do to prevent her.'

It was evident to Lillian she wasn't going to get the support she needed. She ought to have known it was as little use arguing with George as it was with Laura. 'That's all very well, but it's what Philip is up to that I'm worried about.'

'And why should Philip be up to anything?'

For a moment they looked at each other. Then George reached out and gently touched Lillian's unpowdered morning cheek. 'There's nothing to worry about, my dearest. How could there be?'

Three

As her train lurched over the points some ten minutes before it was due into Huddersfield station, Laura closed her book and stood up to peer into the mirror above the opposite seat, hoping there were no smuts on her face. She could not see any, but still dissatisfied with her reflection, she tried to pull the brim of her brown peach-bloom felt hat to a more becoming angle. It was not a very nice hat, and she couldn't think now what in the world had compelled her to wear it – except perhaps a vague feeling that she ought to tone down the effect of the rest of her outfit, which was very nice indeed, although it was saxe-blue in colour, a shade hovering uneasily somewhere between blue and grey. That had been Aunt Lillian's fashionable choice, not hers, but whatever Laura's reservations about the colour, it couldn't be denied that the cut of the garments was superb. Up here, in the wilds of Yorkshire, might it not be considered . . . a little too smart? It was too late to do anything about that now, however. The train, precisely on time and in great clouds of steam, was already panting and hissing into the station, where she had been told someone would be waiting to meet her and convey her to Wainthorpe.

Laura had never before been further north than St Albans, to spend occasional weekends at the home of her college friend, Cicely. This part of Yorkshire they called the West Riding was a mystery to her, despite some conscientious revision of what she'd been taught about the northern woollen trade of which Huddersfield was a great centre, and what role the West Riding had played in the Industrial Revolution. She had listened to Ruth Paston on the iniquities of the old child labour system in the textile mills. She'd read again about those machine-breakers they had called the Luddites, who had believed those first machine looms would rob them of their livelihood. She had also done her best to disregard the comments of all those who had learned she was to pass some time here, to the effect that its inhabitants were hard-headed folk who called a spade a shovel and lived years behind the times.

Now, however, as she emerged from the station in Huddersfield, she was taken aback by an immediate impression of the town's solid Victorian prosperity. Surrounding her were substantial buildings of dressed stone, heavy with importance, and a railway station that would have rivalled London's Euston in its neoclassical splendour. The place was busy with motor-driven delivery vehicles and motorcars, one of which had broken down (as motors everywhere were still apt to do) impeding the passage of several more reliable horse-drawn vans and carts. Smartly painted dark-maroon and straw-coloured double-decker electric trams, crackling and sparking from their overhead poles, rhythmically clanged and swayed their way down the tracks set in the road, just like London trams. And as it became obvious the people in the busy streets were no less well dressed than similar people in any other large town or city, she could see her own fears about being overdressed as ridiculous and rather patronizing.

But then, there came the matter of her mode of transport to Wainthorpe.

She stood at a loss beneath the station's Corinthian columns, her luggage at her feet where the porter had dumped it. No one appeared to be waiting for her. But within a minute or two an elderly man approached, wearing a black coat turning green at the seams, with an old-fashioned billycock on his head, a large red-spotted handkerchief round his neck and a pipe stuck in his mouth. Without removing the pipe, he asked her if she was Miss 'Arcourt, and when she said she was, with an unsmiling nod he picked up her luggage and took it towards – not one of those up-to-date motorcars she might have expected from a rich man with a library full of books – but a little horse-drawn trap. Was this the mode of transport deemed suitable for one who was after all, only to be an employee? An indication that Mr Beaumont, her new employer, was tight-fisted – or merely one of those northerners she'd been warned about, who hadn't yet entered the twentieth century and felt that hardiness was next to Godliness?

Oh, well! Gamely, she clambered up beside the driver, a surly individual whose uncouth accent she had difficulty in understanding, who gave his name as John Willie Sugden and after that seemed to feel he had no need to prolong the conversation further. The trap was open to the elements, and he made no move to pull up its hood, but it was smartly painted, the chestnut coat of the little horse between the shafts was glossy and well-groomed and there were leather cushions on the front seat next to the driver. Morosely, Sugden indicated a folded woollen rug, evidently intended to throw over her knees, and shouted, ''Ey-up, Jinny!'

It was not long before she found those agreeable first impressions of her new surroundings were to be distinctly reversed. Scarcely was the town centre left before – hey presto, the trap was being driven straight into just the sort of heavily industrialized area she had expected, but was still not properly prepared for. Truly, as they drew deeper into it, she began to feel as though she had been plunged into another world. A pall of smoke and vapour mingled powerfully with another, unidentifiable, disagreeably rancid odour. Engineering works, textile machinery factories, dye houses and all manner of other concerns ancillary to the woollen trade jostled with warehouses and corner shops, but overriding everything else were the towering mills – one every few yards along the road, it seemed. Square, fortress-like, many-storeyed and built of soot-blackened stone, they loomed over narrow rows and terraces of little grey houses, darkened with the same grime. A noxious river, the Neller, flowed alongside the road, beside that the canal, and every mill had its big iron gates bearing their name – telling the world they belonged to Bamforths, Hardcastles, Shawcrosses, a litany of repeated names. Each had its own tall, tapering chimney stack, no doubt meant to send the thick belching clouds of smoke and soot issuing from it above the tops of the surrounding hills, though the intention had not been conspicuously successful.

Every now and again flat, tarpaulin-covered wagons harnessed to teams of huge stamping draft-horses pulled in and out of mill gates in front of them, forcing them to stop, the carts' iron-shod wheels grinding on the stony road surface. Top-heavy with enormous loads of big, square bales of greasy wool, their passing left little doubt as to where that odour had come from. Dyers and spinners, the mills proclaimed themselves, weavers, fullers, woolcombers, shoddy and mungo manufacturers . . . *shoddy*? And what could mungo be? she asked Sugden.

'Devil's dust,' he replied grimly, but did not choose

to elaborate and went on puffing away at his evil pipe, not appreciably improving the atmosphere. Laura bit her lip, vowed to keep her own silence thereafter and lapsed into her thoughts, with only the jingle of metal, the creak of leather and the rhythmic impact of the little mare's hooves to keep them company.

As the distance lengthened the Neller valley narrowed, and the rolling hills either side soared ever more steeply up to the bleak moors on top. Small mill towns climbed the hillsides at an angle of forty-five degrees, where pinafored women hung out washing on lines strung across the streets, wearing clogs and woollen shawls wrapped over their heads, fastened under the chin with a safety pin. By now, Laura would have been glad of the fur-lined cape Lillian had insisted she packed. Forgetting her vow of silence, she asked, shivering, 'Is it always so cold up here?'

'Cold? Nay, it's nobbut fresh today. Wait till winter!' Laura pushed her gloved hands further under the rug on her knees, seeking warmth, very glad indeed that she would *not* be here by the time winter arrived. Relenting, Sugden added, pointing ahead with his whip, 'Nearly there, any road. Yon's Wainthorpe.'

It was suddenly upon them, another steep little town, grey rows of back-to-back terrace houses, one above the other, like the rungs of a ladder. The main road ran in a curve here along the floor of the valley, past shops and public houses and a Co-op, with dark alleys and less than salubrious streets in between; a church and at least two chapels, a little market square. Mill machinery hummed and clattered, carts rumbled on the stone setts.

Sugden again pointed with his whip. 'Beaumont's.'

They had reached a humped bridge over the river, as polluted here with the discharge of dye products and factory effluents as it was lower down. A large sprawl of buildings, and rows of low weaving sheds from which issued a deafening racket, were dominated by a five storey mill with a smokestack taller than any of the others in the town, aggressively proclaiming ownership. 'BEAUMONT' was painted in giant white letters from top to bottom of its length, which were reflected in its gently steaming mill dam. An imposing wrought iron arch into a cobbled yard proclaimed the name: Cross Ings Mill. Oddly, in all this stood an old-fashioned, low-roofed dwelling house with open windows and white lace curtains, built on to one side of the mill itself. Was this Farr Clough House, where Mr Beaumont lived?

The question appeared to afford John Willie Sugden a sardonic amusement. 'Ainsley Beaumont? Nay, not him! We've a bit to go, yet. This is nobbut t'mill.' He pointed with his whip. 'Yon's Farr Clough, up on th' Edge.'

Laura was able to catch only a glimpse of a large stone edifice perched near the top of the highest of the hills beneath which the town sheltered before it disappeared from view in the curve of the road, signposted 'Moortop Road'. She looked for the house again, but in vain, as the road made wide upward zigzags, each turn seeming to take them only a little higher up the Pennine slope. The distance they covered could not have been far but it seemed miles away from the valley they had just left. The wind became even keener, flattening the tussocky grass, unhindered by anything other than a few stunted trees and the millstone grit outcrop thrusting its way through the thin soil.

A few black-faced sheep skipped bleating into the heather as they passed, the road became rougher, Laura's teeth rattled and at any moment she was convinced a wheel must come off and overturn them into one of the bright narrow streams of water that gushed down the hills – to end up in that stinking river below, she assumed. Nevertheless, with the ugliness of the industrial sprawl below left behind, and now above the smoke-pall, she began to feel exhilarated, and moved by the sombre grandeur of the scenery which now surrounded her. Of all the people who had been ready to warn her of the inhospitable weather and general discomforts of life in the North, why had none of them ever mentioned the upland splendour of these hills, moors and valleys, their rushing streams? Her dismay disappeared, she felt a quickening in her blood and a sense of expectancy.

''Ere we are, then.'

Abruptly the rough, drystone walls that ran apparently at random over the wild moorland revealed an opening on to a rough road driven along this side of the hill, along which the trap now passed. There was still no sign of Farr Clough House but on a sudden impulse she cried, 'Please stop. I believe I should like to walk the rest of the way.'

'It's all of a mile yet to th'ouse.'

'I'm used to walking, and I need to stretch my legs after sitting for so long.' And to get my circulation going again, in case I might never be warm again, she might have added. 'Please take my luggage on and I'll follow.'

'Suit thissen. It's straight on.'

The wind tore at her hat and the tendrils of her wayward hair whipped across her face as she followed the trap, watching it disappear into the distance. Now that she was moving the wind stirred her blood and brought bright colour to her cheeks, and with it a magic feeling, as though she could run and jump, throw her arms in the air. Although the sky was grey and clouded, darkening the shortening afternoon further, there was a cosmic feeling about the great empty spaces tumbling around her as she walked, listening to the whistling wind and a bird with a piping, plaintive call. Lillian would have felt amply justified to know how cold it was, Laura thought with a laugh. Yet, here and there in that bleak treeless landscape could be seen the occasional whin bush, a splash of sunshine among the black peaty soil and the heather, a definite hint of spring not far away.

The wide undulating track cut through the rough bent-grass, with the ground rising to the ridge of the moor above on the one side, while to her left, sloping precipitately down into Wainthorpe, a plunging road could be seen. No sign of the house yet, and the threadbare soil and the sharp, flinty stones under the soles of her shoes did not make walking any easier. She had to watch her step, so that she didn't at first see the man with the dog who was standing about a hundred yards distant, his back to her, looking down into the valley below. The dog, however, saw her. With a low, snarling noise deep in its throat, it made a wild dash towards her, a long-legged creature with a great square muzzle and a rough-curled black and tan coat, and a turn of speed that brought him within feet of her in seconds. There was no cover and the dog's master did not even bother to turn around, not even when an involuntary scream escaped her. She backed away, caught her foot in a twisted root of heather and fell awkwardly. With a spring, the dog was over her, its feet on her shoulders, pinning her to the ground. Its jaws were within inches of her face when she was aware of someone arriving with a leap and a bound

on to the path beside her, and the dog was pulled off her by
a yank on its collar. She was assisted to her feet with a firm
brown hand.

'I say, I hope you're not harmed?'

'Not for want of trying!' replied Laura without much grace,
for she did not like to be seen at a disadvantage.

A pair of steady grey eyes in a deeply tanned face looked
down with concern into hers, as she stood shakily recovering
and dusting herself down. She had suffered a shock, and might
have a bruise or two, but she didn't think there was more to
it than that. 'You might, however,' she added indignantly,
straightening her hat, 'do well to keep your dog under better
control.'

'And so I might, if he belonged to me.' He threw a glance
to his right and Laura realized her mistake. The man whose
back had been turned towards her was walking away with the
aid of a stick, apparently uncaring of the scene behind him,
and the dog was now loping after him. 'There goes Sim's
master – Ainsley Beaumont.'

It scarcely seemed a good omen for the future that the man
who had engaged to employ her was one who could ignore
such an incident, despite there having been a rescuer to hand.
'Then I must beg your pardon, and thank you.' He waved her
thanks away. 'What sort of brute is that? I've never seen an
animal like it!'

'I dare say you haven't, he's an Airedale – mostly – a dog
bred in these parts, and not renowned for its sweet temper,
though Sim's more impetuous than vicious. He's still not much
more than a puppy.'

'Well, I must take your word for it.'

He laughed. 'All the same, he can hardly be blamed for
what he did, he's on his own ground here, and we're not used
to trespassers.'

'I'm no trespasser,' she returned crisply, gathering her dignity.
'I'm expected at the house. My luggage has gone ahead of
me.'

'Ah. Then it appears I must now beg *your* pardon.' He raised
a humorous eyebrow, and she flushed, suspecting he knew very
well who she was. A tall, loose-limbed man with a craggy,
lively face, he was evidently not one to adhere to convention.
Cold as it was, he went hatless, with the wind raking his crisp

hair. His dress was relaxed and informal, a dark jacket and a snuff-coloured waistcoat, a flowing tie. 'You must be the new lady librarian from London,' he added, confirming her suspicions.

'I suppose the description will serve as well as any.'

'And what are you doing out here, all alone on the moor?'

'Oh, I don't mind being alone, and I simply felt like walking.'

'Did you, by Jove! Well, I can understand that, there's nothing like it, up here, that's what I was doing myself, but in the circumstances I think we'd better be getting you back. I can leg it to the house and get them to send the trap back for you if you don't mind waiting.'

'That won't be necessary, thank you.'

'Then may I offer you my arm?'

'Really, I'm quite all right.' Her knee did feel a little bruised but she was not about to mention that. 'I can actually walk better alone on this surface, thank you.'

'If you're sure, Miss . . . ?'

'Harcourt,' she said briskly. 'Laura Harcourt.' She held out her hand, and smiled.

'Tom Illingworth,' he returned, taking her hand and looking so intently into her face, and for so long, that she began to blush. 'I am very pleased to meet you, Miss Harcourt.'

From the moment Tom Illingworth saw that smile, looked directly into the determined little heart-shaped face and those luminous hazel eyes, all the years he had been waiting suddenly seemed worth it.

He apparently did not live at Farr Clough House, as she might have assumed from that proprietary 'we', but he *had* been born and bred in the valley, here in Wainthorpe. After qualifying as a railway engineer, he had gone out to South Africa to work on Cecil Rhodes' proposed Cape to Cairo railway. Yes, she was quite right in thinking the outbreak of the second Boer War had put a stop to that ambitious project, but after the war was over he had stayed on for several years. He knew he was almost certainly talking too much about himself, but since her interested responses seemed to show she didn't mind, he carried on, deliberately slowing his quick stride as he spoke, forcing them both to walk slowly. He had no wish to arrive at Farr Clough just yet. He was more than content at that moment to be up here, in a world inhabited only by himself and Laura Harcourt, the peewits and the wind.

'So, shall you be going back there?'

'No, I've had enough of South Africa. Well, it's God's own country, Miss Harcourt, for some, which was what it seemed to me, once. I fought there during the war, but afterwards . . . well, let's just say, I stuck it for as long as I could, and then came home like the prodigal son. I was homesick, I hadn't seen my mother for nine years and it seemed like a good idea.'

This was neither the time nor the place to talk about his real reasons for abandoning his dream of settling out there in that ineffable country, with its boundless possibilities. The intention to free the blacks from the yoke of the Boer, and allow them to live under the more moderate British rule had seemed a lofty ideal, but during the war and after, the dream had turned sour. Disillusionment with the empire building of the powerful English-born diamond and gold magnate turned politician, Cecil Rhodes, and his avowed aim of planting the British flag in any country in which a Briton set foot; with conditions in the aftermath of the war; with the scorched earth policy the British army had employed, which had made refugees of Boer women and children; with the disgrace that was the concentration camps in which they were kept. He had become ashamed to be British in that country and could no longer stomach it.

For all that and other, more personal, reasons he did not choose to think about now.

'And what will you do now?'

'For the moment, I'm looking around. This will always be home, the place I return to, but there's plenty of opportunity for railway engineers all over the world. It won't be difficult to find something.' For the moment his face darkened, like a cloud passing over the sun, but then he was smiling again. 'That's more than enough of me. What of you, Miss Laura Harcourt?'

'Oh, me! Nothing so thrilling has ever happened to me.'

'Thrills of that sort are overrated, I can assure you,' he returned dryly. 'What brought you here?'

'The lawyer who has attended to Mr Beaumont's affairs for some years passed on to me that he was in need of someone to catalogue his library, so here I am.'

'His library, oh yes!' The idea seemed to amuse him. 'Well,

don't let him make a slave out of you. The old curmudgeon will, if you don't watch out.'

Before she had a chance to pursue this, the house was suddenly upon them. They had approached it sideways, but the rough road now swung round to bring them to the front elevation, and there it was, set on a kind of natural plateau in the rise of the hill, overlooking Wainthorpe. In front was a small garden of sorts, dominated by a stone-flagged area in front of the house, in which was set a square pool. The low drystone walls that formed the boundaries had crumbled away in parts, so that it was hardly possible to distinguish where the moor ended and the garden began.

But it was the first sight of the house itself which was never to fade from Laura's memory as long as she lived. A fine old three-gabled Yorkshire manor house of dark grey stone and mullioned windows, and a massive oak door over which, carved into the stone, was a coat of arms, and the date 1589. Of the three gabled sections, however, only two remained intact. The third, projecting at right angles some several feet in front of the others, was roofless, windowless, and nothing more than an empty fire-blackened shell.

Open to the sky, the ruin still stood attached to the rest of the house. Creepers tumbled over the walls, and rooks and jackdaws had made their nests in the crannies and corners of the stone. The silence of the darkening afternoon was broken only by their melancholy cawing as the wind tossed them about like bundles of black, ragged feathers, while they rest- lessly settled and resettled themselves on their nests. But for the open windows in the occupied part of the house, and smoke issuing from a chimney, the stone pile might have been one with the stones from which it was built.

Laura laughed nervously. 'Straight out of *Jane Eyre!*'

'Yes, there was a fire here, too, as you see, some twenty years ago.' He added abruptly, 'That wing should either be pulled down, or rebuilt.'

'Why is it allowed to remain like that?'

For a moment his face was grim. 'Who knows? Put it down to an old man's stubbornness – which I'm afraid is something you're all too likely to find out . . . there, I've frightened you when I only meant to prepare you.'

'Thank you, but I'm not in the least frightened.' she said,

not very truthfully, still recovering her wits. This was not like her, Laura Harcourt, who prided herself on her common sense, and took most things in her stride. The sight of the house had simply come as a shock, something she hadn't expected in the least.

At that moment, the front door opened. A woman stood on the steps, the Airedale beside her.

Four

'Good afternoon, Una,' Tom Illingworth said, as they reached the steps. 'This is Miss Harcourt, whom I met on the way here . . . Miss Beaumont.'

'And who else could she be, Tom, unless John Willie left another lady walking up to the house?'

Facing Laura was a young woman of around her own age, slim to the point of fragility, very striking, nearly a beauty. An oval face with a pale skin and remarkable eyes, grey-green, long and assessing; thick, smooth, honey-blonde hair, tightly drawn back, almost as if with the deliberate intention of playing down her attractiveness; dressed severely in a high-necked blue and white striped blouse and a narrow dark blue serge skirt with a tight belt at her waist. She appraised Laura with a quick glance before extending a brief, cool hand. Their fingers barely touched. 'Miss Harcourt – walking all that way! Come in, Grandpa's waiting. And you, Tom? Will you come in for a moment?'

'After yesterday? I believe not, thank you all the same.' Their eyes met, hers judgmental, his look quizzical. 'In any case, my mother's expecting me.'

'As you wish. It's no any use arguing with Thomas Illingworth, Miss Harcourt, he will never change his mind once it's made up.'

A faint smile touched the corners of his mouth. 'I won't willingly break a promise, if that's what you mean. Goodbye, Una. Goodbye, Miss Harcourt, I hope it won't be long before we renew our acquaintance.'

'Thank you once more for rescuing me.'

'Rescue?' Una Beaumont's finely drawn brows rose.

'From the attentions of Sim. I hope his welcome won't lead her to think we're all so uncouth.'

'Oh, he's a fraud, aren't you, Sim?' She bent to fondle the dog and he fawned on her. Laura kept her distance.

Tom Illingworth raised his hand in salute and swung away, disappearing along a half-hidden footpath which sloped away from the house. Some kindling energy departed with him, leaving Laura feeling oddly as though she had been deserted. She wished that he had felt able to accept the invitation to step inside, despite the undercurrents implied in that exchange with the young woman who stood next to her. His easy presence might have bridged the awkwardness which she already felt for some reason lay between her and Una Beaumont.

Following her, Laura stepped into a wide, flagged hall, low-ceilinged and panelled, where a broad oak uncarpeted staircase rose, at the foot of which her bags rested. To one side was an enormous stone fireplace with the same coat of arms carved into the beam above it – this time painted in fading colours, but with the white rose of Yorkshire still distinguishable at its heart. The hall was distinctly chilly: the great fireplace was empty and somewhere towards the back of the hall a window was open, from which came strong gusts of the fresh moorland breeze. Yet everything spoke of solid, old-fashioned comfort. The heavy furniture, built to last, was polished and cared for, almost aggressively so. A shining copper vase of fresh daffodils sat on a black oak table gleaming with years of beeswax and housemaids' elbow-grease, and the stone-flagged floor likewise had a polish that threatened life and limb to the unwary. The large space, as dusk approached, was already lit by several oil lamps. Unseen, a clock with a sweet chime rang out half past four.

'I'll get Jessie Thwaite to take you to your room, Miss Harcourt. Come down when you're ready, Grandfather is waiting for you in his study. Oh, here she is.' A tall, well-made young woman with a fresh complexion, wearing a plain cap and apron, had appeared from the back premises. 'This is Miss Harcourt, Jessie.'

'Pleased to meet you, miss.' Jessie's smile was warm and ready. 'I'll show you upstairs.' So saying, she slung one of Laura's bags on to her shoulder, picked up the other two and set off at a nimble pace, footsteps tapping briskly on the oak stairs.

'Grandfather's room is there,' Una Beaumont said, indicating a door to one side of the hall. 'We eat at six.'

'Thank you.' Laura hastened to follow the fast-departing Jessie up the staircase, on to a landing which stretched unequal arms out either side and overlooked the draughty hall.

The maid was pushing open with her shoulder the farthest

door on the shortest, right-hand side. 'Here we are then.' She deposited the luggage at the foot of the bed and gave Laura an appraising look. 'You'll be wanting a cup of tea now, never mind waiting till six,' she announced forthrightly. 'Sit you down by the fire and make yourself comfortable, and I'll bring some up.'

'That would be nice, if it's convenient—'

'Nay, it's no bother.' Jessie hesitated, then said surprisingly, 'Likely Miss Una forgot what a long journey you've had. She's a bit preoccupied like, just now.' She nodded and departed with a whisk of skirts, leaving Laura alone in the big room.

Like the hall, it was low-ceilinged and black beamed, with a long, low casement window, near which stood a marble wash stand, and was otherwise furnished with shining red Victorian mahogany, glowing like the hide of the chestnut mare which drew the carriage to take George Imrie to his bank every morning. A big, high bed was piled with spotless white pillows, and the brass of the bedstead glittered. There was a smell of lavender, furniture wax, lamp oil and the keen, peaty air that was, like the draught downstairs, billowing the curtains into the room and counteracting any warming effect the bright fire burning in the stone grate might have had. Laura closed it immediately, recognizing that she was going to have to learn to be as appreciative of fresh air as the people who lived up here evidently were. For a moment, she caught her breath at the sight of the ruined wing, projecting out to the back, as well as to the front, and here only a few feet away, casting a shadow over her room, and with an involuntary shiver, she turned her back. And for a moment, she was taken by a tremendous and very unexpected pang of homesickness.

Fortunately for her composure, at that moment Jessie came back with a tray balanced on one arm and hot water in a copper can in the other hand. Breezing into the room like another draught of fresh air, she allowed Laura to take the can from her, although its weight seemed to have caused her no trouble. 'The water's hot. You might like to have a bit of a freshen up before you go down to see the master, I thought.' She set the tray down on a small table by the fire and poured strong tea into a cup. There was buttered toast as well.

'Thank you, that was a kind thought. I'll be down in a few minutes.'

'Take your time. It won't hurt Ainsley Beaumont to wait

for once.' The blunt comment did not appear to convey any disrespect for her master, it seemed merely a statement of fact. Jessie had a bright, intelligent face and a crooked smile that was very attractive. She bent and put a few more coals on the fire from the scuttle, drew the curtains, and before going out, she added, 'I'll see you in the morning, then, Miss Harcourt. I'm off home now.'

'You don't live in, then?'

'Not just now. My Dad's poorly and there's nobody else to look after him. I live with him down in Wainthorpe.'

'That's a long walk.'

'Nay, it's but ten minutes if you take the gainest road, this side. Goodnight.'

'So, the lady librarian has arrived,' said Gideon. 'What is she like?'

His sister shrugged her slim shoulders. 'Very . . . Londonish.'

'Pretty?'

'Tom Illingworth seemed to think so. He met her on the way here.'

Gideon threw her a sharp look, but she was bending over the chair by the fire in which their mother slept, covered by a Paisley shawl, her head askew against the woolwork anti-macassar. Amelia's strong face was relaxed and unaware, her eyelids closed over those dark eyes which could at times flash such formidable fire. One ought not to look at people when they are asleep, they are too vulnerable, Una thought, turning away. Her glance fell on an opened chocolate box standing on the table. She picked it up, inspected the inside and then deliber-ately threw both box and its remaining contents into the fire, where it hissed, crackled and threw blue flames up the chimney.

Gideon raised his eyebrows. 'Tut-tut.'

'Dr Widdop has warned her time and again about eating so many. He's told her how bad chocolate is for her.' Debilitating headaches were the bane of Amelia Beaumont's life, and she was also putting on too much weight. Una sighed with impatience, then gently adjusted their sleeping mother's shawl.

'Better than brandy.'

'Gideon! She hasn't—?'

'No, just joking, joking, Una. But she might if you take away her chocs. Poor old Ma, even she has to let herself go sometimes. You'll be for it when she finds you've thrown her sweeties away.' He lit a cigarette, picked up an ashtray and threw one leg over the arm of his chair.

Una gave him a severe glance. 'What are you doing home so early? You are an idiot, Grandpa will be furious.'

'I've had enough of the mill today,' her brother replied shortly. 'He knows I don't do it often, so don't lecture.'

It was hard being a twin sometimes. Especially when your other half was the one you sometimes didn't exactly care for. Gideon felt that he did not – at the moment at any rate – care for his sister, or not very much. Sense of humour gone missing. Her lips tight and her forehead creased. Forever tap-tap-tapping on that damned typewriting machine. Disappearing for meetings with those hordes of women who were taking the West Riding by storm; those termagants from Huddersfield, Leeds and Halifax, some of them even marching over the hills from the Lancashire boundary, from as far as Manchester, agitating for votes for women. Stirring up the mill girls as well as teachers, shop assistants, housewives, any woman who would listen to their rubbish. Una would be losing her looks altogether if she didn't watch it and that would be a pity. They were the best asset she had, though she would never admit it.

Gideon was not vain enough to equate that thought with his own good looks. He was a charming and easy-going, normally good-natured, though just now rather discountenanced, young man. Slim and lithe, with thickly-lashed eyes like his sister and a boyish lick of hair, a darker blonde than hers, there was nevertheless a masculine strength in the firm chin line and breadth of shoulder. They were indeed a handsome couple. Even their names were paired, in a sense; their mother, ever with an eye on the main chance, having taken a notion when they were born that it would be expedient to christen her first-born after their titled great-grandfather, Sir Gideon Staincliffe Tyas. From which it followed that Gideon's twin should be called after his wife, Lady Tyas, despite her name being Fortunia, though the child had somehow cleverly contrived to get herself known as Una from the moment she could speak.

'Well, Grandpa's come home early, too, to see Miss Harcourt, so you'd better keep out of his way,' she said sharply. Gideon shrugged. He, and his grandfather, knew how hard he worked.

Ainsley Beaumont had no son to follow him in his business,

since his only child, Theo, the twins' father, had died when they were little more than babies, but Gideon had never been left in any doubt that his future was expected to lie in running the Cross Ings Mill. Since that was what he had always expected – and wanted, too – he had seen no reason for not starting work at the mill straight after leaving his North Yorkshire boarding school, where he had done well academically, as well as excelling in games.

But five years later he was restless, somehow the life and enthusiasm had gone out of it. And he was astute enough to know that his present disaffection lay mainly in the deterioration of his normally good relations with his grandfather.

Cross Ings Mill was by far the biggest in Wainthorpe; Beaumont's were respected the length and breadth of the Neller valley, and the business prospered. But how long would this state of affairs continue if Ainsley refused to step forward into the new century? Everything was still done in the old and, to Ainsley, trusted way: he ran the mill himself, scorning to employ a manager, his finger on the pulse of everything. Gideon was fed up with the fact that his grandfather would not listen to him, or let him have his head enough, as he felt was his right. Horns clashed, tempers were lost, daily it seemed.

'Take it easy, lad, you'll get nowt out of Ainsley Beaumont that road,' advised Whiteley Hirst, who'd been his grandfather's mainstay, his office manager, bookkeeper and much more for longer than Gideon could remember. 'I've had to keep t'band in t'nick long enough to know that,' he added broadly. Yes, Whiteley had always been adept at keeping things running smoothly. 'He'll come round all in good time.'

In due course. When he, Gideon, would take over from Ainsley and run the mill. *All in good time.* He was sick of the phrase. He was young, eager and hot-blooded, and patience had never been a virtue of his.

His grandfather was a man who gave out energy and power to a sometimes frightening degree. The sheer force of his personality had always dominated not only the workforce at the mill, but everyone here at Farr Clough. Yet despite his overbearing attitudes, his quick temper, he had never been an unreasonable employer; sins were forgiven if not entirely forgotten. Lately, though, even Gideon had been afraid of him at times. What was the old devil up to? Stamping around the

mill and everywhere else, finding fault with this, that and the
next thing, demanding unjustifiable changes. Quarrelling with
everyone if they didn't immediately jump to his commands
– even with Tom Illingworth. Yes, what *about* that row with
Tom yesterday? Tom, of all people! Which had escalated to
include Gideon himself – *and* Whiteley Hirst.

There was something profoundly wrong, and Gideon didn't
like it. Was Grandpa becoming non compos mentis? It worried
him because he was extremely fond of the old man who had
been all but father to him, and Cross Ings was, after all, the
most important part of both their lives, and he was damned if
he knew what to do about it.

And what – *what* in God's name was he doing, bringing
this girl from London to catalogue a roomful of dry, dusty
books that neither he nor anyone else in living memory had
ever touched?

In his first words to her, Ainsley Beaumont supplied Laura
with the reason why he had walked away from the scene of
the attack upon her by his dog. 'Put yourself directly in front
of me when you speak, if you please,' he said to her without
preamble when she presented herself to him. 'I'm going deaf
as a post in my old age. It's no use you shouting, there's not
a thing I can hear, but I manage well enough at lip-reading.'

He shook her hand firmly and told her to sit down, and
then, regarding her with a steady look, said nothing more for
a long time. Whether he had been entirely unaware of what
had taken place out there on the moor or not, it was impossible to say. If he had, he was making no effort to apologize.

He had been, and still was for that matter, a handsome, if
heavily built man, unsmiling, short-necked, with a dark, strong-
willed face, blue-jowled and with an obstinate cleft chin.
Though his close-cut hair was plentifully sprinkled with grey,
his thick eyebrows were still fierce and dark, and from under
them his shrewd eyes regarded Laura steadily for what seemed
like a very long time. She did not find the regard comfortable,
but she did not flinch.

'So,' he said at last, 'you are Miss Laura Harcourt.' As with
many deaf people, his voice was pitched low. A pleasant voice,
though his vowels, his turn of phrase, remained uncompromis-
ingly northern. 'Well, well, and what makes you want to come

here? I hear you're one of these over-educated young women we hear so much about nowadays.'

'I have just completed a three year course at the Royal Holloway College, if that's what you mean,' Laura replied coolly.

'Overqualified to sort out a few books, aren't you?'

'It makes a change until I get my bearings. I'm not quite sure what I want to do in the way of work, yet.'

'Aye, that's it nowadays, isn't it? Work, as if looking after a man and a family wasn't work enough! I suppose you think you're entitled to the vote, as well, like our Una? No, don't answer that . . . it seems we never do get the better of you young women, going down that road, and I don't mean us to get off on the wrong foot.' He allowed himself a slight smile. Laura, not to be drawn, swallowed a retort and said nothing. 'You'll soon get used to me, Miss Harcourt. Don't take offence.' After a moment he added, 'So, what did Mr Carfax tell you?'

'Nothing more than you need your books cataloguing, and the fees you've offered.' Which had not, she reflected, been exactly generous, and might have affected her decision, had she been in need of something better paid, and not least had she known what sort of employer she was to have.

He made no reply, his hands on the silver knob of his stick. Driven at last by a scrutiny she did not intend to allow to become unnerving, Laura said, 'Perhaps it would be as well, Mr Beaumont, if you gave me some idea of exactly what you need me to do here.'

'Books, as you said, that's the long and short of it. There's a lot of 'em, mind, but seeing as you're a bit of a bluestocking, sorting 'em out shouldn't worry you.'

'What does your library consist of?'

'My library?' He gave a short laugh. 'Well, I reckon it has to be mine on account of I own it, but I've never opened a book out of it yet, or out of anywhere else much,' he said, not without pride. '*Huddersfield Examiner* and *The Leeds Mercury* are good enough for me.'

'Forgive my asking, then, but why do you need them cataloguing?'

'They came with the house when I bought it, lock, stock and barrel, twenty-odd year back, from my wife's father. They've never been touched since. Happen it's time they were seen to.'

An explanation which left much to be desired, Laura thought. 'Are there many?'

'A few hundreds? A thousand or two? I can't rightly say. I've never counted. Not all that many, I shouldn't think.'

'In that case, since I don't like time hanging on my hands, I dare say I shall soon be finished.'

'Take your time. There's nowt got with rush and kick.' As if it suddenly occurred to him he might have been less than welcoming, he added gruffly, 'If I said little in my letters to Mr Carfax, Miss Harcourt, it's because there's little to tell. I shan't bother you much, I'm mostly down at the mill, and we're not a big household – there's only my grandchildren, the twins, and their mother. You'll be treated as one of the family while you're here.'

'Thank you. I've already met your granddaughter.'

'She's got some funny ideas just now, Una has, but she's a good lass, at heart, I suppose.' He added abruptly, 'But there's one more thing. My daughter-in-law, Amelia, Mrs Beaumont – their mother, that is. You might consider her a bit – funny in her ways, like.'

There was a pause. The fire collapsed in a flurry of rosy ash.

'You mean she's mad?'

He gave another short bark of laughter as he leaned forward to pick up the poker and rearrange the coals. 'You're a young woman after my own heart, Laura Harcourt, you speak your mind. No, she's not mad. Saner than most, I reckon, except she likes her own way a sight too much and isn't slow to say so. But I mustn't grumble. I'm nearly seventy and she's taken a lot off my shoulders since my son died . . . she's run this house for nigh on twenty year, so I reckon we can all put up with a bit of stick. But take no notice of what she says, if you can, and don't let her frighten you away.'

He leaned forward for the tongs and replenished the fire with another lump of coal. Sparks flew, as a tall grandfather clock ticked away in the corner, its silvery chime, when it came, identifying it as the one Laura had heard in the hall. The shadow of the old man's profile, thrown on to the wall by the lamp burning on the desk by his elbow, had a fierce, patriarchal cast. He might be the sort of person who would overwhelm one, on the other hand he might be kind. He had his little vanities – and not inconsiderable ones. His good suit was of grey worsted, his brown boots polished like conkers, a heavy gold watch-chain spread across his waistcoat and from it depended a circular gold sovereign case and a gold fob seal.

She stood up, sensing the interview was at an end, and rather glad that it was. 'I'll start first thing tomorrow morning, Mr Beaumont. I promise I won't prolong my duties and subject you to any unnecessary expense.'

'You wouldn't be here long if you did, lass.' He smiled grimly, then gave her one of the long, penetrating stares she was becoming used to. 'Aye,' he said eventually. 'I reckon you'll do well enough, Laura Harcourt. You'll do.'

As if on cue, the doorknob rattled and Una came into the room. 'Have you finished putting Miss Harcourt through the third degree, Grandpa?'

'If you mean have we done talking, we have.'

There was a challenge in the way their eyes met before Una turned to Laura. 'Then come and meet the rest of us, Miss Harcourt.'

Five

When Una pushed open the door to her mother's sitting room, it at first appeared empty, a low-ceilinged room cluttered with too much furniture. Only a single lamp burned, shaded in dark red, and the last of the daylight was further dimmed by ferns, potted palms and heavy plush curtains of a deep plum colour, which were half-parted across the mullioned windows. But as her eyes became accustomed to the gloom, Laura saw that a trousered leg hung over the arm of a wing chair and a woman slept by the fire. It seemed to be a room created for somnolence, a room that spoke of long hours of stifling ennui, of occupants who had long since ceased to have anything to say to one another, where the mantel clock chiming the quarters and the fall of a coal in the grate, the turning of a page or the click of a thimble placed on a table would be the only sounds to break the silence.

Una broke it now by saying, 'Well, is anyone at home here?'

The leg disappeared, and a young man immediately sprang up from the depths of the chair and made his way with a dexterity that could only have come from long practice between balloon-backed chairs and spindly tables laden with knick-knacks.

'My brother Gideon, resting from his labours at the mill, as you see . . . Miss Harcourt,' Una introduced them dryly, bending to adjust the lamp so that it burned more brightly. She turned and looked appraisingly at Laura. 'No, I don't think that's going to do. Everyone else calls me Una and I should be mortified if you did not, and I was compelled to call you Miss Harcourt . . . Laura?'

She smiled, very briefly, but it transformed her. Una Beaumont might not, perhaps, be the cold, sarcastic girl she seemed; or at any rate, not a person to be judged by first impressions − any more than her brother, who looked nothing like someone who had just returned from work at a mill, albeit his appearance was somewhat dishevelled: his high collar was slightly askew, his hair flopped towards his eyes and looked as though he had run his hands through it, more than once. But his tie held a pearl pin, and like his grandfather he had on a suit of the best worsted, which he wore with elegance. He seemed friendly, and his tone was slightly amused as he asked, with a faint drawl, 'Well, then, Laura, and how did you get on with the old man?'

'Mr Beaumont? I'm not sure, but he seemed to think that "I'll do well enough."'

She had evidently correctly caught Ainsley Beaumont's tone. They both laughed.

The woman by the fire, wakened by the sound, sat up with a jerk of her head. Caught napping, she looked affronted at the loss to her dignity, but in a moment she had smoothed her hair and her skirt and was sitting upright, as stiff and unbending as though sleep had never been further away. 'Well,' she demanded, discerning the newcomer, 'and who do we have here then?'

'Come and meet my mother, Laura,' said Una.

Amelia Beaumont sat without moving but after a moment offered a handshake. She had been lying in front of the fire, and yet her hand was cold as a frog's. A heavily built woman in middle age, her curves firmly disciplined in whalebone, she was a commanding figure, handsomely dressed in a snuff-coloured blouse and skirt discreetly trimmed with heliotrope velvet bands. Her dark brown hair, dressed wide, emphasized a skin pale as her daughter's. Otherwise, there was little resemblance between them, or between her and her son, for that matter. She might once have been considered handsome and might still have been, were it not for the uncompromising set to her mouth and the strange, opaquely dark eyes which now fastened on Laura with a long, considering gaze. 'So you're the young woman from down south?'

'Yes, I'm Laura Harcourt, Mrs Beaumont.'

Until her other clothes had been shaken and pressed free of their packing-induced creases, there had been no question for Laura of changing anything but her travelling shoes for bronze-coloured slippers and removing her coat, and Mrs Beaumont's gaze travelled over her, from the shining mass of her wavy hair to the row of tiny, lapis-lazuli buttons on her ivory crêpe-de-chine, French-made blouse. 'Hmm.' Her look made it clear that she did not approve of what she saw, and Laura was inclined to think that disapproval was the least of

it. She was taken aback to see an almost palpable flash of dislike
in those opaque eyes.

'So what are you doing up here, then, miss?'

'Well, of course, I'm here to sort out Mr Beaumont's books
for him.'

'And about time too – that room's a disgrace,' she returned
bluntly. 'But that's not what I meant . . .' She considered Laura
again, but the black marble mantel clock chiming six interrupted whatever else she had been going to say, and she put
an end to the conversation by pressing large, capable hands on
the arms of her chair and standing up in one direct movement.
She needed no assistance from the hand her son put out to
help her. 'It's teatime.'

Everyone immediately made an obedient move towards the
door.

It was strange eating without the strong light of gas or elec-
tricity, but lamplight was gentler, kinder, warmer, leaving the
edges of the sombrely furnished room in darkness while its
golden, flickering light lit the faces of those around the table.
There were just the four of them. The carver chair at the head
of the table was empty, though a place was laid. It seemed the
head of the house at Farr Clough had decided not to join
them on this occasion.

Amelia Beaumont, absorbed in her meal, said little, though
her presence dominated the table. Once or twice as they ate,
Laura looked up and caught those curious eyes on her, and
felt again that she was being judged, and found wanting. She
had never before encountered what she could not but feel was
unwarranted dislike, and for a while she tried to overcome it
by drawing the older woman out, but her efforts were met
with such indifference that her pride would not let her carry
on. Perhaps she was imagining the animosity. Yet Laura could
not suppress a slight shiver. A feeling that behind those secret
eyes, the tight mouth, there was passion, and perhaps something
darker, held in.

She's clever, this girl – or perhaps just socially accomplished
– thought Una, watching Laura try to draw out, first her
mother, then Gideon, who responded warmly as they sat down
to the usual knife and fork affair of cold meats, tinned salmon

and salad, buttered plain teacake and a great array of sweet-stuff, washed down with many cups of strong, dark tea, doubtless not the sort of meal someone from London was used to. Una herself never had much appetite, either, for this vast array of food, especially not after the heavy midday dinner that was always served here at Farr Clough, rain or shine. But no one dared break with tradition, at Farr Clough Grandpa upheld it and was usually here at teatime. It was too bad of him – Una hesitated to say perverse, though that was the thought that passed through her mind – not to appear today, seeing that Laura Harcourt being here was his idea.

At any rate, Gideon was exerting his usual easy charm, enthusiastically expounding a subject he needed no encourage-ment to talk about. 'Yes, I do have a motor – of sorts,' he was telling Laura, 'but discretion dictates that I mostly keep her down there at the mill. She doesn't go so well up the hills, I'm afraid. I would have driven to the station to meet you myself, only Grandpa . . . Well, nose to the grindstone and all that. And anyway, he doesn't approve of cars—'

'Considering the number of times you've broken down on the way up here, he can hardly be blamed for that,' Una commented.

'Oh, well, these dashed hills, as I say – and the old girl *is* second-hand. Never mind, I have my eye on a topping little Wolseley two-seater that's guaranteed for hill climbing, when I can get my hands on the ready to buy it, that is. Tell you what, Mother. You persuade Grandpa to part with a hundred and seventy-five pounds and I'll take you out for a spin when I get it. Even take you down to Ramsden's,' he said, smiling at her but adding for Laura's benefit, 'My mother walks down to the butcher in Wainthorpe three times a week to buy meat, rather than have them send it up.'

'I'll not have Joe Ramsden sending up any old rubbish he thinks fit, not as long as I've got the use of my two legs,' Mrs Beaumont stated. 'You won't get me going down there in one of those dangerous contraptions, neither. What, a hundred and seventy-five pound! You'll never get *that* out of Ainsley Beaumont,' she added with finality, helping herself to another slice of currant pasty.

'Probably not.' He gave an exaggerated sigh. 'Not when he won't even think about motorized lorries for the mill. What do we want *them* for, he says, when we have fourteen horses that don't need petrol at one-and-three-ha'pence a gallon, and neither do they have brakes that fail and run into trams. If he had his way we'd still be using packhorses as they did in Great-great-grandfather Beaumont's time.'

'You've planted the seed. Let it grow and sooner or later he'll come to think it was his own idea.'

'How clever you are, Una!' he replied, smiling, as if the idea hadn't already occurred to him. She responded only with a raised eyebrow.

'Cross Ings Mill has been in the family for a long time, then?' Laura asked.

'Oh Lord, yes. Generations,' Gideon replied carelessly.

Seemingly, this was a subject which either did not interest Amelia or she did not wish to talk about. Having finished her meal, she took it as a sign to push her chair back. 'Well, then, if we've done, Prissy will be wanting to side all this lot and get it washed up. And I've still a lot to see to before I get to bed, so I'll say good night now and leave you. There's a good fire in the workroom, and your breakfast will be at half past seven, Miss Harcourt.' She nodded stiffly to Laura, who made a mental note not to be late. Inflexible routine was obviously the rule in this house and she had no intention of getting on the wrong side of Mrs Beaumont.

The room they retired to was shabbily comfortable, haphazardly furnished, and one the twins seemed to have made their own. Books and papers were everywhere, and a typewriting machine on a table seemed to be the reason Mrs Beaumont had called this a workroom.

Laura was glad to sink into a chair by the fire, unable to feel anything but relieved to be rid of a presence she felt to be domineering and humourless, and she surmised she was not the only one. Yet, as if sensing unvoiced criticism, Una embarked on a somewhat defensive explanation. 'Mother has a lot on her plate, so she's early to bed, early to rise. It's not an easy house to run, and we don't keep a big staff. I expect she's gone to smooth Mrs Macready's feathers. As if one more to cook for will make any difference.'

Mrs Macready had apparently come to Farr Clough when the house had belonged to Sir Gideon Tyas, their maternal great-grandfather, and was still here, despite her old age. 'Doing us all a favour. Working for Beaumont's is a comedown, as far as she's concerned,' Gideon said with a laugh.

'Beaumont, that's a French name, isn't it?' But it was one Laura had noticed several times amongst the recurrent Hardcastles and Bamforths she'd seen above mill gates and other concerns, on the way to Wainthorpe.

'It might have been once, though we've no French ancestors that I know of. We were nothing more than hand-loom weavers up on the moors, until the first Ainsley Beaumont graduated towards owning a small mill in the valley, where the woven pieces could be finished as well. Where the water flowed – plenty of it for powering the mill wheel, and soft for washing the wool. And where there was plenty of room for expansion. Now the whole process of manufacture's under one roof – thanks mainly to Grandpa – though it was an uphill job, as he never ceases to remind me,' he added dryly. 'Beaumonts—' He broke off abruptly. 'Sorry, I tend to get carried away.'

'No, no, please, go on. After all, it's a story to be proud of.'

He shrugged and said he supposed it was, of course, if you thought about it like that, though you didn't often, not when you had been brought up with it. You just took it as it came, got on with the day-to-day running of the mill and accepted its profits as the natural outcome.

If he was endeavouring to sound cynical, he was failing signally; flippancy could not conceal that this was the way to his heart. Laura could see she had touched on a nerve, a passion in him. This cloth-making business was clearly as much in his blood as it was in his grandfather's, inherited from one generation to the next.

'I'd like to know more about it all,' she said, 'don't forget, it's all new to me – and by the way, what is mungo? I asked your driver what it was but all he would say was devil's dust.'

'John Willie? I'm afraid the old so-and-so's disposition doesn't improve as he gets older. What he meant was—' Gideon paused. 'Old rags and wool are ground together to make a lesser quality cloth called shoddy, and an even cheaper one called mungo. Unfortunately it makes a lot of fine dust.'

'That gets into the men's lungs, so they can't breathe,' said Una.

'It's cheap, however. Cheap cloth. There's always a cost.'

'Mostly to folks like Jessie's father. There's nothing done

about it because money matters more. Even Grandpa has a share in one of these mills.'

'Used to have.'

A taut silence fell between them, broken only by the sound of the wind in the chimney. Tread softly, Laura warned herself, though she didn't know why.

'Well,' she said awkwardly, after a moment, 'it's obvious there are more aspects to the wool business than I'd dreamed of. Tell me more.'

It appeared Gideon had a better idea. 'It's far easier to show than to explain. Why don't I take you round the mill sometime and show you the different processes – that is, if you're not afraid of noise, and some dirt?'

'I'm used to both. Stepney, where I've been working lately, isn't exactly famed for cleanliness, or silence.'

She guessed she had surprised them both, but the change of subject seemed welcome, and for a while they talked about the Settlement, the conditions in which the women had been forced to live before being taken in there, and how they were helped. 'Oh, if you knew how hopeless those women feel!' Laura finished, 'when there's absolutely nothing they can do about the position they find themselves in.'

'But it's not only in Stepney where that sort of thing happens.' Una was showing more animation than Laura had seen in her yet. 'It's here, in the valley, in Wainthorpe, in the mills and everywhere. Women work ten hours a day in the mill – when they are not having babies – and have to cook and wash and clean for their husbands and children after they get home – and then have to watch these same children going to work half-time in the mill when they're but thirteen—'

'It used to be when they were only seven or eight, and they worked fourteen hours.'

'So it's all right, then, for children to work *six* hours?'

'I didn't say that, Una. You're deliberately misunderstanding. My sister,' he said, turning to Laura, 'in case you hadn't guessed, is a supporter of rights, for herself and everyone else. Would it surprise you to hear she also supports votes for women?'

'You can't have one without the other,' Una retorted.

So it was true that the flames of feminism which Mrs Pankhurst and her three daughters had set alight in Manchester and were spreading in London like the Great Fire, were leaping here, too. 'My friend Eva Carfax is a member of the WSPU and she has told me how strong the movement is here in the North.'

Quickly, Una asked, 'And you, too? Are you committed?'

Gideon sighed. He was beginning to look bored.

'Not . . . exactly,' Laura said cautiously, unwilling to admit that the extent of her commitment so far had been in occasionally addressing stacks of envelopes.

'That's something we must remedy, then. You'll be surprised how many women around here are involved. All sorts of people. Jessie Thwaite, for instance, is one of our strongest supporters.'

This was no surprise. Jessie was clearly a strong-minded young woman with views of her own. Una, becoming animated, went on to say how she herself helped to draft speeches for the women who worked in the mills and weren't afraid to stand up for what they felt was right, but who didn't feel themselves educated enough to put it into the proper words. She wrote pamphlets and letters to the papers, organized meetings, and most importantly, she produced a small, quarterly magazine called *Unity*, which she wrote mostly herself and distributed, free, as widely as she could in the neighbouring towns.

'In fact, put her in here with a nosebag and a jug of water and you're unlikely to see her for days,' Gideon drawled.

Una ignored him and told Laura there was to be an important meeting in Halifax in a couple of weeks. 'Will you come? We're hoping some of the WSPU leaders will be there, and there's to be a great speaker, a political activist who's on our side. Do come and swell the ranks.'

Gideon ceased to yawn. 'Halifax? I'll drive you over there,' he volunteered.

'What, and risk conking out over the moors?'

'Better than the tram, but it's up to you. There's room for both of you.'

'And for Emmie Broomhead as well, of course.'

He shrugged with a show of indifference. 'If she wants to come – though Emmie isn't interested in all this feminism.' Una raised a cool eyebrow. 'But look here, Una, if you insist on talking suffragettes at Laura, I must remind you she's had a very long day.'

'I'm sorry, yes, I am thoughtless. You must be tired, Laura.'

Laura made polite protests but she could not make them

very convincing. She was quite thankful to Gideon for the intervention. Tonight, of all nights, she had even less inclination for 'talking suffragettes' than usual.

Someone had been into her room while she was out and had banked the fire and, she saw by the stirring of the curtains, had opened the window again. Beyond the dark outlines of Cross Ings Mill almost directly beneath her, the darkness of the hills was pricked by hundreds, maybe thousands of lights from farm, cottage and street, the squares of light from the occasional late-working mill, spreading into the distance towards the red glow that lay above Huddersfield.

Despite the cold, she stood mesmerized, until at last she was forced to shut the window, wash, undress, and climb between icy, starched sheets that seemed to smell of the peaty air which had dried them. She thought longingly of the hot-water bottles always placed in her bed at home and wondered how she would ever get to sleep. But she discovered that a stone hot-water bottle, flannel wrapped, *had* been placed in the huge feather-bed, and under the pile of soft blankets of best Yorkshire wool, she soon grew warm and, exhausted with her long, bewildering day, fell asleep with the breathtaking view she had looked out on still in her mind.

It was not this sight that presently haunted her uneasy dreams, however, but that of the blackened shell of the other part of the house, the feeling that had come over her when she had first set eyes on it, and the knowledge that it lay just the other side of the wall from where she slept.

Part Two

Six

Amelia Beaumont invariably rose at the crack of dawn and by six thirty she was already seated in the small, over furnished sitting room that was her favourite place, in the little corner which was big enough only to accommodate a desk and a chair. But that was all she needed to do her weekly accounts.

A shillings worth of shin-beef, one ox-tongue, a joint of shoulder pork, pig's trotters for brawn, two stone of potatoes, one of flour, three pounds of carrots, one block of paraffin wax to make polish . . .

She was careful to note down every penny before adding it up, after which she wiped the pen and dipped it into the red ink, ruled off, blotted it and turned to a different page. The household accounts, like everything else at Farr Clough, were kept in meticulous order, ready at any time for Ainsley to inspect them, but though she would have preferred him to see the evidence of his trust in her, he always waved the suggestion away. 'Carry on, if it makes you happy to see it all in black and white, but don't bother me with your sums. You wouldn't diddle me, Amelia.'

That was true, and waste of any kind was anathema to her. Amelia had taken thrift in with her mother's milk. Nothing was ever wasted in the Chadwick household, and the same rules applied under Amelia's jurisdiction here at Farr Clough. She was quietly satisfied to see that this week she had even saved a shilling or two. That, and seeing that his house ran as smoothly as his business at Cross Ings, was the least she could do. It was her way of paying Ainsley back for everything he'd done.

She had always known that her escape from skivvying in that low-down old Tyas Arms, being nothing more than the publican's daughter, lay in getting herself married. When Theo had put a ring on her finger – only just in time, before the twins were born – Ainsley hadn't batted an eyelid – not in her presence, at any rate. What he'd said to his son was between him and Theo. For a moment she closed her eyes as the old, familiar pain ripped through her.

But she'd got what she wanted. Folk thought she gave herself airs, but this was only so she could hold her head up in the town – no longer that Chadwick lass from the Tyas Arms, but Mrs Theo Beaumont of Farr Clough, who numbered the wives of the local nobs among her acquaintances.

She dipped her pen in the ink again. *Wages for Mrs Macready, for Jessie, for the new maid, for John Willie and the boy, Zach. A load of best coal cobs, and another of nutty slack, delivered . . .*

All the same, for all his generosity, Ainsley Beaumont wasn't always an easy man to live with. She had had to tread so careful a path it had by now become second nature. He could be wilful and overbearing, he was hard-headed, though not hard-hearted, and it wasn't wise to oppose him. Even though lately some of his actions had been downright daft – more than that, dangerous. He'd got hold of some queer ideas and no mistake, such as getting that stranger from London to sort out his old books, when Una could have been put to do it, and without having to be paid a penny for it, either.

Amelia shielded her eyes with her hand, her elbow on the table. Here it was, not yet seven in the morning, and she was tired. Not physically, but wearied of thinking, worrying, obsessed by fear. What would they say, Wainthorpe folk, if they *knew*? How they'd tattle behind their hands!

She had the beginnings of another headache, too. The headaches were usually a sign, a warning. Please God, not now. She couldn't afford the dark days, the week – weeks, sometimes – sucked out of her life, that the darkness demanded.

The news originated from Cross Ings Mill, gathered momentum and by teatime all of Wainthorpe was buzzing with it.

Accidents regularly happened in any mill, horrific accidents; it stood to reason, in places where there was so much dangerous machinery, and when people working there were not always as careful as they should be in keeping to the rules about unprotected hair and loose clothing which could easily get caught up in the flying and whirling belts and cogs. But this accident had happened outside, not inside, Cross Ings Mill.

Few people went by the dam, and took care not to get too near if they were forced to do so – no telling what there was in that filthy millpond soup. Not for nothing was it known as the slap-dab. Nobody, that is, apart from the little limbs of Satan who larked around there, running and balancing along the wall for a dare, or simply out of bravado; young lads who'd been told in no uncertain terms that they'd know all about it if their mams heard what they'd been up to. It wasn't unknown for one of them to fall in. Once, years ago, a little lad had drowned there. But a grown man?

Who was it? A drunk? A stranger? Surely nobody else would have been such a fool as to let that happen.

'Epidural haematoma due to blunt impact to the head,' repeated Detective Inspector Charlie Womersley. 'And what does that mean when it's at home?'

Three men – the doctor, Womersley and the local police sergeant, Binns – were standing on the path which ran alongside the Cross Ings dam.

'It *could* mean he hit his head on the bottom of the dam when he fell in, but he didn't,' Dr Pike said.

Womersley wished he had been there yesterday after they fished Ainsley Beaumont out of the dam, but that hadn't been deemed necessary at the time. The law routinely required enquiry into the circumstances of any unexpected death, but when the dead man had been identified as a prominent townsman, a wealthy millowner who employed a good percentage of the town's workforce, and had a finger in many other of Wainthorpe's concerns, what had at first seemed like accidental drowning had suddenly warranted somewhat more than investigation by Sergeant Binns.

With Binns's inspector temporarily hors de combat on account of having fallen off his bicycle a week ago, the sergeant and a couple of constables represented all of Wainthorpe's constabulary staff. It wouldn't have done to let it be thought that the enquiry was not of paramount importance, and Womersley, an experienced detective inspector, had been brought in. He had no particular objections: it would merely be a routine enquiry, soon over, which suited him well enough; he was coasting towards retirement and didn't need any major investigations to upset the equilibrium of his last few months.

'Good of you to give us more of your time, Doctor.'

When the body had been found, Dr Widdop, the police doctor, had been snatching a few hours' sleep after having attended a patient for most of the previous night, and his assistant, Matthew Pike, had come in his stead to make the official certification of death. It was the first time it had fallen to him to perform such a task. An incomer from somewhere down south, he was bursting with new ideas. He was also a very positive young man and had had no hesitation in making known to the police his private dissatisfaction with the idea that the death could have been accidental, or even suicide; a conclusion agreed by the pathologist who had carried out the preliminary examination of the body.

He said now, 'The coroner's certain to ask for a post-mortem, Inspector, and I think it'll show he couldn't have fallen in – or jumped, either, if it comes to that. Neither did he drown. He was dead before he hit the water.'

Womersley grunted, uneasily digesting the implications of the statement. 'You sure of that?' The question was rhetorical. Inexperienced as he was, the young doctor wouldn't, he knew, have sounded so emphatic if there had been any doubts, and in any case it was backed up by the pathologist's report.

'He didn't drown,' Pike repeated. 'No water in his lungs. It was that blow to his head that killed him – before he went in. Need I say more?'

'Since he could hardly have thrown himself in, not if he was already dead, it means somebody else was there,' supplied Womersley, who never minded stating the obvious. 'Another fight, I suppose, that went too far, as they do. He was knocked down, hit his head – and died. So we have a manslaughter on our hands.' Anything more, he didn't want to think about.

Pike, a stocky, carelessly dressed young chap with leather patches on the elbows of his tweed jacket and sharp eyes behind thick spectacles, shrugged. 'Maybe.'

Womersley cocked an eyebrow.

Pike added, 'Why bother to throw him in, if he was already dead? Unless they weren't sure he was, and wanted to finish him off, make absolutely certain.'

Womersley looked down at the gently steaming surface of the oily, filthy, stinking dam. He reckoned that even if the old man hadn't been dead before he went in, it wouldn't have been long before he was.

'Or to hide the body, like?' the sergeant offered.

Fred Binns was a wiry fellow with sharp eyes. Suspicious deaths on their patch were rare and he was eager to make the most of this one in the absence of his inspector. All the same, it was just as well they'd decided to send in what he thought of as the big guns – however little Inspector Womersley, middle-aged, slow moving, seemed to fit the description.

'Bodies have a habit of floating, sooner or later, Sergeant,' Womersley pointed out.

The doctor said, 'He didn't sink at all. The air in his lungs would have kept him buoyant for a while, at least until he became waterlogged, but he was found before that had the chance to happen . . . he drifted over there, to what they call the goit, where his body got caught.'

The path they stood on was black, trodden earth, bounded on one side by the substantial wall that surrounded the dam. Along the base sprouted a fine colony of weeds: rough grass, ragwort, nettles, bracken, even a rogue clump of heather. The mill dam itself was an elongated shape, eight foot deep, with steep, straight sides and a bottom lined with stone setts. The goit was a conduit for the purpose of channelling the water from the dam into the mill. Not the clean, beautifully soft water that came down from the hills, essential for washing the wool; this was the polluted waste left behind after the clotted, greasy wool fleeces had been scoured, plus other detritus, waiting to be turned into steam to power the engine. An iron grating prevented the conduit from being blocked by rubbish, and that was where the body had lodged, along with a lot of scummy residue and a dead rat, left behind when the body had been taken away.

This was beginning to give Womersley heartburn. He sighed, reached into his pocket for the mint imperials. 'Not just a fight, tempers lost, then?'

'A fight, possibly, but . . . the autopsy will prove whether he hit his head as he fell, or if something hit *him*. There's a difference. If he fell, the damage to the brain will show at the opposite side to the wound, if not, it'll be on the same side. Medically known as *coup* and *contre-coup* injuries, if it's of any interest.'

'If he was deliberately attacked, it wasn't for robbery.' Womersley brought to mind the details he had familiarized himself with. The dead man's handsome, silver-knobbed walking stick had been left lying on the path. 'And he still had his gold watch chain and sovereign case – with sovereigns still in it, if I'm not mistaken, Sergeant Binns?'

'Aye. His wallet was stuffed with notes as well.'

But it looked as though somebody had made the attempt. The inside breast pocket in the lining of his jacket, where he had kept his pocketbook, had been torn – a long rip from the corner – though oddly, the pocketbook had been left there, apparently intact. It must have been a recent tear – his clothes had been good, and though not new, had been well taken care of. A hole in one trouser pocket had been neatly patched. His boots had metal heel protectors hammered in, to save wear. His socks were hand-knitted, and someone had thriftily and carefully darned over the places in the heels where the wool had worn thin. It was the sort of thing Womersley's wife, Kate, did for him. For all his money, Ainsley Beaumont, like all sensible folks, obviously hadn't believed in discarding his clothes before they'd outlived their useful life.

Womersley looked down at the bloated corpse of the dead rat and suppressed another sigh. It was Saturday morning, the beginning of the weekend and a half day at the mill, which would shut down at twelve thirty. The town market was already in full swing, and later the trams would be packed with Huddersfield supporters bound for the rugby match at Fartown. Rawlinson, the detective sergeant Womersley had brought with him, would be disappointed at not being able to join them all. Womersley was beginning to see his own weekend slipping away. He'd promised Kate to put up the supports for when the kidney beans were ready to be planted out in their garden – Kate's garden, by rights – the overrun and neglected private garden that she'd taken over and made into a profitable little business, growing and selling flowers and market produce. A countrywoman born and bred, she'd made a success of her little venture. To Womersley, the peaceful walled garden and its ancient mulberry tree with a seat running round it had been a revelation. He had never before in his life put a spade into the ground or felt the warm earth crumbling beneath his fingers, or stopped to listen to a robin as it perched on his garden fork, and as he learned more from Kate, he sometimes wondered why he had ever become a policeman, and not a gardener. He had developed a passion for growing sweet peas, and a competitive streak which had enabled him to win several prizes for his blooms. Maybe it was the same competitive streak which had got him to the rank of inspector, in an organization not noted for its quick promotions — so maybe he was a policeman at heart, after all. Certainly, with his passion for justice, he never rested till he'd got to the bottom of things. Those who didn't know him, with his ponderous manner, thought him soft, which amused him, but those who did know him were glad they were not on the wrong side of the law.

He brought his attention back to what was going on. 'Then if robbery wasn't the motive, we'd better start looking for somebody who had it in for him.'

'Who shouldn't be hard to find, from what I've been hearing,' Pike said shortly, getting ready to leave. 'Choleric sort of fellow, our Mr Beaumont. Just about everybody seems to have come up against him sooner or later.'

'Nay, you'll go a long way,' Sergeant Binns protested, feeling bound in all fairness to correct this impression, 'before you find anybody thought that bad of him. Ainsley Beaumont was a hard man, right enough, and a bit short-tempered, but he were fair, if you did right by him. And very respected by t'other wool men. Wait till you see his funeral. I'll be capped if it isn't one of t'biggest in the Neller valley for years.'

Womersley respected local knowledge from a shrewd bobby like Binns, but Pike, who seemed to have his own opinions about the victim, merely shrugged. Womersley said dryly, 'Well, his funeral doesn't look like it's going to be tomorrow, or the next day, come to that. Somebody wanted him out of the road. So we'd best set about finding who. First, who was it found him?'

It had been little Kathleen O'Mara, a ten-year-old who had been taking her father's dinner to him at the mill, as she often did — peas and sausage in a basin wrapped and tied up in a red spotted handkerchief. When she saw the thing floating on the surface of the dam after she came through the snicket on Syke Beck Lane and on to the path above the mill, she'd dropped the basin and stood there crying her eyes out till her father came looking to see where his dinner had got to.

'Hard on the little lass, that.' Womersley had a soft spot for children. He and Kate had not been blessed with a family, to their sorrow. 'She won't forget that in a hurry.'

'She were more upset about her Dad's dinner, and breaking the basin,' Binns said. All she could say were, "Me mam'll kill me." But she'll be all right.' Even Brid O'Mara, ever handy with a clout to the head, having the Irish in her, would understand.

'Dinner time, then, when he was found . . . so how long had he been dead, Doctor?'

'That's a slippery one. Fixing the time of death is not a precise science. That water is still hot when it comes from the mill, and warmth accelerates stiffening, but the body wasn't stiff, so not all that long. Five or six hours at most? The question is: would his body have floated so long?'

'Let's say about starting time, then, to be going on with. Wouldn't there have been folk around?'

'Not a lot use this way to get to the mill,' Binns said. 'They're supposed to go in through the main gates to clock in at the time office, and any road, it's gainer for most folks to use t'other way.'

'So if it was quiet, you'd think he'd be aware of anybody looking for trouble.'

'Not necessarily,' Pike said, 'he was very hard of hearing. He wouldn't have heard.'

Womersley thought about this for a while. 'For anybody knowing that, then, it would have been easy to come up behind him, bash him over the head, lean him against the wall and tip him in.' He pointed to a scrape that a steel-tipped boot heel might have made on one of the dam wall's coping stones. 'And look here.' He pointed to black splotches on the wall, near the nettles sprouting at its base. 'Blood, Doctor?'

'Could be.'

'We'll need a search team. Where's Rawlinson got to?'

'He's coming,' said Binns.

Detective Sergeant Jack Rawlinson, Womersley's assistant, who had been sent into the mill office to make sure Mr Gideon Beaumont would be available to see them when they were finished here, loped around the corner and reported that Mr Gideon had already left. Whiteley Hirst, the office manager, would wait to see them, however.

Rawlinson was young, and keen, and hoped to step into Womersley's shoes when he retired. Womersley hoped so, too, and meant to help him on his way as much as he could. It was a promise he'd made to himself, though the lad's enthusiasm for what he called 'advanced' police methods sorely tried his patience at times. He was a tall, gangling fellow with bony hands and feet, and stubbly, spiky light hair that wouldn't be kept smooth no matter how much brilliantine he used. Despite this, he was something of a dandy – snappy suit, high collar, handkerchief in his top pocket. He was bright eyed and smart, young for the hoped-for inspector's job, but despite his background he had a grammar school education behind him, plus intelligence, and was full of a nervous energy that admittedly sometimes got on Womersley's nerves. The lad was never still. Even while he was listening as Womersley summed up for him what they had been discussing, he was bouncing up and down on his toes like a boxer, his eyes were roaming around the scene, and he could hardly wait until his inspector had finished before pointing a yard or two back along the path, to a depression in the trodden black beaten earth. 'Looks to me like a rock was in that hole not so long since.'

It was a jagged but clean-edged impression, as if a sizeable stone had been embedded in the dense, heavy soil and had only recently been prised out. 'Could a stone that shape have fitted the wound in his head, Doctor?' he asked.

'Possibly. Very possibly. More than likely, I'd say.'

'We could get a plaster cast, Mr Womersley – that hole's a perfect mould.'

'Aye, I reckon it is, but we'll need a bit more than that. Like the rock itself. And if he *was* hit with it, likely it'll be down on the bottom of the dam along with a hundred or two others.' They hadn't been looking for a weapon, of course, but Womersley was mildly annoyed that he'd failed to spot what now seemed patently obvious. 'But all right, lad, a plaster cast's the next best thing.' He nodded to the sergeant. 'Get it seen to.'

Rawlinson looked highly pleased with himself and Pike said unexpectedly, 'They only had to wait, you know – whoever it was did this thing. He would probably have been dead anyway within the next six months. He had a brain tumour.'

Womersley stared. 'Is that right?'

Rawlinson said, 'Well, maybe they couldn't wait that long.'

'All the same. Hardly seems fair, poor devil.'

Womersley looked at the sky and then at his watch. It was a dark, overcast day with no hint of sun. The valley seemed to have closed in on itself. A breeze ruffled the surface of the oily water and the smoke pall over the town seemed heavier than ever. 'It'll be dinnertime soon and they'll be knocking off. We'd best go and see this Mr Whiteley Hirst, Rawlinson.'

He walked back along the path, followed single file by the others, and once in the mill yard, they separated, the doctor and Sergeant Binns heading towards the town, while Womersley and Rawlinson walked towards the mill.

'Before we go in,' Rawlinson said, 'especially in view of what we've just heard, I should tell you there was a dust-up in the office about a week back, a big row between Whiteley Hirst, Ainsley Beaumont and his grandson, Gideon – and a chap called Tom Illingworth that lives in yon house over there with his mother.'

'Who told you this?'

'Chief clerk, name of Edwin Porteous. He followed me out of the office and told me.'

Womersley raised his eyebrows. 'Now why should he bother to do that?'

'Just what I asked myself,' said Rawlinson.

Seven

Gideon and his sister had taken uneasy possession of the small formal parlour by the front door, rarely used except for company. They sat, unusually silent, as if that would allow them to believe the blow they'd received and still couldn't credit. It was an obvious relief to both when they heard Jessie Thwaite answering the front door, and then the murmur of a voice they recognized as that of Tom Illingworth.

Tom would know what to do. Ever since he'd taught Gideon to ride his first grown-up bicycle when he was ten, Gideon had looked up to him as the elder brother he had never had, and often sought his advice. Once, he had thought he might become more than brother, when Grandpa had decided he ought to marry Una. However, Tom's patent lack of interest apart, Una had soon put a stop to that. She might look as fragile as one of the harebells on the moor, but she was tough, knew her own mind and had other ideas. Despite everything else he was feeling, there flashed across Gideon's mind the question: what of those other plans of hers, now?

Tom came into the room, asking, 'What's the matter with Jessie?' As well he might, having seen the maid with her lips pressed tight together, her cheerfulness gone.

He looked around the room, mystified. Una was sitting bolt upright, as if she were frozen into the position. Gideon was standing with his back to the fire, one hand shoved into his pocket. 'What is it? What's wrong?'

'You haven't heard, then? The accident, down at the mill?'

'Accident, what accident? I've been in London for a few days and only just got back.'

'Your mother hasn't told you, then?'

'She's out. I didn't wait to see her, I came straight up here. It's not – it's not my uncle – not Whiteley, is it?'

'It's not Whiteley Hirst, Tom, it's Grandpa. He's had an accident. He's dead.'

'Dead?'

'They found him floating in the dam, drowned, about dinner time yesterday.'

'Good God. In the *dam*? I don't understand.'

'No one does,' Gideon said tiredly. 'They think he must have fallen in.'

'*What?*' Ainsley Beaumont had walked past the dam every day of his life since he was thirteen, and probably before that he had been one of the little daredevils who had balanced along the top of its wall. An accident was surely an impossibility. Even had he tripped on the path, it was unlikely he could have tumbled over the three foot wall which surrounded the dam.

Gideon was looking like a lost, hurt and bewildered schoolboy, the confidence knocked out of him. The rudder had gone from his ship and he was off course. 'What now?' he asked in a dazed manner. 'What do we do? Where do we start?'

Tom clasped his shoulder. 'One thing at a time. Just tell me, what happened?'

'He left home for the mill as usual, but never arrived. They say he fell into the dam. I'd been in Leeds all day – to see Greenbaum's about half a dozen pieces they claim were not up to snuff, which is a damn lie, of course, and I . . .' His voice trailed off. 'I didn't get back until mid-afternoon, after they'd found him.'

'Does Miss Harcourt know?' Tom asked, surprisingly.

Gideon exchanged a look with his sister, as if wondering for a moment who Miss Harcourt was. 'Laura? Well, of course. Oh, here she is.'

For a while Laura hesitated in the doorway. 'I came to see if you wanted some tea.'

Una shook her head. 'Please come in, Laura.'

Laura went to sit beside her and touched one of the cold hands, though she felt little warmer, herself. The news had shocked her. She had been here little over a week and scarcely more than met Ainsley Beaumont. Once or twice he had looked into the library and pronounced what she was doing as 'champion', but for most of the previous week he had been in London for something they called the wool sales. She was not even certain whether she had liked him or not, but in the face of such tragedy what did that count?

Although the dusk was falling rapidly outside and the

claustrophobic room felt to be closing in on them, no one had thought to light the lamps. Tom saw to them now and as the light bloomed, there was the sound of an engine, and on to the flags outside the house a motorcar drew up, a rather splendid vehicle from which a bulky figure emerged, goggled, capped and voluminously overcoated. A few moments later the family doctor, Dr Widdop, came in, bringing with him an unmistakable air of reassurance and solidity. Una's face seemed to unfreeze a little and Gideon almost imperceptibly squared his shoulders.

Having been divested of his protective gear in the hall, the doctor looked less bulky, though he was still an impressive and prosperous-looking figure in a good suit, the cloth of which might have been woven in Wainthorpe, but had certainly not been tailored there. His boots had that perfectly fitting, hand-made look, and he wore a gold ring. He had a wise, worldly face.

Nathan Widdop had in fact been born into a wealthy family of Neller valley textile machinery manufacturers, but having no interest in engineering, he had trained as a doctor, set up his practice in Wainthorpe and married the district nurse. When his father died he had sold his share of the business to his two brothers and continued to live among the local inhabitants, working harder, with longer hours, if the truth be told, than most of them. He had never, however, seen the necessity to divest himself of what he regarded as the small comforts of life, and though his native accent had been almost lost somewhere in the hospital corridors and medical schools where he'd received his training, and his clothes and his car were objects of ironic amusement to his patients, he remained a well liked, even loved, family doctor. He often gave untenable advice, but he didn't press for his bills, and it was not unknown for a load of coal to be delivered when children were ill, or a few shillings to be left on the kitchen table for a needy family after one of his visits. Between them, he and his wife had brought into the world most of Wainthorpe's babies, including Gideon and Una.

'I'm so sorry I couldn't get here sooner.' He shook hands with Tom, and with Laura when introduced, giving her a shrewd look, then bent to kiss Una and put an arm around her shoulder. She shrank a little, as she was apt to do from bodily

contact, but allowed his hand to remain. 'My dear, this is a
bad business, a bad business.' He looked tired and uneasy. He
had spent the night before last attending to a woman enduring
a long and difficult labour in one of the poorer houses in the
rabbit warren of narrow streets, yards and alleys at the end of
the town, and then last night he had again been called out at
midnight to the lingering deathbed of an eighteen-year-old lad
suffering from TB. Conscious all the time of the abominable
death of his old friend.

'How could such a thing have happened, Dr Widdop?'
Gideon asked.

The doctor looked from Gideon to his sister, ran his finger
round his collar, where a faint rash showed, and rubbed at a
similar patch on the back of his hand. 'I think we should all
sit down. There is something I have to say, which may . . .
where's your mother, Gideon?'

'Upstairs. She's been very upset since we heard – you know
how she is – but Una's persuaded her to lie down.'

'Then we won't disturb her. I'll go up and see her later.'
They exchanged a long look and a nod. The doctor looked
again around the circle of bewildered faces. 'Do you have any
brandy?'

Gideon waved towards glasses and a decanter on the
sideboard.

'For all of us, then.'

'I don't want any brandy,' Una said, with a shudder.

'You need it, however. Shall we sit?'

They waited uneasily until Gideon, glad of something to
occupy himself with, had poured and dispensed the drinks and
they had all taken their first sip – apart from Una, who drank
hers off as if it were medicine. He then told them in a few
short words that Ainsley had been seen by him in a professional
capacity six months ago, that eventually a brain tumour had
been diagnosed, and he had been told he did not have more
than a possible six months to live.

The silence when he had finished could have been cut with
a knife. 'But he told no one,' Una whispered at last. 'He didn't
seem ill. How could he have kept such a thing to himself?'
The brandy which she'd drunk too quickly had brought two
spots of hectic colour to her pale cheeks and her eyes were
over-bright.

'That was what he wanted. No fuss. And perhaps in the end he found his own way of going.'

With a sharp tap that was almost a bang, Gideon put the glass, which he had scarcely touched, on to the polished table by his chair. He stared at the doctor. 'You are not saying what I think – that he did this thing *deliberately*?'

Widdop said bleakly, 'Gideon, he didn't have much to look forward to. You know your grandfather and I, friends that we were, didn't always see eye to eye, but I have to say that in this he may have had a point.'

'What point? What point could there be in something so – so *crass* as that?' He fell into a furious silence but brought out at last, in a sudden rush of anger, 'Well, if it's true what you say about a brain tumour, it could explain why he's been acting in such a deuced peculiar way lately. But to drown himself . . . No! I don't believe it. I'll never believe it. You know as well as anyone he was one to face up to things. He didn't know the meaning of fear, and he would *never* have taken the coward's way out. I don't think the idea would even have occurred to him.'

'None of us know how we would react to that kind of thing until it happens,' Widdop said with weary experience.

'He was an old man,' Gideon went on as if the doctor hadn't spoken, 'and if he was as ill as you say, might he not have taken a sudden turn for the worse when he was walking along the dam-side, perhaps leaned against the wall for support, lost himself and toppled forward into the water?' He was clutching at straws, but then he stopped. How likely was it that an old man like Ainsley, sick into the bargain, could have managed this acrobatic feat?

Unexpectedly, Una put in her support. 'Throwing himself into that filthy dam? Not Grandpa, not in a month of Sundays.' She exchanged a look with Gideon. 'My brother is right.'

'Of course I am. For one thing, if he'd wanted to do such a thing deliberately, he would have stuffed his pockets with stones or something, to make certain, like that woman did last year, when she threw herself into the canal. I don't care how unlikely it seems, an accident's the only explanation.'

The doctor said quietly, 'It's possible, you know, that he chose to take his life in a moment of aberration, or despair, not allowing himself time to think. However, accident or suicide, we shall have to wait for the autopsy.'

'Autopsy?' Una looked slightly sick.

'A post-mortem. I'm afraid the coroner . . . in such cases . . .' He paused. There seemed to be something else he was reluctant to say. But he remained silent and after a moment he rose stiffly. 'I must see your mother before I go. Stay where you are, I know her room.'

Eight

The Cross Ings offices were squeezed into a corner of the main building and entered through a small lobby, off which opened a further two doors. From behind the larger came the busy clatter of the mill machinery. In the opposite door was a flap marked 'Enquiries'. Rawlinson gave it a smart rat-tat, and after a moment it shot up and the head of a scrubby-haired adolescent lad with a pimply face appeared like a jack-in-the-box. 'Morning. Oh, it's you again!'

'Tell Mr Hirst we want to see him, lad,' said Rawlinson severely. The flap was shut; a minute later it opened again and they were told to come into what was evidently the general office.

In a very small space was a little table with a typewriting machine standing on it and a chair in front, two large cupboards and a shelf on which was ranged a row of books, all of this leaving very little room even for the occupants to move around. At present, the clerks were seated on tall padded stools fitted with backrests at a high, sloping desk that stretched from wall to wall beneath a big window offering a view of a road winding up on the opposite hill towards the moors. It was a pleasantly wooded prospect in which several largish villas could be discerned; it was obviously the best side of the town, where many of the mill masters and other notables presumably lived, with the view of it unimpeded from this vantage point by any mill chimneys. It appealed to Womersley's sardonic sense of humour to think its own view would necessarily overlook the town itself and the grimy Neller valley, though perhaps the satisfaction of knowing it was all theirs made up for this.

In the office, an elderly man seated at one end of the desk was rolling an old-fashioned, round ebony ruler, rather like a piece of broomstick handle, down the columns in a ledger, then ruling them off in red ink, and didn't bother to raise his head. The boy stood in the middle of the room, staring at them. The third occupant, a rotund man with curly black hair, probably in his forties, wearing a navy-blue serge suit, shiny

at the seat and elbows, was busying himself at one of the
cupboards. 'Mr Hirst?' said Womersley, extending a hand before
he saw the man was grasping a hefty ledger marked 'Daybook'
and was unable to respond.

'This is Mr Porteous, the chief clerk,' said Rawlinson
hastily.

Edwin Porteous had a heavy, doughy face, and curranty
eyes. 'Sorry, you'll have to wait for Mr Hirst. He has somebody
with him at the moment.' A heated interchange issuing from
behind the closed door he indicated with a fat white hand
confirmed this. 'Sounds like they'll be done in a minute,
though,' he added as there came the rattle of someone's hand
on the knob.

Placing the book he had extracted from the safe on the
desk, he nimbly eased himself into the seat that was comfortably hollowed out by his ample posterior. 'And you can get
back on your buffet and stop gawping, Arnold,' he said sharply
to the boy. Arnold went back to his own stool in the corner,
picked up his pen, nibbled the end and stared out of the
window. Porteous opened the ledger, and paid them no more
attention. The elderly man went on adding up his columns.
The voices from the next office continued, and Womersley
and Rawlinson waited.

A row such as Porteous claimed he had previously overheard
coming from the room next door would clearly have been
audible; even now, with voices raised but nobody actually
shouting, it was still possible to distinguish an angry word here
and there. Presently the door flew open and from it emerged
a short, middle-aged man, swarthily-complexioned and with
thick, heavy dark eyebrows drawn together. His aggression was
bigger than he was – the very pencils in the top pocket of his
brown smock seemed to bristle. 'Aye, then, we'll have to see
who comes out on it best, won't we?'

'Cool off a bit, afore tha' does owt tha'll regret, that's my
advice,' replied the man who had followed him out. 'Tha's
picked a fair time for all this and right, what with all we have
on just now.'

'I'm sorry about Maister Beaumont, but that's got nowt to
do with it.'

'It has for us. So think on!'

The man left abruptly, banging the outer door behind him,

and Whiteley Hirst said apologetically, dropping the Yorkshire, 'I'm sorry about all that. Come in, will you?'

The bookkeeper and office manager was a very big man; his height matched Rawlinson's, and he could have given Womersley, who was no lightweight, several pounds, but for all that he was soft-looking, with a doleful face and bags under his eyes, giving him the appearance of a sorrowing bloodhound. An old, furrowed scar running deeply across his forehead added to the impression. The handshake he offered was surprisingly firm.

'Who was that?' Womersley asked.

'Apart from being a natural troublemaker, you mean? Name of Quarmby, George Quarmby – warehouse overlooker, a trades union man. Strong Labour supporter. Not to say a right pain in the arse, to be frank. Does all he can to encourage women to join the union, what's more.'

'That's bad,' Rawlinson said.

Womersley shot him a warning glance, but Hirst had not noticed. 'He's a good worker, though, I'll say that for him. Only reason I've seen he's kept on.'

'Office manager' seemed to be a loose term. The way he spoke suggested Hirst enjoyed authority beyond that, one extending over the workers in the mill. 'Just now, he's agitating with these other hotheads from Huddersfield about a concerted strike for more pay all along the valley. Strike? Ainsley would turn in his grave.' He paused. 'Aye, well.' Slightly embarrassed at his inept choice of words, he waved them to a seat.

The bookkeeper's office was just as sparse and utilitarian as the other. There were two desks which, being lower than the long one in the outer office, offered no pleasant distractions by way of a view from outside. Two or three wooden chairs stood by a large table marked with what looked like dye stains. On the table were piled long tufts of wool samples, twists of yarn, a pair of delicate scales and swatches of cloth, an open order book, and – startlingly incongruous in that office – a modern telephone. It was a dark little room, lit by gas. So dark that even at this time of an admittedly overcast day, two mantles were lit on one of the brackets, their yellowish light not contributing to the cheerfulness of the place.

When they were seated, Hirst himself sat down heavily in the swivel chair at his desk. 'Well, who could have thought it, all this? A bad do and no mistake, a right bad do. How can I help you?'

'Tell me about the day Mr Beaumont died,' Womersley said. 'Was he expected in?'

'He was, and it was a surprise to me when I came in at half past seven – I'm always here before the rest of the office staff – and found he wasn't already here.'

Apparently, it had been Ainsley Beaumont's custom all his working life, to walk down Syke Beck Lane from Farr Clough House, taking the short cut halfway down to bring him out by the dam, which he would walk alongside to arrive at the mill well before the engine started. He took care always to be in the vicinity of the mill yard where his workers could see him as they clocked on at half past six. Everybody at Cross Ings must have been aware of this routine, which only varied if he had made other business arrangements for that day. 'Nobody could say he didn't set a good example!' Hirst said. 'When he hadn't turned up by nine o'clock I sent up to Farr Clough to enquire, but they said he'd had his breakfast and left, only a fair bit later than usual. It did make me uneasy, but there'd been a lot of that lately, him acting funny like. And then, they came to tell us they'd found him, in the dam.' For a moment, he looked quite overcome.

Rawlinson said, 'We shall need to look into his papers, his books and stuff, Mr Hirst. Where's his private office?'

'Private office? The only private office at Cross Ings, lad, is over yonder.' He indicated the second desk, at right angles to his own. 'I know when to make myself scarce if there's anything I'm not expected to hear – though there's never been much of that, it's my job to know all that goes on,' he added, his pride obvious. 'To tell the truth, though, it's not a very satisfactory arrangement, place needs modernizing and we're all on top of one another, you don't need me to tell you that. It's served well enough up to now but if we go on expanding as much as young Gideon reckons we should . . . there's talk of pulling down my sister's house next door to build more offices . . . Any road, you'll find the books in that safe, if that's what you want – *and* all in order.'

'Did anybody owe him money?' Womersley asked.

'There's always money owing for pieces that have been bought, till the end of the month, that is.'

'I don't mean that sort of money. Bad debts.'

Whiteley Hirst raised a sardonic smile. 'Nobody that doesn't pay on time gets credit at Cross Ings. I can guarantee his business affairs here were in good nick, it's what I'm here for, and you're welcome to see the books at any time. If it's anything of a private nature, well, that'll be up at Farr Clough, where he lived.'

'Or did he owe anybody else?'

'Not as I know of.' His eyes went from one to the other. 'There's summat you're not saying. He didn't do away with himself, if that's what you're thinking, I can tell you that. Anybody that knew Ainsley would tell you the same.'

Womersley said nothing and Hirst threw him another penetrating look and said bluntly, 'And he didn't tummle into the dam, neither, did he?'

'No, Mr Hirst, it's looking very much as if he might have died as the result of a fight, after which he was thrown into the dam.'

The silence that followed was suddenly overlaid by a deeper silence, the cessation of sound as the machinery in the mill was switched off. Almost simultaneously, the loud hoot of the mill buzzer sounded, accompanied by a dozen more across the town, signalling half past twelve, followed by the scrape and clatter of boots and clogs on the cobbles in the mill yard as the millhands rushed for home like greyhounds out of a trap, panting to leave the muck and toil of the mill behind, if only for a day and a half. Sounds from the outer office suggested the clerks there were packing up, likewise.

There was a knock and Porteous poked his big face round the door. 'I'm off then, now, if there's nothing else?'

Whiteley Hirst blinked and came to life. 'No, that's all right. You get off, Edwin. See you Monday.' Porteous's little black eyes darted from one to the other, then he nodded and left.

'What are you talking about?' Hirst said at last when the outer office door had banged behind him. 'Nobody would have done such a thing as that to Ainsley.' He might as well have said nobody would have dared.

'Well, it seems he was killed by a blow on the back of his head. And no, it's unlikely to have been a fall,' Womersley said, forestalling the comment he saw might be coming. 'It looks like somebody had a grudge against him, a score to settle, something like that. Any trouble of that sort lately?'

It was the first, obvious question and often brought an immediate answer. Murder rarely happened out of the blue, something had to have led up to it and usually friends, family, neighbours or workmates, somebody or other, would be well aware what it was all about, and have a good idea who was likely to have been responsible.

But the manager shook his head.

'Come on, Mr Hirst, you had some words with him yourself a couple of weeks back? You – and young Mr Beaumont . . . that's Mr Gideon, right? Angry words, a right old row in fact.'

'How did you come to know that? No, don't answer. I suppose it must have been all over t'shop in half an hour, it were loud enough.' His speech was becoming broader, slipping into its native accents as he became more agitated. 'Everybody knows we were always fratching, Ainsley and me, but it didn't mean owt, I've worked here ever since I left school and there's not much I don't know about the business, it's just how we were. We never fell out for more than five minutes. I'll admit this was a bit different, though. There was Gideon and young Tom Illingworth – he's my nephew – in it this time . . .' He paused to rub a hand down his face, pulling its lugubrious folds even further down.

'Go on, Mr Hirst.'

'Ainsley had some sort of idea to bring Tom into the business, which were the daftest idea he'd ever had and I told him so to his face. Tom is my sister's lad, he's a qualified engineer and he knows and cares nowt about the wool trade. But Ainsley always had a taking for the lad, helped him with his education and that. Tom just laughed when he heard what Ainsley wanted.'

'And that was all?'

'Not by a long chalk, it weren't. Ainsley told him he were an ungrateful young pup, after all he'd done for him, and that made Tom get his rag out – not easy, but when he does . . . I didn't like it myself. Ainsley had never needed anybody else in the business before . . . and why should he now, especially when he had Gideon coming up? Then the lad himself had to go and chip in, and ask where he came in on all that.'

'And what did Mr Beaumont say to that?'

'He told him right sharp to hold his tongue. That fair set t'cat among t'pigeons, and Gideon shouted some more at his granddad and then stamped out. He can have a rare temper on him an' all, sometimes, he isn't a Beaumont for nowt, but it's soon over, just like it was with his granddad, bearing no ill will. He's a bit impetuous at times, that lad, but he has his head screwed on. He's right, Ainsley should have given him more rope. He forgot he were running this place on his own when he were Gideon's age.' He sighed again. 'Well, choose how, it were all over summat and nowt and if you're thinking one of us held a grudge about it and then took it out on Ainsley, you've another think coming.'

It seemed eerily quiet without the noise of the machinery rumbling in the background. 'What would you say, Mr Hirst, if I told you Mr Beaumont knew he was a dying man?'

'Dying?'

'According to the doctors, he'd been diagnosed some time since with a tumour on his brain that meant he couldn't have lived for much longer, anyway.'

If the information about the way Ainsley Beaumont had died had been a shock, this had shaken Hirst to the core. He was again left speechless, the blood draining from his heavy face. 'A tumour?' he repeated at last. 'Diagnosed? You mean he *knew*?' After a moment, he added, 'Well, that accounts for it, that and a lot more.'

'Accounts for what, Mr Hirst?'

'When we were having that set-to, he shouted at Gideon, "You can do what you like when I'm dead and gone, but till then, I'm still here, think on!" It's what folks say, I know, but I tell you, without the word of a lie, it fair gave me a turn, coming from Ainsley. He was never one to think that road, never mind say it.'

He gazed, upset, at the scratches and stains on the bare surface of the wooden table. 'Killed? Oh God, I don't know what they're going to make of that, up at Farr Clough.'

'Mr Hirst, I'd be obliged if you'd keep all this to yourself for the time being.'

'What? Not tell the family?'

'I suggest you let them remain in happy ignorance for the time being. I'll see them myself tomorrow.' This afternoon he would need to go back to Huddersfield to report to his superintendent. 'It'll come better officially, and there's no point in upsetting them before we have to'

'Well,' Hirst began indecisively. 'I don't know. They'll want to know. She'll—'

'I'm not asking you, Mr Hirst, I'm telling you. Just keep it under your hat for now, right?'

'All right, if that's what you say.'

Nine

Everyone took the tragedy in their different ways. Gideon, preoccupied and withdrawn, spent so much time down at the mill that he was hardly visible, while Una, although fighting off a heavy cold, buried herself in the back room amongst her papers, taking refuge in her work for the Cause, working as if the deadline for the publication of the next issue of *Unity* was something she had to meet under threat of execution. Laura was left much alone in the evenings after her day's work in the dusty library. She was trying to finish as quickly as possible, feeling that her presence in a house of mourning must be intrusive, but meanwhile, was there anything she could do to help? she asked Una. She wasn't sure that she could be of much use, though . . . all the business seemed to be done on the typewriter, which she had no idea how to operate.

'Oh, you'll soon pick it up,' Una said impatiently. 'I have a stack of letters to be sent out about that meeting next week in Halifax and I need the envelopes addressing, so we'd be glad of your help, wouldn't we, Jess?'

Jessie, who often stayed on to help after her day's work was done, said, 'One thing you can do is come down with me instead of Miss Una when I take this petition down into Wainthorpe.'

'Rubbish, Jessie, I'm perfectly well. It's only a chill,' Una said.

'Caught tramping up and down the streets in pouring rain, just to distribute leaflets.'

'We have to let people know about the Halifax meeting.'

'It's a raw, damp day out there. You go standing out in that lot and you'll be asking for it.'

Laura, standing the following day with Jessie outside one of the mill gates at closing time, to get signatures on a petition to be sent to Parliament – votes for women, naturally – reflected wryly that if her friend Eva could see her, she would congratulate herself on being right, having known all along that sooner or later Laura would succumb and be persuaded to strike a blow for women's freedom. She drew her scarf tighter. If she *was* here through new-found convictions, instead of through default, she would have felt less miserable, frozen to death as she was.

At least she had seen something of Wainthorpe and gained a considerably more attractive impression of it than when she first passed through it in the trap with John Willie Sugden. Mills there were, of course, large and small, and at the poorer end of the town, a crooked maze of narrow, grimy streets, yards and alleys. As for the rest of the place, she had noticed some good buildings, plenty of shops, a big elementary school and a small park where the town brass band played in the summer. And always, wherever you were, high on the hillside, looking immensely far away, was Farr Clough, a black silhouette standing out against the dark grey background of the hill behind it.

But she'd had little time for more than a cursory look around, and now dusk was falling and the mill due to close. Laura's task was simply to stand holding the petition clipped to a board, while Jessie stood on a box waving her arms and shouting to exhort the women to sign as they came out of the mill, still in their black pinafores under their shawls.

In the end, they obtained thirty-nine signatures, though Jessie said it was only a drop in the bucket. Laura was surprised to find herself quite exhilarated, though afraid at one point that the situation might turn ugly, as so many encounters did. Some of the mill girls made rude comments and joined the men in jeering at them, but most of them wished them good luck as they lined up to sign, which Jessie judged a marvel in itself, since they were at the end of a gruelling day and many of them must have been anxious to get home in order to make their husband's and children's teas.

They were just packing up – numb about the hands and feet, but flushed with success – and Jessie was inviting Laura to take a cup of tea with her and her father on her walk back up to Farr Clough, when a rattling sort of motorcar that turned out to belong to Dr Widdop's assistant, a young man called Matthew Pike, drew up behind them.

'Glad to see you,' he said, quite evidently having known they were going to be there. 'Hop in.'

Jessie seemed not at all averse to this. Nor was Laura, for

though his motorcar was very far from the last word in luxury, it was a long way up to Farr Clough and a cup of hot tea wouldn't come amiss.

He was quite young, this doctor, spectacled, gingerish, untidy and every bit as energetic as Jessie. He congratulated them on the success of their venture and seemed altogether very anxious to assert his support for women's liberation, though how much of this was due entirely to his beliefs, and how much due to his wanting to impress Jessie, might be open to interpretation, Laura felt.

The shock of losing the master of Farr Clough, the man whose presence had dominated all their lives, had not robbed Amelia of her antagonistic approach. She and Laura met in the hall the next day, where Laura was exchanging a few words with Gideon before he went down to the mill. To all intents and purposes, Amelia seemed to have completely recovered from the hysterics she had fallen into on hearing of the accident at the mill.

'You'll be leaving us now, then, Miss Harcourt,' she stated bluntly, without any attempt at finesse.

'The job isn't finished,' Gideon said before Laura could reply, looking hard at his mother, 'and I hope Laura will agree to stay until it is.'

'Oh, we can forget that. Nobody ever bothered with the library before, and I doubt anybody will want to, now. There's no need for it.'

'On the contrary, it's something that ought to be completed.' This unusual show of authority from her son halted Amelia for a moment, then she simply turned and walked away in her usual stiff and unbending manner. 'Well, will you stay and finish, Laura?' he asked.

If that was what he wished, she was willing to do so. 'I don't want to upset your mother, but I confess I feel I ought to finish what your grandfather wanted.'

'Who knows what he wanted?' He shook his head. 'The truth is, I haven't the faintest idea. All the same, I reckon sorting those books was long overdue. You're doing a splendid job, and maybe we can open up the library again and make proper use of it. Please, I hope you'll stay – and take as long as you like.'

*   *   *

Facing the garden, and the prospect of the valley below, the library could have been one of the most attractive rooms at Farr Clough, though that was far from the impression it had made on Laura when she first entered it. A pair of library steps, a few straight chairs set around a huge central table as if for a meeting, drugget on the floor and not a picture or an ornament in sight. A tightly buttoned grey and brown tabby plush armchair, looking like an uncomfortable afterthought which had just been brought in, stood near the black marble fireplace in which a fire had been lit, large enough to roar halfway up the fireback when it should get going, though the chimney at that moment had thought otherwise, and was protesting by throwing intermittent billows of smoke into the room.

Unlike the rest of the house, where Mrs Beaumont's good housekeeping was so much in evidence, the room had clearly received no attention. It smelled overwhelmingly of musty old books which obviously hadn't been touched for years. They lay on the shelves anyhow, thick with dust, not always in neat rows with their spines facing outwards, but sometimes stacked in tottering piles, or leaning drunkenly against each other.

Someone had provided paper, pens and ink, and a large protective apron had also been left on the table. Setting to work, Laura had soon found some of the books almost too big to lift, as if reluctant to relinquish the same positions they'd occupied for generations, their titles as dry and dusty as the books themselves, and their contents surely of no interest to anyone but the scholars who had written them.

Today, with the fire going nicely, she had decided to forget Amelia Beaumont's animosity and tackle the last wall of shelves. She was a strange woman, almost impossible to imagine her as the twins' mother, physically or otherwise, although she might once have been beautiful, or at least striking in a strong, dark, gipsy-looking way. Perhaps they took after their father. No one ever spoke of Theo. There wasn't a single photograph of him anywhere in the house . . . but then, they didn't seem to go in much for family photographs – there were some of the twins, principally one with their grandfather, and one of a rather beautiful woman in a ball dress with a long train, holding a fan, with feathers in her hair, who must be Lady Tyas, their great-grandmother.

Perched on the very top of the library steps, to the accompaniment of sneezes, she was dusting the space left by *Delineations, Historical and Topographical, of Yorkshire*, asking herself crossly why Mr Beaumont had not simply employed a housemaid to tidy up his old books, when she noticed a roll of paper which had slipped behind the next few books, tied around with a black silk ribbon.

She descended the steps and untied it, and when she had spread it out on the table and weighted it with books to prevent it curling up again, she found the roll comprised several foolscap pages pinned together, closely written on both sides. The handwriting was backward-sloping, as if the writer might have been left-handed, and it was also embellished with confusing twirls and elaborate curlicues to the downward loops, all of which made it extremely difficult to decipher. After a while she found she was able, with concentration, to see that it appeared to be a work of fiction. Intrigued, and nothing loath to be relieved of her dusty job for a while, she settled down before the fire in the armchair – more comfortable than it looked – to read the rest of the story, the handwriting becoming easier to read as she became accustomed to it. It was dated 1887, and entitled: '*A FOOL'S PROGRESS*'.

There is an old superstition that says only a fool would venture out toward the Devilstones on the moors on a Friday, especially on Friday the thirteenth. And never in February, when snow is blowing up. Call me a fool right enough, I should have remembered that. I, Ben Kindersley, had known Castleshaw Moor from the hour I first drew breath, and I knew as well as any man living what a God-forsaken spot it can be in February. But I had just reached nineteen and my blood was hot with anger, and I was past reasoning.

It was but a matter of a basketful of a dozen or so broken eggs, nothing more, that brought things to a climax. Shattered my resolution to stay on the farm until I was twenty-one, by which time I had hoped I should have seen my way clear to be earning a penny for myself and have come to some understanding with my father. But what happened with the eggs altered everything. Big strapping lad that I am, I am sometimes clumsy. Anyhow, I dropped the basket as I passed it into my sister Mary's hands, and the eggs broke, every one of 'em, and spread all over the stone flags on the kitchen floor that the girl, Lottie, had just scoured. At which Father turned puce-purple till I thought he would have an apoplexy.

It wasn't really the eggs, of course, although we hadn't so many we could afford to throw them on the floor, and they'd been intended for use in a custard pie and some other celebration dishes that night for my birthday. We'd had words earlier in the day, Father and I, when he'd caught me reading for a few minutes after our dinner at midday, when he thought I should already have been at work again, and I'd forgotten to curb my tongue, and things had been said between father and son that would have been better left unsaid. Afterwards, he turned away in his usual surly manner and went on with what he was doing, and I turned the other way as well, and went on with what *I* should have been doing, and the matter might have been pushed aside for the time being, as such matters usually were, with things being left unsaid, resentments left unspoken, to simmer and fester, had it not been for what happened later with the eggs. For some reason this simple accident caused me to make another smart retort when Father cursed me for laughing at the mess which the cat, Betty, and the dog, Vixen, were even then making short work of.

'Don't thee back answer me, tha gurt gormless 'a'porth o' nowt!' he shouted, reverting to the broad accents of his youth, which Heloise had tried so hard to eliminate. 'Tek thi 'ook, and don't let me see thee till tha's come to thi senses!'

I should not have taken that as I did. I knew well enough that he merely meant that I should get myself out of his sight for a while, find myself a job in the stables, or mending the drystone walls of the sheepfold that were sore in need of attention, anywhere until he cooled down. There was nowhere else I could have gone, save out on the moor, or into the dark space above the hayloft where you needed a candle to see by. We were a crowded homestead and North Brow, once a handloom weaver's house as well as a farmhouse, was scarce big enough for all of us. Besides myself, my father and my three sisters, there was Lottie, the servant lass, and Ephraim, the cowman. Lottie had a box bed in the kitchen and I, because there was nowhere else in the house, shared that space above the hayloft with Ephraim. I didn't object to this, except for his snores after he'd had a sight too much ale on market days. It was quiet, and warm, and I'd fixed myself up a shelf where I could keep the one or two books I had, and where of a night I wrote by candle the bits and pieces I had such hopes of one day. My father alone had a room to himself, the one he'd shared with my mother when she was alive, and later, with Heloise. What had once been the loom chamber with the long window to give light when my grandfather's father had woven pieces which he carried to Huddersfield Cloth Hall to sell – until the advent of machinery took all the pride and profit out of it – had become the place where my sisters, Prue, and Mary, and Lisbeth slept. Oh, and there was the little corner off the landing with a curtain drawn across it where a bed had been wedged for Lucie Picard. I must not forget Lucie Picard.

She found me in the stable next morning after that row with my father, long before it was light, rubbing our old mare Nellie's nose, with my belongings already in the carpet bag, and of course, being Lucie, she knew at once what I was going to do. I should have been a sight more careful, made less noise, doused the lantern.

'Take me with you, Ben.'

'What?'

'You're running away. I want to run away, too.'

'Don't be daft, Lucie. I'm off to try for a job on *The Manchester Guardian,* and if I can't get one, happen one in Leeds, or even London. What could I be doing with you, there? Besides, I'm walking, and you wouldn't last five minutes on the moor.'

'We could take Nellie.'

'Nay. I can't do that. Nellie stops where she is.'

I won't deny I had thought of it, but that was as far as I'd got. It would break my heart to leave my patient old friend. We'd known one another since I was a nipper, but pinching a few victuals from the pantry to keep body and soul together was a different matter from making off with Nellie. They'd never manage without her. Leaving the old mare would hurt me almost as much as leaving Lucie – but then, I was going to come back one day for Lucie, though she wasn't to know that, since I hadn't told her, for I didn't know when it would be.

'You're a hard one, Ben Kindersley.' That I was not, and well she knew it, and she tried to plead, putting her little hand on my arm, a slip of a thing just gone seventeen years old, with a mane of bright curling hair, looking up at me with those great eyes you could lose yourself in. 'Please.'

Lucie was like that – determined to get what she wanted and sometimes wild with it. Well, she was Heloise's daughter, wasn't she? But with her it was only because she couldn't wait to try out the wonderful things she was sure the world was waiting to offer her, whereas Heloise had been sly and calculating and with no intention of trusting to luck – which was how she'd got hold of my father, after our mother died. She had been a governess at a big house in Saddleworth, living a wretched life at the mercy of their cold Christian charity because she had been taken in, along with her fatherless young daughter, and had to pay for their goodness by swallowing slights and insults, which was against any Frenchwoman's nature. She'd seen her chance and made a beeline for my father, Joe Kindersley, as soon as she'd heard he was a widower. For all she was hard as a flint, she had pretty ways when she wanted to show them. That was how she'd got my father, something he'd come to regret, I know, as we all had – except for the fact that she'd brought Lucie with her. Everybody who knew her loved Lucie, even Prue, to a degree, for she was winning and affectionate. And I? I loved her best of all.

She put her hand again on my arm 'Take me with you, Ben, please. I don't want to stay here, not without you.'

'Nay, Lucie.' I would not, much as I wanted to. Indeed, I could not.

I threw her off, with as much roughness as I could summon. I left her in the barn and set off for the last time past the mistle where the beasts were lowing softly, waiting to be milked, and past Vixen in her kennel who strangely made only a faint whimper, as if she knew what I was up to. Once out on the track, I made fair progress, but I hadn't gone more than a few miles when the snow began, which I much misliked. The moor was no place to be when it snowed. It fell in thick, soft flakes that soon lay on the track like a blanket and settled into the crevices between the black rocks, where if it went on and the wind rose it would soon form itself into drifts that could be up to twice the height of man, as I'd seen many a time. I turned a bend in the track and stopped for a minute for a last look up to the spot where the farm, North Brow, stood gaunt above me now. And there she was, running and struggling and gasping, with naught but her shawl over her head.

I waited till she reached me, then I took her by the shoulders and shook her till her teeth rattled – Lucie, whom I had never once even raised my voice to before! – and she let me, saying not a word. The wind had brought some colour to her pale cheeks, and tendrils of her bright hair escaped from her shawl, and though she kept her head up, she began to shiver. The rage went out of me as suddenly as it had come, and I took from the carpet bag the waistcoat her mother had stitched (hoping to ingratiate herself with me, I had no doubt) and put it on her, then I took off my coat and draped it round her over that. I had on a thick leather jerkin underneath and I was still warm from my walking, and from my anger, and did not feel the cold, not then. But still, I cursed to myself, knowing what I should rightly do, which was to take her back, while knowing that now I had made my bid for freedom, I could not stomach to slink back, like Vixen with her tail between her legs.

However, it was either that, or press on, and try to reach the road to Oldham, and thence to Manchester. There was an inn I knew where we might beg some sort of shelter, even in a barn, until the way was passable. But Lucie was spent, and frozen. She had no pattens on, nor even shoes to her feet proper for that weather, so I picked her up, and threw her over my shoulder.

She was no heavier than any of the sacks of grain and meal I was used to lifting. I could carry a double load, any day, and I'd been familiar with this track ever since I could walk, but what with Lucie, and the carpet bag slung over my other shoulder on Grandpa's stick, and the conditions underfoot, my foot slipped and in trying not to lose hold of her, I fell heavily. Lucie, my bundle and I landed in a sprawl on the hard ground under the snow. I heard it crack, my leg, and when I tried to stand up, I found it would not bear my weight, and the pain was red-hot in my thigh – as well as another sharp pain some-where in the region of my breastbone when I drew breath to ask Lucie if she was all right.

She had sustained no damage, thank God, and was picking herself up even as I asked.

I broke out in a cold sweat and rued what had brought us

into this: my temper, which is slow-burning, but all the hotter for that. Despair threatened to overwhelm me, but it was Lucie then who helped me, giving me her frail shoulder to lean on, as we limped towards what shelter there was by a group of great boulders, Lucie who snuggled up to me to give me her warmth and spread my coat over both of us, Lucie who held me whenever I passed out on another wave of pain, and spoke comfort to me whenever I came round.

It was there, an hour later, lying in the lee of the rocks, with the snow almost covering us like the babes in the wood, that Ainsley Beaumont found us. He lifted us into his covered trap and took us – not in the direction I had hoped to go, which was where he had come from, having been in Oldham on business the night before, where he had stayed – but along the road towards Huddersfield and his own home, here, to Farr Clough House. I was not conscious of the way we were going, then, and not in any condition to dispute it if I had been. Indeed, I was not conscious of anything much for a long time after that.

This was almost certainly not fiction. Ben Kindersley and Lucie Picard were real people, and this was their story. Who were they and where were they now? Why had he written, and hidden, this manuscript? Or perhaps it had not been deliberately hidden, but had simply slipped behind the books and been lost. Laura went on reading, hoping the next pages might tell her more.

I, who have scarcely had an illness in my life, took a fever occasioned by my cracked ribs pressing on the lung, or so said the doctor that Ainsley Beaumont fetched. There were days and nights when I did not know myself or my surroundings and I am still as weak as a kitten. So here we must remain, I suspect, until this cursed hip of mine heals. It was badly broken and Dr Widdop told me gravely that I must be prepared for the possibility that it will always remain a weakness. I, who have thought naught of walking a dozen miles over the rough moor into Huddersfield, and a dozen miles back, may never be able to walk that far again. Such are the consequences of my temper – for me, and for Lucie. She is very much on my conscience. I have not yet bethought myself what to do about her.

Mr Beaumont will not hear of us leaving until I can walk at least in some comfort, though he made a stiff business of quizzing me pretty thoroughly as to how the two of us came to be lying out there in the snow.

'So you thought you could just walk into the offices of *The Manchester Guardian* and present yourself and be taken on, then?' The idea seemed to offer him some grim amusement.

'I did not expect to be taken on as a journalist, sir, but I was prepared to do any sort of job, only I never reached there.'

'And what possessed you to start out in the midwinter – and you a farmer's son? I should have thought you'd know the right side of the weather.'

'I'm not that sort of farmer's son, sir. At least, I know the weather as well as anybody but—'

'All right, all right, I've no doubt you had your reasons. But what about the lass? What are you going to do about her? She can't go with you into the sort of life you have in mind. What thought did you give to her?'

He cocked a wry eyebrow, and I felt myself flush hotly at what he must be thinking, but I couldn't bring myself to tell him the truth, that it was Lucie who had followed me when I left, that she wouldn't be said nay, that she hated the farm more than I did, or so she said. Well. That was hard, because I didn't hate the farm, nor anyone in it, not even my father, if it came to that – just the farming way of life, which I was never cut out for, although all the world seemed to be of the contrary opinion, purely on account of my size and the breadth of my shoulders and the muscles that made short work of all the heavy jobs that come with a farm. Whereas all I could see was my life stretching before me, toiling and moiling to little purpose, when all I wanted to do was write about what that good man Parson Havergill and I talked about in those long hours beside his fire, him teaching me my letters and giving me books to study and newspapers to read. 'You'll get there one day, lad. Just bide your time, bide your time and pray, and the chance will come when the Lord deems you ready for it,' he told me. Which advice makes me downright ashamed now to recall, as if I had abused his trust.

'Well, you can stop here as long as it takes, you and the lass. She seems happy enough here,' Mr Beaumont said, dealing cards. He enjoys a game of cards, especially if he wins, and I like the companionship playing with him brings, though I sorely miss the stimulation of conversing with Mr Havergill. Mr Beaumont is commonsensical and not averse to an argument but he has no leanings towards discussion and debate for its own sake.

'Then I hope it doesn't take long, sir. I don't know how I can ever repay you for what you've done as it is. If it hadn't been for you picking us up, we'd have been dead now, Lucie and me both.'

'And what else should I have done then, left you there to freeze to death? Nay, I'm not that heartless! I couldn't hardly leave you lying in the snow, but I'm not a charity, neither. Happen we can find clerking or summat of that sort for you down at Cross Ings, till you see your way forrard.' As usual, he covered his kindness by brusqueness. 'But frame yourself and get set up as soon as you can, think on? It's not right you being on your own up here all day with these women.'

What did he mean by that? Did he think I had designs on the servants? There wasn't one of them under forty, even the nursemaid who had up to then been looking after young Mrs Beaumont's twins. Surely not Mrs Beaumont herself?

I should not like him to think that of me, but he need have no fear. The idea of me and Amelia Beaumont is laughable. Theo, his son, is welcome to her. She is a loud, coarse woman, with a tendency to veer from one mood to the other, as different from Theo as he is different from his father. The nurse, before she left, was a gossip and told me Theo's mother, Charlotte Tyas, came from the local gentry while she, Amelia, was the daughter of a publican. Theo is a pretty-boy kind of fellow, likeable enough, but he looks down on the mill, where he's forced to earn his livelihood with his father – a painful parallel with my own situation, although since he is of age he could do something about it, if he so wished. But then, he would not be cushioned by his father's money, which is evidently important to him.

Ainsley has only ever had a son, and has been without a wife for many a year, and maybe that is why he is so taken with Lucie. His eyes light up when he speaks of her. 'She must stop here,' he said last week. 'Happen she can make herself useful, looking after the bairns, now that nursery maid of theirs has taken the huff and gone.'

And who could blame Lucie for accepting the offer? Unlike the nursemaid, she takes no offence at Amelia's moods and is very good with the babies, and in return Amelia professes to make a pet of her and has even passed on some of her dresses, which are not suitable and make her look too much older than her years for my liking. But Lucie is happy and that must be all that matters.

All the same, Ainsley Beaumont is deluding himself. Lucie will no more stay here for long than she would have stayed at North Brow. For one thing, to the other folk who live here, even to young Mrs Beaumont, she is as alien a being as her mother was at North Brow. There is no doubt some jealousy among the maids of her beauty, suspicions of her cleverness and the Frenchified ways her mother taught her. But Ainsley Beaumont doesn't see that, or that Lucie is young and her head soon turned.

I should have foreseen what would happen. There is now only one thing for me. Benjamin Kindersley . . .

Laura turned over this, the last page, but the other side was blank. The last two words on the previous page were not meant to be the beginning of a new sentence. The narrative had run right down to the foot of the page and evidently not wishing to leave his signature isolated on the back of the page, he had squashed it in at the end of the line. There *was* nothing more.

Her curiosity had been thoroughly aroused and she was disappointed that the story had ended in that abrupt way, with no satisfactory ending. She hoped she might find more, the rest of it, as she worked, though that was probably unlikely, and maybe just as well – she thought it quite possible she had stumbled across secrets the family would not wish to be made public. Until she decided whether or not to speak of what she'd found, she rolled it up and retied the black silk ribbon, put it back where she had found it and went on with what she was doing.

She had not been at work more than ten minutes when Tom Illingworth arrived.

Ten

'Come out for a walk,' Tom said as he came in. 'I've had business in London for the last week, tiresome business – after which, I need some fresh air to get buildings, traffic and all that out of my head.' He paused. 'I'm afraid, last time I called to make your acquaintance again, I walked into all that sorry business . . . Come on, with all that's happening, you need to get out of this house. A good blow will do you good as well.'

It sounded very much like an order, but the rain of yesterday had ceased, the sky was bright and the idea of some fresh air was appealing. 'All right.'

He set a punishing pace towards the tops, along the ancient stones of a road where once, he told her, Roman legions had marched across the treacherous Pennine passes from Chester to York – the same track, long afterwards, that was used by packhorse trains with their panniers of wool from the scattered outlying sheep farms and weavers' cottages. Up here, there was a bird's eye view of the world, with glimpses of shining silver below that were distant reservoirs. Further still above them, on the high passes, snow still lay. The silence was complete, apart from the occasional bleat of a sheep and the sad cry of a curlew. Once they disturbed a dark shape, flying up out of the heather at their feet, startling them with its hoarse kok-kok-kok, but it was only a moorcock.

The wind carried their words away as they walked and, tired of trying to hold on to her hat, Laura took it off and let the wind blow through her hair as it would. Presently, dropping down a little below the brow, they found a sheltered spot where they could sit for a breather on a rocky outcrop that made a natural seat. They sat in silence, looking out over the wide view beyond, over the flat plains of the red rose county, the old enemy, Lancashire.

After a while, he said, 'This was one of Ainsley's favourite spots.'

'You were fond of him, I think?'

'We all were, perhaps more than we knew. He was good to me as a boy, and he's been like a father to the twins. His only son, Theo, was lost in that fire, you know. They were barely two years old.'

She had not known this, no one mentioned the fire, the cause of that blackened ruin, whose shadow she still tried to avoid seeing when she drew her curtains at night. Perhaps because it was a constant reminder – to Ainsley Beaumont of the loss of his only son, to the twins for a father they were never to know, and most of all, perhaps, for Amelia Beaumont, losing her husband and the father of her babies so tragically. 'That's – awful, dreadful. How did it happen?'

'An accident with a lamp, I'm told.'

'And Theo died? How terrible. Was anyone else hurt?'

'The rest of the family were saved.'

It was not altogether satisfactory as an answer. The fire had happened twenty years ago, about the time the account Ben Kindersley had been writing had stopped. It was on the tip of her tongue to tell Tom about finding those hidden papers and the abrupt way in which the story had ended, to ask him if Ben and the girl, Lucie, had also been victims, but she was not sure she wanted to know that they had perished so horribly.

Before she could make up her mind to ask, he said: 'It's hard to believe he's dead. He took a fancy to me when I was a boy, lent me money to get educated, to "better myself" as he put it – though I don't think becoming an engineer and going off to South Africa was quite what he had in mind! I was a disappointment to him. It seemed he expected a better return from his money.' He laughed shortly, then broke off a wiry stem of grass and twisted it tightly round his finger, staring into the distance. 'The reason I've been up and down to London – one of the reasons – was to see about another position, a railway venture in South America.'

'South America?'

'It's unlikely I shall take the offer. For one thing, they want me to put money into it – the sort I don't have. But neither shall I do what Ainsley wanted of me.'

'Which was?'

'Oh, some bee he had in his bonnet, involvement with the mill.'

'Maybe you were not a disappointment to him, after all, if he thought enough of you to offer that.'

It was some time before he answered. 'More a matter of conscience, I think. My mother and he—' He threw her a quick look. 'She was one of his mill girls, you see, but . . . well, let's just say they go back a long way.'

Laura wondered if she did see. What was he trying to tell her, that he was more to Ainsley than just a young man in whom he had taken an interest? It was hardly a thing she felt one could ask. 'Well, I don't suppose I should care to be offered a job just to appease someone's conscience, either.'

'If my mother didn't resent it – and she didn't – why should I? All the same, I'm sorry we parted in anger over that, as we did.' There was still a slightly bitter edge to his tone, and he fell silent, but after a few moments he sprang suddenly to his feet. 'Oh, forget all that. Dark thoughts for a lovely day. Don't let's waste it.'

Winter up here would be as treacherous as the bleak environment Ben Kindersley had so vividly painted, but today the sky was blue and the hills on the opposite side of the valley even bluer, soft and hazy, and in the pretty copses and cloughs further down the valley where the trees grew, spring could be seen in the greening of the branches; the wind had blown the dust of the library from her mind.

His sombre mood seemed to have been cast off and he smiled as he looked down at her, saying, 'I've told my mother about you and I said we'd drop in for a cup of tea – is that all right?'

That sounded like another fait accompli, but she smiled. 'Yes, I'd love to meet her.' She let him pull her to her feet.

They turned back the way they had come, and then, she couldn't help it, she'd picked up her hampering skirts and was running as fast as she could over the tussocky grass, the wind in her hair, until at last she was out of breath and had to stop and lean, panting, against a large boulder. Tom caught up with her easily, and stood in front of her, leaning in with his hands stretched out, imprisoning her between his arms against the rock. 'My, Miss Harcourt, that was a turn of speed!' His eyes danced.

'Childish of me, but I've wanted to do that,' she panted, 'from the first day here. And now I have a stitch.'

'Breathe deeply and it will soon go.'

He didn't move away, but stood where he was, looking down into her flushed face, still amused.

He was laughing at her and she didn't mind. Laura knew she looked like a gypsy but she didn't care. She held her side, until at last the stitch went, and then she broke away.

Presently, they struck a downward track, beside a trickle of clear brown water singing over pebbles and then joining a beck flowing strongly between a ferny cleft in the rocks before disappearing from sight. The beck lent its name to the track that became Syke Beck Lane, which was the road leading into the town. As dizzy as the drop appeared from the top, it was nothing compared to when you were walking it. Laura, more than once, had need of Tom's hand on her elbow as the unmade road twisted and turned between houses built wherever there was space enough to tuck in a small row of two or three, with little back lanes between. Lower down came one or two small shops, wedged in between the houses: a fish and chip shop, a small front-room establishment selling knitting wool, and next to that, a wooden building that sold newspapers, sweets and tobacco. The name above the door was W. Thwaite. Jessie's father, Tom said. It was a lifeline, set up for him by some fund from his chapel, since he'd been forced to give up work at the mill.

Directly opposite the shop, a snicket in the low walls led to a pathway sloping towards the sprawl of Cross Ings. Its dam gleamed, oily and now sinister. It might be some time before that path was regularly used again, Laura thought with a shiver, and was relieved when Tom, without giving this obvious short cut a glance, kept to the road, which eventually brought them to the main gates of the mill.

'When I first arrived here, I thought this was Farr Clough, where the Beaumonts lived,' she said as they approached the house in the mill yard.

'They did live here, once. It was the family home, right up until Ainsley had married and moved into the Tyas residence.'

It was tucked into a corner, with one wall adjacent to the mill – no Farr Clough, but a good house, with nothing to say against it, except that where once its windows had offered a view across the Neller valley, this was now obscured by the erection of newer buildings as the business had grown.

'Mother, I'd like you to meet Miss Harcourt . . . Laura.'

'It's good to meet you, Laura.' Sarah Illingworth was small and quietly spoken, but for all that there was a strength and calmness about her that immediately reminded Laura of Ruth Paston. 'Though I wish it had been in better circumstances.' A momentary shadow crossed her face. 'Well, never mind that for now, come and sit yourself down.'

Tea was set in the best room, and Mrs Illingworth had been baking. The warm smell of it pervaded the house and the results were spread on the table, plus a tea service patterned with violets, all daintily set out on a hand-embroidered cloth with a crocheted lace edge.

'What must you think of me?' Laura cried suddenly, catching a glimpse of herself in the big mirror attached to the sideboard. 'I couldn't keep my hat on in the wind, Mrs Illingworth.'

She had no comb and had lost most of her hairpins, but Sarah was able to oblige. 'Such bonny hair.' She reached out to touch one of the wayward curls as Laura smoothed and patted and managed to pin it up somehow. She glanced at Tom, and something seemed to pass between them. She had nice hair herself, Tom's mother, thick and wavy, with no grey as yet in its brown.

There were framed studio photographs on the sideboard: on the one side Tom as a small boy, standing to attention, spruced up for the photograph; on the other his father, Henry Illingworth, sitting stiffly self-conscious in a wing collar and bow tie, his hair plastered down and parted in the middle, his moustache turned up and waxed at the ends, while Sarah, in a dark stuff dress and a little velvet hat, was standing with one hand on his shoulder, the other resting in a velvet muff, across which a spray of flowers was pinned.

Sarah noticed her interest. 'My wedding photograph. Tom's father had the same job my little brother Whiteley has now.' She laughed. 'Silly, but that's how I still think of him – we were a big family and there's twenty years and more between us.'

After tea, they sat by the fire in the cast-iron fireplace, a ginger cat snoozing on the soft wool rug. It was peaceful, in spite of the incidental noises from the mill yard, and a low and continuous humming noise, a slight throbbing from behind the wall against which the sideboard stood, causing a tiny vibration of the stand on which a painted ostrich egg reposed, presumably one brought from South Africa by Tom. The sound was, of course, the pulse of machinery from the mill to which the house was attached. Neither Tom nor his mother appeared to think it worthy of mention, obviously too used to it to notice.

'I like your house, Mrs Illingworth.'

'It's not a bad little place, but they'll pull it down, now Ainsley's gone. They want the space.'

'Then you'll have to stop being so stubborn and let me provide you with something better,' Tom said. 'But I think you underestimate Gideon, Mother.'

'It wasn't Gideon that promised I could go on living here as long as I wanted after your father died, it was his granddad!' she reminded him. 'Ainsley Beaumont and I have known each other many years, Laura, that's why he's let me stay on here.' For a moment, there was a faraway look in her eyes.

'And so he should have, when you think of what you did for him!'

'Well, Tom, it didn't turn out so badly, it seems.'

She said no more, and picked up a piece of crochet work. The shadows gathered as they talked, the lamp was lit, and the complicated pattern of the circle she was working grew under her quick fingers, but now and again it seemed to Laura that the look she gave her son was uncertain.

At length, he pushed his chair back. 'I'll walk you back, Laura, but we'd best be off before the light goes. That road's not the easiest in the dark.'

'Mrs Illingworth, thank you so much for the tea. Will you let me come and see you again before I leave?'

'It'll be a pleasure. I'm only sorry you can't stay up here longer.' She hesitated for a moment. 'How are you getting on with Amelia Beaumont?'

Laura made a rueful face. 'I'm afraid she hasn't exactly made me welcome.'

'Aye, well—'

'Mother, I don't think—'.

But Sarah went on quietly, 'Don't take too much notice of her, Laura, she's not a happy woman. She should have married my brother, but Theo Beaumont was a better proposition, I reckon – not that it's ever made any difference to Whiteley. He's been devoted to her for over twenty years. All right, Tom, I'll say no more. It's been grand seeing you, love,' she said, kissing Laura's cheek. 'I never thought—'

'I'll bring her again, Mother,' Tom said. 'That's a promise.'

On the following day, the lamps were already lit by mid-afternoon when Jessie brought a tray of tea into the library, with a request from Mr Gideon that when she had drunk it, would Laura kindly join him and Miss Una in Mr Beaumont's study.

'He's not down at the mill today, then?'

'No. They've been with Mr Broomhead, the solicitor, all day. Tom Illingworth's with them now, as well.'

She set the tray down and left. Laura sipped her tea as the rain rattled on the window. That halcyon day yesterday on the moors looked as though it might have marked the ending of the fine weather. All day, the wind had swept heavy rain in sheets, inhibiting any wish to venture out into that boggy expanse. The view from the window was dismal indeed, obscuring the town. She drank her tea quickly, and then went to the study.

'Thank you, Laura, do sit down. You, too, if you please,' Gideon added to Tom, who had pulled a chair forward for Laura, touched her arm briefly, then moved away, to stand with his hands in his pockets, looking out of the window, seemingly absorbed in the prospect of the bleak landscape.

Gideon introduced their family solicitor, Richard Broomhead, father of Emmie, a balding, middle-aged man with a portly stomach and a rich, fruity voice, which he used as if he had forgotten he wasn't reading the lesson in church.

The twins arranged themselves either side of him behind their grandfather's desk, giving an impression of confrontation. A disagreeable feeling in the room made Laura feel very glad Tom was there. He now sat on the wide sill, his back to the window, and offered her an encouraging nod which gave nothing away.

Gideon came straight to the point. 'We have a copy of Grandpa's will here. It's a new one, made only last week. Mr Broomhead, will you . . . ?'

Broomhead's mouth was a sour, disapproving curve. He

addressed himself to Tom and Laura: this will Mr Beaumont had left superseded the one dated some five years previously, which document had been lodged with Broomhead's firm of solicitors – who, he emphasized even more disapprovingly, had dealt with all the business for every Beaumont, and for Cross Ings Mill, for decades. It was, of course, quite within Mr Beaumont's rights to have appointed another firm to draw up this new will. 'Though I have no idea why he should have gone to such lengths,' he added shortly, with more than a hint of umbrage in his tone.

'Didn't want all Wainthorpe to know what he was up to,' remarked Gideon carelessly.

A short, icy silence followed. 'That was uncalled for, Gideon.'

'Oh Lord, I'm sorry – I didn't mean—' Gideon could have bitten his tongue out. In a few thoughtless words, he had just maligned the professional integrity of the man who had acted for Beaumont's for as long as he could remember. He wouldn't easily be forgiven for it, though in actual fact it was a well known fact that little remained secret for long in Wainthorpe, even professional secrets. It would have been better not said, though. To cap all, the man was pretty Emmie's father. 'Please forgive me, Mr Broomhead,' was really all there was to say.

The solicitor inclined his head and after a while went on, stiff-faced.

'There is no need for me to read it out, verbatim. Suffice it to say that equal shares in his business and what is left of his private fortune after certain bequests, are to go to his grandchildren – Una and Gideon that is. There is an annuity to their mother. Also a legacy to his bookkeeper, Whiteley Hirst, and a sum of money to Sarah Illingworth, plus the house she now lives in.' Tom folded his arms.

'And,' he then read out, holding up his hand in expectation of interruptions and turning to where Tom sat, '"the same sum of money I lent him, disregarding the fact that he has now repaid it, I leave to her son, Thomas Henry Illingworth".'

Tom laughed shortly, seemingly not very surprised. 'Which I shall not take.'

'That's up to you of course, Tom,' Gideon said quickly, 'though I don't know if you can refuse it.'

'Of course I can, and I will. I cannot speak for my mother.' They looked at one another, Tom adamant, Gideon troubled.

'Take it, Tom, he would have wanted you to have it.'

Again, Gideon had said the wrong thing. 'What has what *he* wanted got to do with it?' Tom asked, suddenly cold. 'And why leave money to my mother? Did he think he had need to make up for what he did? I tell you, she has reason to be *thankful* for that. She married my father, and a better man there never was. She has never repined over what might have been. Anything else she did for him—' He stopped and took a deep breath. 'I'm sorry, forgive the display of temper. I had better go before I say more.'

'We haven't finished yet,' Una said. 'Go on, Mr Broomhead, please.'

'"And to Laura Harcourt, of London,"' Broomhead read, '"fifteen thousand pounds."'

Laura felt herself turning rigid with shock in the silence that followed. 'Is . . . this some sort of practical joke?'

'Wills are not subjects of practical jokes, Miss Harcourt. This one was drawn up by some London lawyer who,' the solicitor added with some distaste, 'has apparently advised him before.'

'London? What is the name of this firm?' Laura asked tightly. She was trembling – and not only with the shock of what she had just heard. Her cheeks flamed.

'They are no doubt a perfectly respectable firm—' began Broomhead, backtracking a little.

'*What* firm?' Laura insisted, getting to her feet.

'One by the name of Carfax, Arroway and Carfax.'

'I might have known! But why? Does he not say *why* he has left me this money?'

'We thought you might know,' Una said coolly. Laura's cheeks burned even deeper.

'He did not say,' replied Broomhead. 'Perhaps these other solicitors have been told.'

'Thank you. If you will all excuse me, then,' Laura said in a choked voice, and all but ran out of the room and into the hall.

She had scarcely put a foot on the first stair, when the study door crashed open, and then shut, and Tom was there behind her, his hand on her arm. 'Stop, Laura. Listen to me. I think I know, I can guess—'

'I'm sure you can! No, Tom.' She put her hands to her ears as he tried to speak again. 'Please.'

'You must not let this upset you.'

'I am not upset. I am furious.'

'I can see that,' he said, his mouth twitching despite himself. Her colour was still high, her eyes sparkling with rage. The pins were coming loose in her slippery hair and a rebellious lock had slipped over one ear. 'But who with? Not me, I hope?'

'With everyone. I have been made a fool of for too long.'

The amusement left his face. 'I would never make a fool of you, Laura. Just please listen to me and let's talk it over calmly.'

She was too stirred up to think of being calm. All she wanted, for the moment, was to be alone. She shook him off and ran up the stairs, her footsteps loud on the bare treads. This time he did not attempt to detain her.

'I'm afraid,' said Mr Samuel Tewson, chief clerk at Carfax, Arroway and Carfax, 'that Mr Philip has already left, Miss Harcourt. He's taking an early lunch, then I believe he meant to go on to the Saturday exhibition at the Academy. Mr William is still here, however, fully recovered now, I am happy to say. If you would like to see him, instead?'

'No, thank you Mr Tewson, it's Mr Philip I want to see. Do you know where he's lunching? And is he alone?'

Having made this precipitate journey to London, Laura was not to be put off. Saying nothing to anyone, simply leaving a note, she had, early this morning, walked down Syke Beck Lane, taken the electric tram to Huddersfield and caught the first available train, sustained by the fury she had felt ever since she had heard of the astounding bequest to her. Making her way independently down here, she had felt more truly alive than she had since first going to Wainthorpe, propelled by her own actions, rather than submitting meekly to the unexplained whim of someone else.

'Yes, he is lunching alone,' Tewson replied cautiously. He

liked Miss Harcourt. She had often come along here to the office with Mr Philip and Miss Eva, when they were all children. A pretty child, and what a handsome young lady she'd turned out to be! But very forceful, very determined, like all of them, nowadays, it seemed. Looking at her sparkling eyes and flushed cheeks, he had a plunging feeling of trouble ahead. Not only for Mr Philip, but without a doubt for Samuel Tewson as well.

For weeks now, he hadn't slept well, not slept well at all. Besieged by doubts and covered in shame. Feeling that not only had he let his employer down, he had let himself down, too. He couldn't think what had come over him, that day when the letter had arrived, during that time when Mr William had been unfortunately absent, struck down by the gout and temporarily residing in Bath. A letter from Mr Ainsley Beaumont, it had been, a client whose business with them was limited – although, such as it was, it reimbursed them handsomely, it had to be admitted. And now he, Tewson, was about to compound his guilt by leading Miss Harcourt, a young lady who clearly wasn't going to take no for an answer, to Mr Philip.

On that day during his father's absence, that day which had lodged so particularly in Mr Tewson's mind, Philip had read the letter with its extraordinary request which had come from Ainsley Beaumont. He had previously met this gentleman, shaken hands with him, but any dealings with him had been his father's province, as was the correspondence between them; their meetings, always arranged for when the old man came to London to deal with wool business, had been conducted in private with Mr Carfax senior. But Philip, in his father's absence, was responsible for the firm's business and must therefore deal with this request.

The letter was straightforward enough, requesting that a certain proposition be put before Miss Laura Harcourt. The writer, Mr Beaumont, was quite specific as to her name, but as he had not deemed it necessary give any more particulars, it was obvious that there were certain matters regarding Miss Harcourt to which Mr Carfax senior was privy. In the normal course of events, Philip would have waited until he could refer the matter to his father, but this was not something he was prepared to do after that name had jumped out from the page at him. *Laura?* Why Laura? What had Mr Ainsley Beaumont to do with her? And why the secrecy regarding the terms of her employment?

Clearly, he needed to inform himself about the background, beginning with all the correspondence between Mr Beaumont and the firm, which was kept in a small bank of drawers lodged in the outer office.

'Do you have the keys for these drawers, Mr Tewson?'

'I do, Mr Philip.'

'Pass them over, will you?'

'Those drawers, Mr Philip, are private to your father. He never allows anyone to open them but himself.' As you well know, his severe look said.

'Dash it, don't be obtuse. How can I carry on the business without access to all the proper information? Give me the keys, there's a good chap.'

The old clerk began to look agitated. 'I'm sorry, you know, but I can't. It would be as much as my job's worth.'

Philip tried to stare him out. 'Are you refusing, Tewsey?'

'Yes, Mr Philip. Not without your father's say-so.'

Tewson had been with the firm since before Philip was born. He kept humbugs in his pocket for the children when they came to see their father. He wasn't far from the age when he would retire, and he was obviously ill-at-ease with this conversation, but he remained adamant. He knew the business inside out, his loyalty was paramount, and as far as Philip knew he had never breached a confidence or done a single untoward thing in his hitherto unblemished career with the firm. On the other hand, when he had opened the post that morning, as he customarily did, he must have seen the letter which had come from Ainsley Beaumont, and so must be well aware what Philip wanted.

'No, I'm sorry,' he said, adamant.

Philip cogitated. He had no doubt Tewson was as familiar with the background to all this as his father was. Drafting letters, wills, agreements, conveyances and all the rest in his fine copperplate handwriting, he necessarily knew everything that went on in the office. Philip doubted he would tell him what he wanted to know. The old codger was stubborn as the devil when he wanted to be, but Philip liked him and had no wish to antagonize him, or to force him to do something against his own will and the orders of William Carfax. He could not blame Tewson. His father was a martinet, as Philip had good reason to know and be wary of.

'Very well, then, I must wait until I get my father's permission.' He was by no means certain of the outcome in his parent's present irascible state of health and temper, which gout was apt to inflict on a person, but for the moment he could not think of anything else he could do.

'Thank you, Mr Philip.'

The morning routine wore on. An hour or so later, Tewson, famous in the firm for never forgetting the slightest thing, came into the office to make certain, he said, that he had got right something he had clearly understood perfectly well barely an hour ago. 'You see, I'm having to be very careful, nowadays,' he admitted, looking exceedingly uncomfortable at having to make this unexpected and rather shamefaced admission. 'My memory isn't what it was, I'm afraid. Dear me, I worry sometimes that I might even find myself forgetting to lock up properly.'

'Well, it comes to us all, I suppose.'

'Indeed, Mr Philip.'

When lunchtime arrived, the clerk announced with equal unexpectedness that he would go into the park to eat the sandwiches Mrs Tewson had packed for him, and which he usually ate at his desk. 'Such a beautiful day. A pity to waste it indoors.'

Philip waited until five minutes after he and the other clerks had gone, then tried the drawers. The top one, the lock of which controlled the others, opened straight away. He grinned. Good old Tewsey! Nevertheless, it was the guiltiest moment in Philip's otherwise blameless life as he extracted the papers he wanted.

When Tewson came back he was sitting with his feet up on his father's desk, reading the newspaper. But his thoughtful expression wasn't due to the fluctuations of the stock market, or the sensational report of a more than usually alarming eruption of Mount Etna and a warning that further possible eruptions could result in a disaster on the scale of Pompeii; or even the sensational report of passengers being flown across the Channel to Paris in under four hours. He was endeavouring to accommodate the staggering implications of what he had read in that correspondence, and running over in his mind the consequences of doing what Mr Ainsley Beaumont had suggested.

Well, he had done what his conscience told him to do, his father was now back in harness, his temper and gout temporarily assuaged by the curative waters of Bath, and it did not seem to have occurred to him yet to ask why Philip, without needing any more explanations, had so easily agreed to Mr Beaumont's odd request to put that proposition before Laura. Then, last week, Mr Beaumont himself had come into the office and Philip had been requested to add his signature to a new will he had made. Followed by the shock of that telephone message, yesterday, telling them that the old man was dead. Had the old boy had some inkling of his impending death? Had Laura's arrival at Farr Clough House anything to do with it?

This, he thought, was what came of dissembling, even if only a little, of not revealing to Laura that Mr Beaumont had specifically asked for her, but letting her believe the request for someone to deal with his library had been a general one. Philip was left with an uneasy feeling at the pit of his stomach.

He had just rounded off his lunch with a generous portion of the jam roly-poly and custard that was a speciality of the little chop-house where he liked to eat, and wondering if he ought to have given in to the soporific temptation in view of his proposed dutiful visit to the Academy, when he looked up and saw Laura herself threading her way between the crowded tables towards him. At the sight of her face, her colour high and her sharp little chin raised, his heart felt as heavy as his stomach.

He stood up and kissed her cheek. 'Laura! This is an unexpected pleasure! What are you doing here? How did you find me?'

'It seems your plans for the afternoon were well known in the office.'

'Ah, yes. Yes, of course, I did mention them to Tewson. My, you're looking well,' he added nervously. 'Yorkshire must suit you. I've just finished my lunch, but may I offer you some – or some coffee – while you tell me all about it?'

'Never mind Yorkshire, Philip. Or rather, we must mind it – that's what we have to talk about, don't we? I don't want any coffee, thanks, so let's go somewhere else, where you can tell me just what is going on. Somewhere private.'

Eleven

It had turned very warm for the time of year and the heat rose from the pavements in the stuffy London streets. All over the city, the parks were blossoming, and on the Embankment the planes with their silvery flaking bark were thrusting out new green leaves. Everyone was rushing and hurrying along as usual, as if they had a train to catch, even though it was Saturday, but there were smiles on people's faces, somewhere an organ grinder played and the flower sellers were doing a brisk trade in bunches of tulips and mimosa.

Laura felt hot and bothered in the saxe-blue tweed travelling costume, and the brown velour-felt hat was anathema to her amongst all the frothy spring hats other women were wearing. Despite this, she was fully attuned to what she had to do. Philip was destined for an acutely uncomfortable half-hour, if she had anything to do with it.

'Now, Philip,' she began in a very severe voice, as they reached an empty seat on the Embankment. 'Why didn't you tell me?'

Philip sat down beside her and looked across the river. A Thames steamer hooted, trams clanged behind them, a sandwich-board man advertised boots for four shillings a pair. 'What do you want to know, Laura?'

'Oh,' said Laura, with a sigh, 'I just want to know the truth, Philip. Why has Mr Beaumont left me that enormous amount of money?'

She did not ask him why Ainsley Beaumont had sent for her. That was now quite obvious to her: the work on the library had been a smokescreen, a ridiculous reason for getting her to Wainthorpe and Farr Clough, where no doubt he could look her over and decide whether she was worthy of his bequest. '*You'll do, Laura Harcourt,*' he had said. You'll do. Not to fulfil the non-existent need to catalogue his library, but to be the recipient of his . . . his *charity*! That was the word which had burned in her brain ever since she had heard the solicitor, Broomhead, read out the will. The word choked her. Charity.

But *why*? Yet she knew where her thoughts were inevitably leading, perhaps towards the answers to questions which had plagued her all her life, though she suspected the truth might not be as palatable as she might have wished.

Philip was staring down at his gleaming polished boots, looking mightily as if he wished himself elsewhere. Ever since he had dealt with Ainsley Beaumont's request, he had been only too aware that he might well have overstepped the boundaries of his temporary responsibilities and it had given him uncomfortable moments. But whenever he thought of *why* he had done it, he had felt better – until yesterday, when it became very evident that he might have made a grave mistake. He was not, however, about to make another. He remained silent until he could find the diplomatic answer to her question. But the truth, not diplomacy, was what she wanted. And who was he to know what that was?

'Laura, I am not the person to tell you.'

'Then who is – your father?' He shook his head. 'Oh, really, Philip, someone must know!'

He looked very downcast at the accusing way she was speaking to him, and she began to feel a little guilty, and was glad as she watched him to see a firmer resolution come to him, more like the old Philip. She was sorry that she had hurt his feelings – he had, as usual, meant well.

'I wouldn't have upset you for the world, you know – you, of all people, Laura.'

She leaned over and kissed his cheek gently. 'Forget me, Philip. I've told you before, we can never be anything to one another. I mean it.'

'You've met someone else,' he said flatly, sensing a difference in her.

She couldn't answer that. Instead, she said, 'Well, Philip? What's it all about?'

'Look.' He felt desperate. 'I'll tell you all I know, but I warn you, it isn't much.' He reached out for her hand, more to reassure himself than her, and she didn't draw it away. It was white again now, the oval nails smooth and rounded with delicate half-moons. 'There's no compulsion on anyone,' he began, 'to give the reasons for why and where they want to leave their money. So . . .'

* * *

Laura's unexpected arrival home a couple of hours later caused a great stir of excitement in Chetwyn Square. It was five o'clock and Lillian arrived five minutes after Laura, pulling off her light chiffon scarf and wafting waves of Floris 'Bouquet'. Screaming with delight when she saw Laura, she embraced her with joy and stood back to examine her, with a look on her face that fought not to say 'I told you so', which was quickly replaced by one of dismay when she learned that this was to be only a flying visit.

'Are you going out this evening?' Laura asked, though the question was rhetorical. Lillian considered an evening at home as the mark of social failure.

'Well, the Endicott's have reserved theatre seats . . . but my dear, it's *Julius Caesar*! I must confess I will not be entirely sorry of an excuse to miss that.'

'I wouldn't ask, but I have something very particular I want to talk to you and Uncle George about, and I'm going back to Wainthorpe by an early train tomorrow.'

'Tomorrow! Then we certainly cannot forego this evening with you. I'll see what Mrs Denning can do for us in the way of something nice. I know there's a chicken . . .'

'Oh, pot luck will do.'

'It won't do for me, or your uncle. I'll see about it now.'

It was good to see him again, her Uncle George, a spare, careful man, deceptively unassuming, and the rock of her childhood. She was grateful that neither he nor her aunt seemed to notice her reticence amidst Lillian's ceaseless chatter about mutual friends and acquaintances, accounts of the social whirl she lived in, which kept the conversation going throughout dinner, during which she fended off difficult questions about the Beaumont family and her work in the library, and concentrated on telling them about the wonderful scenery of the moors, the air like wine, the water like silk . . .

George, too, talked about his two latest acquisitions and invited her comments on them: a spare Japanese print he had hung above the copper-tiled fireplace, and the delicate Satsuma porcelain jar with fu-dog handles which now stood on the mantel. But it was not until they were settled in the drawing room with their coffee that he said directly, 'Now then, what's all this, Laura? What's gone wrong, that makes you come back so unexpectedly?'

It had not occurred to Laura that the flow of conversation might have been covering worry on their part, until she saw the concern with which they were now both regarding her.

'Mr Beaumont is dead. He wasn't a young man, but he had been told he had a brain tumour and it seems he might have taken his own life, though his grandchildren refuse to believe it was anything other than an accident.'

'Oh dear,' Lillian said, inadequately, adding hurriedly, 'How shocking! I'm very sorry indeed to hear it. Frightfully difficult for the family, of course, but will you have any need to go back, now?' Despite herself, she was flushed with pleasure at the possibility and smiled at Laura who was sitting stiffly in her chair.

'I haven't finished the work I went up there to do, yet.' Laura bent to put her coffee cup, the thinnest of Japanese eggshell china which you could see right through, carefully on to the low table next to her chair. 'He has left me fifteen thousand pounds.'

This time there was a stunned silence.

'Fif– Fifteen thousand pounds! But why?'

'You might well ask, Aunt.' Laura had not meant to show resentment so plainly, but she had been controlling herself too long and now it welled up inside her. She transferred her gaze from Lillian to George. 'I think you should have told me long before this what my connections with Mr Beaumont were.'

'Oh, but—' Lillian began, hands fluttering, patting her hair, smoothing her corded silk skirt, thoughts chasing themselves across her face.

George hushed her with a touch on her arm. 'Laura, my dear, we knew of no connection.'

'Well then, of the circumstances of my adoption.' It sounded too formal and hard, but she could not help it. Then the questions came tumbling out. 'Why was I never legally adopted, why did I not take your name? Who were my parents? Who were Mr and Mrs Harcourt?'

George looked as though he might be more comfortable with a desk between them, explaining as if to one of his clients some complicated part of their money affairs. He went to stand with his back to the fire, a hand under his coat tails, looking unusually troubled. 'You want the truth?' he asked gravely. 'The truth, my dear Laura, is that we don't know. You should ask Philip's father, you should ask William Carfax. It was he who arranged that you should come to us, and the conditions.'

'Philip has already told me that.'

George raised his brows. 'And what else has Philip told you?'

'Only that his father, on the instructions of Ainsley Beaumont, negotiated the adoption of an eighteen-month-old child, and that he was instructed to do no more than to arrange for someone to take her in.'

Lillian made a little sound of distress. 'Take you in? Oh, Laura, how can you say that? We so wanted a child, and you were like a gift from God. We didn't *take you in* like a bundle of washing! We loved you from the start.'

'I know that. Of course I know! How could I ever have doubted it? But why did you not tell me?' It was this which hurt her more than she could say . . . that other people had known, while she, the one it concerned most, had been kept in the dark.

George said, 'Dear child, that was the agreement. That we should not seek to adopt you legally, that we should not make enquiries as to who your parents were. Would you have been any happier had you known this? William Carfax once let slip to me that your parents were from Yorkshire, but more than that he would not say. I have always believed he did not know more, in any case.'

'That is what Philip believes. But what about me – am I then never to know, either?'

'Is it so important?' Lillian said in a low voice. She was having difficulty in fending off tears and George went to sit on the sofa beside her.

'It is important to me,' Laura said, 'of course it is. Who were they, the man and woman in the photograph? The ones you let me believe were my parents?'

Lillian's face crumpled. She bent her head. The soft lamplight struck gleams from her bracelets, the silver in her hair. 'That was my idea, but it doesn't signify . . . they were just people I used to know, and they *were* killed in that train crash. Their name *was* Harcourt. I thought it better . . .'

'How *could* you?'

There seemed nothing more to say, and in the end Laura

crossed the room and knelt on the carpet in front of them, taking hold of her aunt's trembling hands. 'I'm sorry, I'm so awfully *sorry*, but don't you see how much it means to me to know who I am?' It was she who was on the verge of tears now, she who had determined to remain unemotional throughout.

'You are our daughter, that's who you are,' Lillian said, with a barely suppressed sob. 'Or so we have always regarded you.'

'And I have never wanted anything more. Except to know who I am, where I've sprung from.' She could see their hurt, that they felt it a betrayal she might want to be something other than their beloved daughter, when it wasn't like that at all. 'You have to understand that I desperately need to know just what Ainsley Beaumont has to do with me. He must always have known about me, but he left me alone all my life and only sent for me, knowing he had not long to live, wanting to see what sort of person I was, before he left me any money. Why?'

'Oh, money!' Lillian said, recovering. 'So easy to give. Is it meant to make up for neglecting you all these years? Well, you don't need it.'

'No, but I shall take it, all the same. And use it. I know exactly what to do with it.' She watched her aunt warily.

George took a cigarette from a box. Lillian closed her eyes. 'Oh, I might have known! That house in Stepney I suppose.'

The reaction was what Laura had expected, but her hackles rose. 'Please don't try to persuade me otherwise. I've made the decision and I don't change my mind once it's made up, or not very often.'

'Well, Laura, I haven't lived with you for nigh on twenty years without learning that!'

'I'm a disappointment to you. I see I should not have opinions of my own.'

George paused in the act of lighting his cigarette. 'Now then, you two. If that is how it stands, and Laura's mind is made up . . . Lillian, my dear, it wouldn't be our Laura if she contemplated doing anything else with it, would it? Why don't we take a glass of something to celebrate the Settlement's good fortune?'

For a moment neither his wife nor Laura said anything. Lillian sat twisting the little lace handkerchief that was now no more than a damp scrap.

'Oh, George! Oh, Laura!' she said at last. She rose and tear-fully kissed Laura, and then laughed shakily. 'What am I to do with you both?'

The tension in the room eased. George held up the brandy. 'But – see here, Laura – you must not, I repeat *not*, worry yourself over this situation, do you hear? Leave it with me. I'll see Carfax and get the truth of it, if there is any truth to be known.'

Laura shook her head. 'No, you just told me you've always believed he didn't know any more than he told you, and from what Philip has said, that seems likely. I don't think there's anything more to be found there. I've gained nothing by rushing down here. The answer to all this lies in Yorkshire, with the Beaumonts.'

With the Beaumonts, and in their past, she thought. Somehow, who I am, who my parents really were, is all tied up with that past.

In Wainthorpe, Whiteley Hirst tossed in his bed, bathed in the sweat of a nightmare, consumed by terror. He could smell smoke and hear fire crackling on the other side of his bedroom door. It was shut tight but any moment now the flames would burst through and he would be trapped. Nothing could with-stand the inferno that was behind it. He tried to move but his bonds became tighter; he was tied to the bed with an invisible criss-cross of threads, a helpless Gulliver. He made an almighty effort but his limbs refused to obey him. He had to get to the window and smash it, jump out. Too late, the flames were here, roaring in like dragons and tigers, the flames of Hell and retribution. He would burn in Hell. His body was already on fire, his blood boiling . . . he shouted for water, for someone for God's sake to throw him into the dam and quench the flames . . .

He woke, and for several minutes lay as motionless as if he *had* been tied down, totally unable to move. He felt weaker than a kitten. His nightshirt was as soaked as if someone *had* tried to douse his burning body. He hadn't had this dream for years.

Twelve

Breakfast in the Imrie house was a silent affair the next morning. George immersed himself in his Sunday newspaper, Lillian played with a piece of toast and Laura ate a boiled egg without being aware of what she ate. The restless, uneasy night she'd spent, tossing and turning, tormented by thoughts she had not allowed to surface before had left her with a dull headache.

'More coffee, Laura?'

'No, thank you, Aunt.'

The doorbell rang. A minute later the starched parlourmaid entered. 'There's a Mr Illingworth to see you, Miss Laura.'

Tom? Laura scraped back her chair and jumped up, almost spilling her coffee. Tom Illingworth, here? She looked round for escape. There was none. Her aunt and uncle were eyeing her strangely. 'Well then, I suppose you'd better show him in, Nancy.'

Lillian, caught *en dishabille*, was in a panic. 'Who is this?' she hissed. 'Not in here, Laura!'

'Oh, he won't mind.' He was already halfway through the doorway, looking uncharacteristically spruce and correct in a dark suit and a stiff collared shirt. 'What are you doing here?' she asked, catching her breath.

'I should have been with you yesterday. I should never have let you come alone.'

'Hadn't you noticed,' she said tartly, 'that I managed to get myself here without assistance? No doubt I can get back to Wainthorpe, too, in the same way.'

'Laura!'

She threw her aunt an imploring glance. She had not intended to be rude, but dared not show more warmth. Not after the thoughts that had come to her during the night. And besides, she did feel annoyed with him, justifiably so, for following her here as if she were not capable of taking a train from Yorkshire to London without male protection. He must have been up since the crack of dawn, to catch the first train – though perhaps he had stayed overnight, she corrected herself, catching sight of the small overnight bag he carried.

'Oh, then you *are* going back?' he was saying.

'Of course I am. Today, as a matter of fact.'

'Good. Then we can return together.'

They eyed each other warily.

'Well.' Lillian's escape route was blocked by the pair of them in the doorway. There was an awkward silence. 'Will you take some breakfast, Mr . . . ?' she asked, pointedly frowning at Laura.

'Thank you, I've had breakfast,' Tom answered, smiling at her. 'But the coffee smells exceedingly good.'

'I'm sorry. I'm so sorry, Aunt Lillian, Uncle George, Mr Illingworth.' Laura made hurried introductions to her aunt and uncle, explaining briefly who Tom was.

Lillian poured coffee, murmured an excuse and fled to make her toilette, leaving George and Laura to entertain this unexpected visitor, returning half an hour later to find her husband and Tom getting along famously and Laura not appearing to be contributing much to the conversation.

George, being committed to meeting friends for his usual Sunday morning ride in the Park, had to leave. He shook hands warmly with Tom, hoped they would meet again, and Laura followed him to the door to say goodbye. 'Come back home to us soon, my dear, but promise me you won't do anything precipitate,' he said, looking gravely down into her troubled face.

'Do I ever?' she answered, attempting a joke, and he smiled a little.

'All the same, I feel obliged to put it to you, Laura. You are impulsive and don't always consider the results of your actions too carefully.' He hesitated. 'This young man. He appears to be someone you can trust.'

It was not a question of trust, but something else entirely which was troubling her, but not even to her uncle could she say what this was.

When she went back into the dining room, Tom was saying that he and Laura must be leaving shortly too, if they were to catch one of the limited service trains which ran on Sunday.

'Why don't you stay for a day or two, Mr Illingworth? Laura could show you the London sights,' Lillian suggested with a brilliant smile, as if Tom were a backwoodsman who had never set a foot further than his own front door.

'I'm sure Mr Illingworth is anxious to get back to Wainthorpe,' Laura said coolly. 'Are you not, Mr Illingworth?'

Lillian looked from one to the other and gave a little sigh. Who was he really, this young man? He was pleasant and had excellent manners, he looked prosperous – his shirt and tie were impeccable – but what did he mean to Laura?

Sunday morning in Wainthorpe was cold, though sunny. Since the mills were shut down, for once the wind had had the chance to blow away the seemingly permanent cloud of sullen smoke and smuts the Neller valley normally crouched under. It was the morning for a brisk walk, for tackling the steep incline up towards Farr Clough House, Womersley decided, mindful of his wife Kate's hopeful suggestion, after she had twice had to let out the waistband of his trousers, that he should perhaps take more exercise. 'First, we need to make a call on Dr Pike.' He'd been altogether too darned close-mouthed, Womersley explained, merely hinting at those enemies he seemed to think Ainsley Beaumont had. 'It's occurred to me since yesterday that he might be less reluctant now he's had time to think about it.'

'Didn't strike me as that sort. To change his mind easily, I mean.'

'We can but try.'

The town was oddly quiet without the ever-present throb of machinery, the familiar grind of iron-rimmed cartwheels and the clatter of clogs on setts. Best boots and suits were the order of the day, for those who possessed them, Sunday clothes and Sunday school for the children. The streets had been cleared of Saturday night revelry, and the market place of the rubbish left behind yesterday, with only the hint of camphor from the stalls' naphtha lamps lingering. Along Briggate, the strains of a rousing Methodist hymn issued from the chapel on the corner, and from the Temperance Hall came the mellow notes of the Wainthorpe brass band, practising for its first open air concert of the season in the park.

Matthew Pike lived-in with Dr Widdop as his assistant, and Widdop's house was situated on that side of the valley which faced Cross Ings Mill. A gleaming, dark red motor car stood outside the front door, and a notice directed patients to the surgery round the side of the house. Womersley ignored this and rang the brightly polished brass front door bell. A woman in a crossover pinafore, with iron-grey hair pulled back into a bun, answered the door. This must be the redoubtable house-keeper Sergeant Binns had warned them about. 'Don't take any old buck from Ada Crawshaw,' he'd advised. 'She's an old maid, with a face like a wet weekend, but her bark's worse than her bite. She's looked after Dr Widdop champion since his wife died two year back.'

She seemed to take great pleasure in informing them Dr Pike was not available, that he'd been called out. After which, she made to close the door.

Anticipating this, Womersley already had a hand out to hold it open. 'Dr Widdop, then?'

'Don't you know what day it is? Only day he's allowed a few hours off? We don't keep surgery hours on a Sunday, only emergencies.'

Womersley replied that it *was* an emergency, and showed his card. She sniffed when she saw they were policemen, but after a minute gave in and reluctantly told them she would see if Dr Widdop would spare them a few minutes, though she left them on the doorstep, closing the door with a firmness just short of a bang, and giving the impression they shouldn't hold out much hope.

Rawlinson's eyes travelled enviously over the polished vehicle at the foot of the steps while they were waiting. 'A de Dion-Bouton,' he said with awe. 'I hear tell that one of these days every Force in the country's going to have motors – not like this, of course, but still—'

'One of these days pigs might fly. If transport's what you're after, you'd best go back to being a PC,' Womersley said testily. 'They'll give you a pushbike.'

Rawlinson accepted the rebuke without comment. The old man's dyspepsia was obviously bothering him again.

The housekeeper came back. 'All right, he'll see you. He's in the surgery, you'd best come through this way. Wipe your feet.'

The surgery was built on to the side of the house, with a corner of it partitioned off as a place where the doctors dispensed their medicines, revealing through the glass partition shelves stacked with jars and bottles of coloured liquids, powders and pills. There they found Widdop, rubbing calamine lotion on to his hands. 'Physician, heal thyself,' he remarked wryly, 'only I can't – nervous rash I get from time to time. Sorry, I can't shake hands.'

'Looks nasty,' Womersley sympathized. The rash was also on his neck, above his collar, though not as red and raw-looking as it was on his hands. 'What brings it on?'

'Who's to say? Overwork, sleepless nights? And one tends to worry about one's patients . . . I lost one yesterday, father of a big family. Poor souls, what's an itch compared with that?' He looked down at his hands, where the lotion was drying chalkily. 'And then again, when Ainsley Beaumont died, I lost a very good friend too,' he said quietly. His face was momentarily drawn with grief but, professional that he was, he put it aside. 'Which is why you are here, I suppose?'

He waved vaguely towards the only other chair apart from his own desk chair, but Rawlinson's long legs meant he could perch easily on the edge of the leather upholstered examination couch. He leaned against it and opened his notebook with a snap.

The surgery did not match Dr Widdop himself, his elegant clothes, his cultivated vowels. He looked and sounded as though he ought to be in Harley Street rather than running a working class practice in a Yorkshire woollen town, in this tired looking room with its scuffed desk and the musty smells of medicine and disinfectant. But he was entitled to personal luxuries if he could afford them, and especially if he worked as hard as he was reputed to do. He had the sort of kindly and avuncular manner which invited confidences, and it struck Womersley that the shabbiness of the surgery might well be the result of a deliberate intention not to overawe or intimidate his patients.

'I believe Mr Beaumont was also your patient, as well as being a friend?'

'He was. Dr Pike informs me he's told you about the tumour he had? Yes, well. He had been suffering from severe headaches for some time, though he'd neglected to come and see me for longer than he should have done.'

'Dr Pike believes Mr Beaumont was murdered.'

'So he does.' Widdop looked at Womersley over the top of his spectacles. 'Well, Matthew Pike's a bright young feller, you know. For a southerner,' he qualified, smiling at the mild jest. 'And what do you think, Inspector?'

'The pathologist's first examination appears to back that up, so I see no reason to doubt it at this stage. I came here to see Dr Pike about one or two things, though I expect you can provide the answers just as well. But tell me, how was it possible Mr Beaumont could carry on with a tumour in his brain?'

'Sheer willpower, for one thing – up to now. He refused to admit that's what it was – insisted it was nothing more than bad headaches.'

'How did he cope with the pain?'

'Pills from me, plus aspirin, and quack remedies from the herbalist. Ate them all like dolly mixtures. I tried to get him to consider surgery, told him of the successes and advances with surgical techniques that are available nowadays, X-rays and so on, but he wouldn't hear of it. He even waved away my suggestion of another opinion.' He shrugged, looking troubled. 'I told him he was a stubborn old fool, and he said he'd been told that often enough, but there were things he had to set right before he allowed himself to let go, as he put it. I suspect by that he meant satisfying himself that young Gideon would be able to carry on at the mill without him. He needn't have worried. The boy's a different cut of cloth to his father.'

The housekeeper came in with a tray of coffee and banged it down. 'We've only these few biscuits left,' she announced, eyeing the two policemen as if they were there on purpose to eat the doctor out of house and home.

'Never mind, I see you've given us a treat with your ginger snaps, Ada, so that'll make up for it. Thank you very much.'

She sniffed, but a rosy colour suffused her face, making her look quite human. 'They're right enough, I reckon.' The door closed quite quietly after her.

Widdop smiled. 'She doesn't mean anything. How do you take your coffee?'

With plenty of milk and sugar was how Womersley, who rarely drank coffee and preferred tea, liked it. He waited until it was dispensed before he prompted, 'What did you mean about Mr Beaumont's son?'

'Theo, oh yes, Theo. He died, still a young man, when his children were barely two years old. They're twins, you know, Gideon and Una. It's always a tragedy to lose a son, especially your only one, and one you expected to follow in your footsteps, even though Theo was a reluctant heir, as you might say. His mother was a Tyas, and so was he, through and through. She died when he was a child, but she lived long enough to have passed her own ideas on to him.' Widdop leaned comfortably back. He didn't appear to mind the interruption to his day of rest, indeed he seemed to welcome the chance for a bit of gossip, which was lucky – in Womersley's experience casual gossip could often turn out to be more useful than answers to direct questions.

'Theo was a likeable enough young chap,' the doctor went on, 'but when he grew up he made a fool of himself. Like his father, he married the wrong woman – though only because it was a case of having to.'

'You're saying Ainsley Beaumont's marriage didn't turn out well?'

'It had been an understood thing that he was going to marry Sarah Illingworth, Sarah Hirst that was. They'd had some sort of a minor tiff and while he was still smarting, he met Charlotte Tyas, who made it plain she was very willing to marry him. It was a temptation, I suppose, one up on all his fellow millowners, going up in the world – the Tyas name and Tyas money. They were the aristocracy of the district, you know, and it blinded him so that he wasn't as cautious as usual – nor as clever as he thought! He should have made certain of the money before he married her. Turned out her father was up to his ears in debt, so the boot was on the other foot. Ainsley bought Farr Clough House – which had been in the Tyas family for generations – from Sir Gideon, who went off with his wife to live in Scarborough on the proceeds.'

'The woman Ainsley Beaumont was going to marry . . . Sarah Illingworth, I think you said? That would be Thomas Illingworth's mother? Lives in the house by the mill?'

'That's right. After Ainsley left her for Charlotte, she eventually married Henry Illingworth.' He paused and picked up a pipe, packed and lit it. 'All water under the bridge. But then, what did Theo do but repeat his father's mistake – only he married below rather than above himself, got one of the Wainthorpe lasses into trouble so he had to marry her; publican's daughter from the Tyas Arms. Flighty young piece, Amelia was then. She'd have been a lot happier if she'd married Whiteley Hirst. He would have kept her feet on the ground.'

'If that's the manager at Cross Ings, we've met him.'

'The same, Sarah's brother. He was always after Amelia, still would be, if she'd give him the chance. But she was too dazzled by Theo. Big mistake on her part as well, to marry him; it left her like a fish out of water – neither one thing nor t'other. Some still say of her in Wainthorpe: "She's nobbut Amelia Chadwick, what's she got to be uppity about?" But she made the best of it – wouldn't allow herself to be patronized by the Tyas set Theo mixed with, and managed to carve out for herself a respected position as Mrs Beaumont of Farr Clough, and I admire her for it. It means a great deal to her – at a cost. She was always highly strung and—' He stopped abruptly. 'I'm forgetting myself. Mrs Beaumont's my patient, too, and I mustn't talk about her.'

'He died young, you said, her husband.'

'Theo? Yes, lost his life in a terrible accident. A fire at Farr Clough, in the wing that he and Amelia lived in. He died saving his children.'

Womersley waited for him to expound but Widdop, perhaps feeling he'd said too much, was not inclined to elaborate. Nothing he had so far heard had brought Womersley any nearer to answering the question of who might have disliked Ainsley Beaumont enough to attack him, and then tip him into the water, and Widdop was probably better able to give them that sort of information than Pike, a virtual newcomer to Wainthorpe, might have done, yet something told Womersley to call a halt. The doctor evidently enjoyed a certain amount of gossip, but he had also been a friend of the dead man, and maybe he'd only go so far.

This did not seem to have occurred to Rawlinson. 'What sort of a man was Mr Beaumont? Apart from being a successful businessman and a hard taskmaster?'

Widdop lifted off his spectacles and steepled his chalky hands together while he thought for a minute. 'Both of which he was. But anybody with influence has a responsibility to do things for the common good, however resented, even if it makes them unpopular, don't you agree?'

Womersley was not so sure that he did. He regarded it as a dangerous philosophy, to believe that the end always justified the means. 'Such as what, exactly, Doctor?'

Widdop smiled and shrugged, but his eyes were serious. 'Well, he had no time for those he regarded as troublemakers, for instance. Certain folks tried to make him out as an unfeeling employer for this, which wasn't true. He certainly didn't suffer fools gladly, but there's many in this town have reason to be grateful to him, though he never made a song and dance about what he did.'

'Specifically?'

Widdop picked up his pipe and tobacco pouch from the desk. 'Oh, now, that's not for me to say.'

'Well, then, troublemakers, as you call them,' Womersley prompted. It was Widdop who had broached this, after all. 'Anybody especially who might have had it in for him?'

'Again, not for me to say. But I'll tell you one thing.' He suddenly looked tired, and older. 'My friend Ainsley had a bleak future to look forward to. Whoever killed him did him a favour.'

The brisk climb up to Farr Clough House left Womersley with no breath for talking. If there was to be much of this sort of thing, in the absence of the sort of transport Rawlinson dreamed of, he'd have to see about hiring a pony-trap or something of the sort.

He stood back and took stock of the house when they reached it. So this was the home of Ainsley Beaumont, and that blackened ruin the place where his son had lost his life. A tragedy now twenty years old, the doctor had said. Today it was tragedy of a different kind with which he had to face the family. 'Come on,' he grunted to Rawlinson, who could scarcely take his eyes off the ruin. 'Let's be having you, Jack. Get this lot over.'

Gideon Beaumont, however, was still proving to be elusive. The request to see him elicited the answer from the buxom young woman in a starched apron who answered the door that he had gone out some time since.

'When will he be back?'

'Dinner's on the table at half past twelve.' As if it were unthinkable that even the young master would dare to miss the appointed time for meals.

'That's not long to wait, then.'

'That motor of his allowing.' She had a strong, handsome face and a no nonsense air. 'Miss Una's in, though, and Mrs Beaumont.'

'I'd rather wait to see Mr Beaumont, first.' Womersley wanted to talk to them both, and to the servants, too, but rich aromas of roast meat were wafting through to where they stood on the step. He'd get no cooperation from anyone in the run up to serving the Sunday dinner. 'Is there anywhere we can wait, Miss—?'

'Jessie. Jessie Thwaite. You'd best come in.'

She showed them into what was evidently a library, though not Womersley's idea of what a library ought to be – they should have leather chairs drawn up to roaring fires, shaded lamps. This was a miserable room that wouldn't encourage anyone to stay there and read. It looked as if there was some sort of clearing up job in progress. On most of the shelves the spines of the books were neatly lined up and seemed as though they might have received a recent polish, but more lay in dusty, untidy piles. Writing implements and folders containing papers were spread on the big table.

He decided to give the heavy, uninviting armchair in front of the empty grate a miss. The other chairs were straight-backed, upholstered in some stiff, shiny black stuff with the horsehair emerging in places, and they looked hard, as he found they were indeed when he had drawn one to the window and lowered his comfortable frame. He popped in a mint and sat back, while Rawlinson, hands in pockets, bobbed about examining the books, grimacing. Apparently not to his taste. Womersley closed his eyes.

Rawlinson found himself a chair at last, sat back with his legs stretched out, his hands stuck in his pockets. His position offered him a glimpse of that part of the house that was the ruined wing. There was a story there, about that fire, he was sure, a story behind the bare facts Doctor Widdop had been unwilling to go beyond. It had been a tragedy which was part of the background to Ainsley Beaumont's life, and Rawlinson was determined to find out more about it. What he was, how he had acted, and why, must have contributed to the reason he was now dead by another's hand. The old man's death hadn't come about arbitrarily, whatever Womersley might wish to think. The inspector professed himself not at all interested in the newfangled scientific tools which were being developed and used to solve crimes – he was barely convinced about fingerprints as evidence, for God's sake! – much less in the psychology of criminology, the twists and turns of the human mind that caused one person to take the life of another. He was more at home with the sort of crime common in this neck of the woods: a fight between man and wife when one or other of them was hit with the poker or stabbed with the bread knife; or someone killed in a drunken brawl after a Saturday night booze-up, when bottles were thrown across the streets and anyone might get caught in the crossfire. Rough-houses like that were common enough, especially amongst the hard drinking Neller valley descendants of those fighting Irish who had come over the sea and provided labour to build the canals. All the same, he'd been a good copper in his day.

The inspector sighed gustily, his chin sunk on his chest, his eyes closed. Rawlinson grinned affectionately and let him doze.

Womersley, however, wasn't asleep. He had the enviable facility of being able to close his eyes to his surroundings while sifting through his thoughts, without dropping off. Besides, the temperature of the room prevented any inclination to doze, not to mention the horsehair pricking him right through his trousers. After a while, some slight sound outside caused him to open his eyes just in time to see a young man, handsome in knickerbockers, tweed jacket and windblown hair, his cap in his hand, arriving by means of an agile leap over the garden wall. So it looked as though Gideon Beaumont hadn't taken his car to get to wherever he'd been, after all. A strong, slim young man, his cheeks flushed with exercise, he came into the room a minute later.

For a moment, out there in the hall, when Jessie had told him who was waiting to see him, Gideon had debated whether to go into the library immediately or not. He was hungry, dinner was in the offing and the prospect of talking to the police was not one he welcomed, after the last humiliating hour he'd just spent.

He'd walked down into Wainthorpe to catch Emmie Broomhead as she came out of morning service at St Mary's, the Anglican church where her father was a churchwarden. Propping himself up on the wall opposite the church, he waited, holding on to his patience while the last hymn was sung, the organ voluntary was played, and the congregation had filed out and shaken hands with the vicar. Broomhead had come out at last, followed by Emmie, on the arm of Stanley Priestley, the smarmy fellow who was articled to her father.

'Morning, Mr Broomhead, morning Emmie. Stan.'

Broomhead nodded shortly and Emmie gave him a cool smile. Stanley smirked. When Richard Broomhead then made as if to pass on and Emmie, without much hesitation, followed suit, it needed nothing more to tell Gideon that the Beaumonts – himself in particular – were no longer on the Broomhead social register. The solicitor had evidently taken serious offence at Gideon's incautious remarks when the will had been read, and the aspersions against his professional character (though they were damned well true! It was hardly a secret in Wainthorpe that Dick Broomhead could sometimes be less than discreet after dining with his cronies down at the Liberal Club – it was certainly why Grandpa had that new will drawn up by someone else.) That Broomhead was the sort to hold on to a grudge was no surprise either, but Gideon had thought better of high-spirited Emmie, being so easily swayed by her father's opinions, taking her cue from him and worse, buttering up to soapy Stanley, whom she'd hitherto professed to despise.

He had been well and truly snubbed. Well, to the devil with that! thought Gideon, hurt and affronted.

He'd come down here this morning meaning to thank Emmie for the pretty little note of sympathy she'd sent him when she'd heard that his grandfather had died, surprising him as well as touching him, for he was not unaware that Emmie liked to receive rather than to give, and wasn't renowned for her scholarship, either. She'd clearly made an effort, her handwriting had been childishly painstaking, and there had only been two spelling mistakes. He knew she had thought him a good catch. Now, after his thoughtless, though unintended, insult to her father, she'd been encouraged to have second thoughts. At any rate it was evident she wanted to punish him.

Then let her! There were other fish in the sea. Gideon didn't bother to prolong the agony, said a curt goodbye and stormed off up the hill back to Farr Clough at a punishing pace. And on the way there he recovered his temper surprisingly quickly.

His attachment to Emmie had been another thing of which his grandpa had not entirely approved. He'd pooh-poohed it as puppy love, and told Gideon he could do better for himself than a spoilt little ninny like Emmie Broomhead; he could more profitably seek to ally himself with one of the richer families in the Neller valley. Gideon now found himself admitting that Ainsley had probably been right, in that as in many other things. He was sore, his pride was hurt, he felt bitterly humiliated, but he didn't think his heart was broken.

When he reached the top of the lane he paused and looked back at the mill and the spread of the buildings below, idle today, not running.

For as long as he could remember, Cross Ings Mill had been part of his life. He had known from a child every dark, greasy corner − where the cockroaches scuttled of a morning when you put on a light, and where the wool-dust blew and clung tenaciously to every greasy pipe and window frame; where the dirty fleeces were sorted at the top of the building by men wearing blue and white checked 'brats', which covered them from head to toe in an endeavour to keep them protected from the deadly woolsorters' disease, anthrax. From the noisy engine house where the boiler that powered the mill's machinery was stoked with coal, to the grease-works where the lanolin was extracted from the waste water after the sheep's wool had been scoured. From the stinking wash-house, through the noisy carding and combing, and the spinning, to the weaving sheds where the shuttles flew across the power looms and the deafening noise was like a thousand devils.

Never mind Emmie, this was more important. Ainsley had been a young man once, as young as he was, and he had become master of Cross Ings. And yes, by Heaven, so would he.

Thirteen

'You've come to tell us we can go ahead with the funeral,' he said directly to Womersley when he entered the library, after Womersley had introduced himself and his sergeant. He could otherwise see no reason for the police to be here.

'Before we come to that, will you ask the rest of your family to join us, sir? They'll want to hear what I have to say.'

For a moment it looked as though he were about to demand further explanation, this youthful heir to the Beaumont tradition. He was young, very young to be burdened with what recent events had thrust upon him, but Womersley recalled that both the doctor and Whiteley Hirst had spoken well of him; there was intelligence and a firm set to his jaw that spoke of his ability to cope when he had overcome the initial shock his grandfather's death had brought, thought Womersley, himself a good judge of young men's potential. Gideon left the room and came back, accompanied by his mother.

An imposing woman, Amelia Beaumont, plainly dressed in severe but well-cut mourning, a jet brooch at her neck. Womersley tried, not very successfully, to reconcile what he saw with the picture Widdop had painted of the light-minded young woman Theo Beaumont had married. Flightiness was not a quality he would have associated with this guarded, unsmiling and outwardly utterly respectable woman. He rose from where he was sitting and moved to offer the tabby-covered chair when she entered, but she obviously preferred to subject herself to the torment of the unyielding horsehair, and he stepped back, rebuffed.

She was followed into the room by her daughter, a tall, slender young woman, also in black, accompanied by a fierce-looking and somewhat malodorous cross-breed Airedale, who fortunately sat obediently when commanded and put his square nose on her feet. Gideon stood with his hand on the back of her chair. There was no point in beating about the bush, no way in which he could lessen the impact of what they were about to hear. Womersley gave it to them straight, translating the medical language of the report of their grandfather's death, in so far as he understood it, into plain English, and indicating what this might mean.

An appalled silence fell when he had finished.

During the last melancholy few days they had all been trying their best to accept the unacceptable manner of the head of the family's death as an unfortunate accident. Some sort of freak accident perhaps, but an accident nonetheless. The idea of Ainsley committing suicide had obviously never been considered as a serious possibility by any of them. But now, there was this staggering revelation, which they were prepared to believe even less. Una sat with her eyes fastened on him, her very silence a refutation.

Gideon, too, was speechless. He had gone very white. For all his outward self-confidence, the lad needs to grow a thicker skin, Womersley thought.

Before they came in, he had asked for water to be brought. Rawlinson, ever alert, saw this was the moment to pour out a tumblerful. Mrs Beaumont shook her head, so he handed it to Una. She took it from him automatically and he watched her, a little smitten, as she held it without drinking, as though she didn't know what to do with it. With her fragile looks and smooth, honey-blonde hair she might have been beautiful, had she not been spoiled by her disdainful manner; her eyes were fine and clear, but when she looked at you so directly, Rawlinson saw condemnation in them. Don't shoot the messenger, he wanted to say. He thought she might well be capable of it.

Mrs Beaumont had received the news with nothing more than a deep indrawn breath, yet Womersley's professional antennae told him that it had shaken her badly. Her lips were pressed together in a tight line and he saw in those dark, opaque eyes a hint of passion, the stirrings of anger. Her brows were drawn together, as if with the beginnings of a headache.

'I can't take this in,' Gideon burst out at last. 'First we are expected to believe it wasn't an accident, but suicide, and now you're trying to make out Grandfather was . . . deliberately killed.' He patently couldn't bring himself to say the word 'murder'. 'What are you trying to do?'

'I'm sorry.' Womersley understood the lad's bewilderment. He explained again, patiently, what the autopsy was certain to reveal, with its unavoidable conclusion that Ainsley Beaumont had met his death by the hand of another.

Gideon was not given to real anger as a rule, yet he felt the heat rushing into his face, a pulse beating in his head, finding in himself a belligerence he had not known he possessed. He had an irresistible urge to smash his fist into the face of the mild mannered inspector who was telling them this thing. 'I can only say I hope you find who it was before I come across him,' he said violently. 'If I do, I swear I'll kill him!'

'You're upset, sir.'

Gideon realized he had been shouting. He said, only slightly less calmly, 'And what did you expect?'

Womersley did not respond. There was a fierceness that ran like a thread through them all – through Ainsley, if everything they had heard about him was true – through Gideon, and even Una. Especially perhaps, the dangerously silent Mrs Beaumont. Even the drooling dog had a malevolent look in its hot eyes. There was nothing he could do to lessen the painfulness of the situation. He said shortly, 'Well, to practicalities. The first thing we need to do is go through your grandfather's papers.'

'Why?' Una asked sharply, brittle as a piece of glass.

'It's necessary in a case of this sort, Miss Beaumont,' the sergeant explained.

'I would rather call it an intrusion,' she returned, giving him an icy glance. The beauty he had been conscious of was less admirable when she became so sarcastic and haughty. 'Anything you need to know, we can tell you, without the need to riffle through his personal affairs.'

She drew a deep breath, as if prepared to carry on, but Gideon, making a huge effort, had pulled himself together, and he gave her a warning glance, aware that he himself had said too much, wary of how she might provoke them. The police didn't know what they were up against. Even when they were young children, he himself had been bested by Una when she was in this humour, when she stood up for her 'rights'. But Womersley gave her no chance to continue.

'I'm afraid it doesn't work like that, Miss Beaumont. Questions don't always reveal everything. Things that may seem unimportant to you may strike us very differently. I'd like you to appreciate,' he went on, 'that what brought this about is, at present, as much a mystery to us as it is to you. We need to look at every aspect of your grandfather's life, his circumstances, his family, the people he knew – and not only any enemies, but also his friends, that we can talk to – and hope that will lead us to find out who was responsible. I simply need you all to cooperate, answer any questions we may put to you truthfully, talk to us about anything you, or we, think might help.'

It was a long and oddly formal speech for Womersley, and surprised Rawlinson even more than the others, but they heard him out, though Una's face remained tight with resentment.

'So you see,' Womersley continued, 'that's why I need to look over his papers, his will. For a man in Mr Beaumont's position, especially, his will is important.'

'If you must,' said Gideon flatly, looking determinedly away from his sister. 'Whatever papers there are, you'll find in my grandfather's study.'

'Show me where that is, if you'd be so kind.' Womersley stood up. 'We shall need to talk to you all more fully, and to the servants, but meanwhile we'll leave you to get on with your dinner while the sergeant and I are busy. I don't want to disrupt things any more than we have to.'

Una Beaumont looked as if the thought of eating made her feel physically ill. 'I shan't be taking dinner. You'll find me in my workroom if you want me, Inspector. I have a deadline to meet.' She stood up.

'Deadline? Are you a writer, Miss Beaumont?'

'I write pamphlets, leaflets, Sergeant. I publish a quarterly magazine. *Unity*,' she added, as though they must know it. Neither of them did. Oh Lord, thought Womersley tiredly. He might have known. *Unity* had never come to his notice, but he had no doubt it was the same sort of publication as many others which had. Una Beaumont, then, was one of these attention-seeking women who were demanding the vote and equality for everybody, those pesky women he suspected Rawlinson secretly admired, though he'd more sense than to make his views publicly known.

'I may go, now?' she asked with a cold little smile. 'I *am* very busy, but I have no desire to be obstructive, and I'll answer any questions if it means you get the coward who took such advantage of my grandfather.'

'Murderers of this sort don't think of themselves as cowards,'

Womersley told her dryly. 'Only how to get away with it without being found out. But thank you, I'd appreciate your cooperation.'

Rawlinson sprang up and opened the door for her as she marched out, her head held high, followed by the dog which gave him a savage glance as he passed. He was thankful it was nothing more.

Mrs Beaumont watched her go, then stood up herself. She had been silent throughout, following the conversation but keeping her feelings to herself behind those unfathomable eyes, and now she said merely, 'Ask, if there's anything you need.'

'Thank you, Mrs Beaumont.'

Gideon held the door open for his mother and then showed the policemen into the study. Although the master was no longer here, the routine of the house had gone on and a fire had still been lit, warming and lighting the comfortable room. 'You'll find all you need to see in the desk. There's not all that much. He didn't believe in paperwork.' He opened a drawer. 'Here's a copy of the will, it's quite short.' He stood stock still for a moment, in command of himself now. 'He made it only last week, and of course it supersedes the old one he'd made. But Mr Richard Broomhead, our family solicitor, confirms that it is fully in order.'

Womersley accepted the long envelope, intrigued by the ambiguity, as Gideon extracted an expanding, concertina-type wallet from another drawer and put it on the desk, saying, 'You'll see what I mean after you've read the will – and this. This is self-explanatory.'

It was soon very evident that Gideon had spoken the truth: the master of Cross Ings had not complicated his affairs with paperwork, not even with a diary – he evidently kept his appointments in his head, believing he would not forget them – nor were there any personal letters or anything of that sort. In the top drawer was the detritus which accumulates in any desk drawer: pencil stubs, a worn down rubber eraser, a tiny tin box of new pen nibs, several old keys of various sizes: door keys, clock keys and so on. Half a dozen little round cardboard pillboxes, some with a herbalist's label, some with that of Widdop's surgery, all of them empty except one, half-full of small pink pills.

In other drawers Womersley found bank statements and a passbook, and after a quick glance passed this over to Rawlinson. 'Take a look at that.' He pointed to the withdrawal of five hundred pounds in cash, two days previously.

Rawlinson whistled. 'That's a heck of a lot of money. What did he want that much for? Was that why the killer left him with all his other valuables? He simply got what he was expecting – money to keep him quiet, like?'

'Blackmailers don't kill the goose that lays the golden eggs,' Womersley grunted, going on to sift through the rest. Deeds for 'a small plot of land on Syke Beck Lane and the building thereon, for the purposes of trading as a newsagent and tobacconist'. A large envelope containing proposals for building a row of two-up-and-two-down houses, also off Syke Beck Lane; letters thanking Ainsley Beaumont for heading a subscription list towards the building of the local fever hospital; an acknowledgment for a privately donated sum towards the construction of a proposed new reservoir; and a record of yearly payments into a Goodwill scheme to provide assistance for Wainthorpe's widows and orphans.

This, then, was that other face of Ainsley Beaumont, the private man Widdop had obliquely referred to, a man of good intent. Perhaps that cash he had withdrawn had been used for a similar philanthropic purpose, Womersley reflected, finally turning his attention to the will.

The bulk of his personal estate and the Cross Ings business was to be shared between his grandchildren and a generous annuity had been left to their mother. A tidy sum was bequeathed to Whiteley Hirst. Gifted to Sarah Illingworth – the woman he had once intended marrying, according to Widdop – was the house she now lived in down at Cross Ings, and to her son, Tom Illingworth, the return of an already paid debt. He speculated about that, even as his eyes were travelling to the surprise which came at the end of all this. To Laura Harcourt, of London . . . His lips pursed into a low whistle.

'And I wonder who *she* is,' he said aloud, 'Laura Harcourt, of London?' There was no indication in the will, just her name and the city.

'Someone he – er – met, on his visits to the capital?' suggested Rawlinson with a grin.

'Happen so.' Beaumont had lost his wife early in his marriage

and had never married again. A discreet and convenient arrangement would have been understandable in the circumstances: a
woman in the capital, one he could visit when he chose.
Playing safe, away from home, gossip and possible repercussions.
All the same, it took your breath away – fifteen thousand
pounds, regardless of the extent of the millowner's wealth, for
that sort of connection!

He leaned back in his chair, thinking, watching the play of
firelight on the long case clock in the corner. Lovely old
moonphase clock it was, with its rich walnut case and a brass
face. Just as he was sitting here, so had Ainsley Beaumont sat,
in this comfortable, slightly shabby room, concocting his
schemes while it steadily ticked the minutes and hours away.

By then Rawlinson had come to the end of the only folder
in the concertina wallet Gideon had presented to them. 'Before
we jump to conclusions, I think you should read this.' He
passed it over. 'Seems to be in date order, starting at the back.'

The binder had a spring spine which nipped the contents
together. Letters. Dozens of letters, written over many years,
which had passed between Ainsley Beaumont and the same
firm of London solicitors, Carfax, Arroway and Carfax, who
had drawn up the will, some of them dating back nearly twenty
years. Duplicates had been kept, painstakingly copied by the
sender, of each of the original letters to the firm, along with
their replies; together they provided the answer to the question
of who Laura Harcourt was, which was not the one which
had first sprung to mind. Amongst the early letters to Mr
William Carfax, nearly twenty years previously, was the request
to find adoptive parents for an eighteen-month-old child, a
little girl named Laura, and from Mr Carfax were regular reports
charting her progress and well being, right up to a more recent
letter that Ainsley had written, presenting Mr Carfax with a
decidedly odd request: that he should endeavour to persuade
Miss Laura Harcourt to accept a paid position to sort out his
library, putting it before her in such a way that she should not
suspect she had been specially earmarked for this task.

Not a London mistress, then, but almost certainly a child
whom Ainsley Beaumont could not, or would not, acknowledge.
The letters showed that over the years, he had evidently been at
some pains to ensure that the relationship which existed between
them was concealed from her, but – probably because he had

discovered he was a mortally sick man – he had decided he now
wanted see her and make amends: hence the request about the
library – and the new will. Was Miss Harcourt, the one who'd
evidently been working on the books in the library, still here at
Farr Clough House? If so, they would need to speak to her. It
would also be interesting to see what the members of the family
thought about that bequest and what, if anything, they had
known about her. And if any of them, perhaps especially Laura
Harcourt herself, had known about the will before Ainsley met
his death.

As Rawlinson pushed the file back into the wallet, something
prevented it from going in easily. Fumbling inside, he withdrew
a little brass key, too small for a door, the kind which might
fit a drawer or maybe a document case, and small enough to
have been dropped into the file accidentally and never found.
He shrugged and dropped it into the desk drawer alongside
all the other unidentified ones.

At the same moment, a maid came in with a tray, not Jessie
this time, but a very young girl with fair hair and a quick
blush, shyly saying that Mrs Beaumont thought they might
like a sandwich while they worked. There had been plenty of
beef left on the joint – none of the family had eaten anything
much. And would they like some tea, or a glass of beer to
wash it down?

Neither man had eaten anything since breakfast, apart from
a couple of Ada Crawshaw's ginger biscuits, and the smell of
roast beef had been tormenting Rawlinson for an hour. His
opinion of Mrs Beaumont went up a notch at the offer of this
hospitality.

For that first journey Laura had made to Huddersfield, George
Imrie had booked her a first class ticket in a Ladies Only
compartment, but she had been in too much of a hurry on
her way back down to London to think about such niceties
and had booked her fare, uncaring that she had been given
second class. Tom was fortunately also travelling second. At
King's Cross, they found an empty compartment, where they
sat on facing seats, watching the other passengers embark and
hoping for the privacy which first class might have helped to
ensure.

Laura wore black borrowed from Lillian, since she had none

of her own to wear in a house of mourning. Because the clothes had belonged to Lillian they were inevitably elegant and modish, and at least lighter than the stuffy, and by now despised, saxe blue tweed, but black was not a colour Laura ever wore and in it she felt sallow and unattractive. She rested her head on the back of the seat, elbow on the window sill, a hand shading her eyes. The whistle blew, and with a jerk the journey began; she closed her eyes, trying to obliterate the nightmares of the previous night. But sleep would not come, it was as elusive as it had been last night. Between periods of snatched, troubled dozing, she had lain awake, worries chasing each other, hardly knowing where dreams ended and coherent thought began. And now they moved behind her eyes again: images of Ainsley Beaumont and the horrible way he had chosen to die, as awful in its own way as the way in which his son had lost his life; flashes of the house, Farr Clough, and the fire that had left that stark ruin; Amelia's unconcealed animosity towards her . . . and Tom. Oh yes, Tom.

It was not until the train had gathered speed and left the northern suburbs of London well behind, when they were steaming north and safe from any other passengers showing a desire to share their compartment, that she felt a light touch on her arm and opened her eyes with a start to see him leaning towards her. She must have dozed, after all. 'I'm sorry, did I wake you? I didn't realize you were asleep.'

'I wasn't.' She shook herself thoroughly awake. 'Just dozing.'

'What's all this, Laura?' He sounded cool, different. 'I thought we were friends.'

'Of course we're friends.'

'Then you and I must have different perceptions of friendship. If that frozen politeness you've been showing is evidence of it. All this "Mr Illingworth"! Something is wrong, what is it?' She tried to speak but could find no way to begin. He gazed sternly at her, but as he saw her difficulty he relaxed a little. 'Something you found out yesterday, was it?'

The train swayed jaggedly over a set of points and she put a hand on the window sill to steady herself. It left a greasy grey smudge on her black glove which she tried to rub off, only making it worse, but it gave her time to collect her thoughts. 'I still don't know why I was sent to Yorkshire on a fool's errand. But I am beginning to have my suspicions. It seems that not only did Mr Beaumont leave me that money, but it was he who arranged for my adoption as well.'

'Ah,' said Tom. She had rushed off in such a hurry, before she'd had time to cool off, and he was very sorry indeed that he had allowed himself to be dismissed so easily. He admired her spirit but he was sorry she could believe he had made a fool of her. 'Leaving you that money matters so much?'

'Why does everyone ask that? Strangely enough, it does, to me! If – if I am a child of his, some illegitimate offspring, if he had a conscience about me—' She stopped herself in time. She had been going to say, 'As he had about your mother.' And that brought back the worst of last night's nightmares, the question about Tom's birth, which she had no right to ask. She wanted to shut the answer out, not to have to acknowledge what might be true.

'So that's it,' he said softly. 'What a terrible girl you are for jumping to conclusions! My dear Laura, Ainsley was not your father, any more than he was mine.'

She stared at him blankly.

'And hear this . . . yes, he let my mother down, and after that she swore she would never marry, but then she met Henry Illingworth and fell in love again, long after she had thought she might never have a child. But she did, she had me. Henry Illingworth was my father, don't imagine anything else.'

The foolish, though agonizing, thoughts that had tormented her fell away, as if cobwebs had been swept from her brain. 'Ainsley was not your father. He was not mine. Then who—?' she began urgently.

At this inauspicious moment, the train hissed and steamed into Peterborough. The platform was crowded, and they sat tensely as people began to get in and move down the corridor. One or two looked into the compartment but didn't pause, until at last someone put a hand on the door. Perhaps it was Tom's scowl which made him move away. He obviously wanted their privacy invading as little as she did. But when the man had gone and others were still glancing into the compartment, he suddenly crossed to her side, drew her into his arms and bent his head towards her. The shock left her breathless, and it was instinctive to struggle, but he held her tight against his chest and hissed in her ear, 'Don't pull away. This way, we'll be left alone.'

He was only just in time. An elderly lady half-opened the door, saw them and with an outraged exclamation withdrew. The train started up again, the corridor became clear and Laura, shaken, pulled away – though he did not allow it instantly – her face flushed. 'That's enough fooling,' she said sharply.

But one look at him convinced her that he was not fooling now, that she had imagined the glint of laughter in his eyes. He sat back on his own seat with his arms tightly folded, his brows drawn together in a dark frown, and for a moment she wondered if what he had just done had been to prevent further questions. He did not seem to like himself at all today – after all, how well had she come to know him in such a short acquaintance? Perhaps not as well as she had thought. He looked dangerously near, just feet away from her in the carriage, and her cheeks still burned.

'I apologize for my uncouth northern manners, but at least we can now continue our conversation uninterrupted. Where were we?'

Aware that she was twisting her gloved hands together so tightly her fingers hurt, she took a deep, steadying breath. 'Who, Tom? Who is my father?'

'What difference would it make if you knew?'

'Unless you've never known who you are, where you come from, you'll never know how much! But since all this seems to be no secret to you,' she accused, 'why have you never told me?'

'It wasn't my secret to tell, and I didn't even know you would *want* to know. You seemed happy enough, the way you talked about your aunt and uncle—'

'That's got nothing to do with it! I love them dearly, they've been everything to me, and still are, but . . . oh, don't you *see*?'

There was a measurable pause. 'Of course, I do see, Laura,' he said at last. 'Very well, then, Ainsley Beaumont was not your father. You were in fact his granddaughter. Your father was his son, Theo.'

Theo. Ainsley's unmentioned son.

'And my mother?' she whispered. Please God, not Amelia, who couldn't even bring herself to use Laura's given name. Her thoughts raced. If she was Theo's daughter, by someone other than his wife, then of course it would explain Amelia's animosity . . . and why she had been given away for adoption.

A woman such as Amelia would never have accepted her husband's illegitimate child. But . . . 'Who *was* my mother?'

After a while he said, 'She was a young girl, a very lovely girl, called Lucie.'

Laura stared out, unseeing, while the uninspiring Midlands landscape sped by. 'Lucie Picard,' she said eventually.

It was Tom, now, who was at a loss. 'How did you know about Lucie Picard?'

After a moment, in a voice that trembled, she told him in as few words as possible how she had found the account Ben Kindersley had left hidden behind the books in the library. She skipped over the details. That was not what she wanted to talk about. 'The fire . . . did she . . . did she die in the fire, too?'

'No.' At least Lucie – her mother – had been spared that. Was she – could she still be alive? The hope died before it was born, when he said gently, 'She died several months later, within a day or two of your birth.'

Laura fought back an almost unbearable sense of disappointment. 'How did the fire start?'

'I don't remember the details, if I ever heard them, I was too young. I believe a lamp was accidentally knocked over, some curtains caught fire and by the time the fire brigade could get up to Farr Clough – it's a bad road for horses at the best of times – it was too late to save the wing. I suppose it was miraculous that the whole house didn't go up, but you must have seen the hoses they keep by the fish pond and the well in the backyard. And the pump.'

Yes, Laura had seen all that, and appreciated the reason for it. No owner of a woollen mill could be unaware of the terrifying prospect of fire and its dangers, to life as well as to property.

'What I do know is that Theo – your father – was a hero. They say he ran up a blazing staircase to the room where the twins were sleeping and threw them from the window to those waiting below, before he was overcome by the smoke.'

This, too, her father's death, was a horror she would have to face, perhaps one she had always in some inexplicable way sensed, right from the very first sight of the ruined wing. He was a hero, then, but she understood now that her own birth was the reason his name was never spoken. 'What about Amelia?'

'Already safe, outside. The fire had started downstairs. My uncle – Whiteley Hirst – was at Farr Clough that night, playing cards with Ainsley. It was he who got Amelia outside while Theo was fighting his way upstairs.'

'And Ben Kindersley?'

He frowned. 'I don't know anything about this Ben Kindersley. I'd never even heard of him until you spoke his name. Remember, I was only a little boy at the time. In fact, I knew nothing of Lucie's existence, either, until after the fire, when Ainsley brought her down to live with us, me and my mother – and my father, who was still alive then.'

She absorbed this in silence. 'Ainsley took Lucie to live with your mother? How could he have asked such a thing of her? After what happened between them?'

'She's the last person to harbour a grudge forever, nor was Ainsley, come to that. I suspect he might have regretted what happened between them, but . . . well it was all water under the bridge, and after a while they managed to become friends again. Knowing her, I'm sure he believed she was the one person he could turn to when he found himself in a dilemma: he was responsible for Lucie, who was alone, expecting his son's child, but she couldn't in the circumstances have stayed at Farr Clough.'

'Do you think that's why Ben Kindersley left?' Laura said slowly. If he had known what was going on between Lucie and Theo, it might account for the abrupt way that manuscript of his had ended. 'Did he leave before, or after the fire?'

'I don't know, but if it was after, it looks very much as though he abandoned Lucie.'

That did not sound to her like the Ben Kindersley of the manuscript, the boy who had carried Lucie in the snow across the moor, who had loved her so dearly. 'What was she like?'

His face at last relaxed into a smile. 'Look in the mirror.'

'I don't mean that.' It gave her a small spurt of pleasure to hear that she resembled her lost mother but – 'What was she like, as a person? She must have been very sad at that time, unhappy.'

'Perhaps so. To me, she was just someone the grown-ups had decided would live with us, someone who was there when I came home from school, helping my mother in the house. I never quite understood why she was there, but ten-year-old lads aren't curious about those sort of things. And it wasn't for long, after all. She only lived three days after you were born.'

Three days. Poor Lucie.

He said, 'I do remember you, though, a little. You stayed with us until Ainsley took you away. My mother was heartbroken. She had always wanted another child, and she had come to love you very much.'

Laura liked that. But Ainsley – her grandfather, as she must now think of him – how could she ever forgive him? 'That's what all that charade with the library was about, wasn't it? He wanted to look me over, to make sure I was fitted to inherit some of his money, though he could surely have arranged to meet me in some other way. All that time—' She choked a little.

'Try not to judge him too hardly, Laura. He had his reasons.'

'How else can I feel? The best thing I can do now is to collect my things and leave Farr Clough. Amelia has made no secret of the fact that she doesn't like me and I can understand why. She is probably afraid for her children's inheritance. Well, I don't intend giving it back! I don't want that money for myself, but I happen to know where it can do some good.' A thought struck her. 'Do *they* know who I am, too, the twins, I mean?'

'No – unless Amelia has told them, which I doubt.'

This story, so important to her, could well be one the family might regard as a disgrace, a blot on the Beaumont name, and she had no wish to reopen old wounds. 'They might well not accept me, but take their mother's side. She dislikes me – but all the same, I think it's time to clear the air with her,' she said with some spirit.

'Don't confront her with it, Laura. Be warned. She can be . . . unpredictable, at times.' He paused. 'She was the reason you were sent away from Wainthorpe in the first place.'

'But I wasn't living at Farr Clough – your mother was looking after me.'

The train was steaming to a halt, and he stood up, reaching into the rack for his overnight bag before turning to face her. 'You were sent away because Amelia tried – unsuccessfully – to snatch you away from my mother.'

'What?'

Perhaps Amelia was mad, after all. Laura said slowly, 'She

knew who I was, of course, immediately I arrived at Farr Clough. As your mother did when she met me, didn't she? And you, Tom? How long have you known that I was Lucie's daughter?'

He saw the colour rising to her cheeks. 'Dear Laura, I think I knew the moment I set eyes on you. As I told you, you are the image of your mother.'

But that wasn't why he had fallen in love with her.

Fourteen

Mrs Macready was in the kitchen, beating eggs and sugar together for a cake, with the yellow earthenware bowl crooked in her arm, when the policemen came in. She was sitting down to do it, an old woman who looked frail as a withered leaf, but who still regarded the kitchen as *hers*, as it had been in her glory days, when she had been cook for the Tyas family. She waved them away with a skinny hand when they came in. 'Away with ye. What would I know about poor Mr Beaumont dying?' Her Scottish accent, thick as porridge, she clung to as a matter of pride, though she hadn't been back to her native land since she'd crossed the border to work as a tweeny in England when she was thirteen. 'The grave claims us all, sooner or later. I'll not be long afore I follow the master.'

Jessie remarked in an affectionate aside, 'Take no notice of her, she enjoys being an old misery.'

This was so evidently true that Womersley felt he could legitimately abandon questioning the old woman unless it became absolutely necessary. With some relief, he turned his attention to the other servants, although he realized her dreich lamentations probably hid a genuine sorrow. She had, they were told, worked for Ainsley Beaumont for more than twenty years and known him for longer.

It soon became apparent that it was Mrs Beaumont, with the help of the capable Jessie, who ran the house between them. The little fourteen-year-old maid Prissy was willing, but as yet inexperienced, and the gormless but good-natured lad, Zach, sixteen and strong as an ox, didn't appear to have a lot up top. John Willie Sugden, the handyman, was almost as old as Mrs Macready. On the morning in question, they had all been up and about before breakfast, busy around the house, the young maid cleaning out the fireplaces, the boy chopping firewood and filling coal scuttles, Mrs Macready frying eggs and bacon. None of them had left the house that morning, including John Willie Sugden, who had been busy seeing to the pony.

'Did the master use the pony and trap that day, then?' Womersley asked him, recalling that Whiteley Hirst had said Mr Beaumont usually walked down to the mill.

'No, but the owd 'oss needs seeing to, choose how. He were allus considerate, Mr Ainsley. I'm under t'doctor for me rheumatics, and mostly he walked down to t'mill and back, 'less he wanted to go somewhere else, like, same as he did t'night afore. Wanted me to retire, he did. Retire! What should I be doing wi' retirement?'

Womersley asked, 'So where did he go that night?'

'I dropped him at t'Liberal Club. But he told me to pick him up at t'mill, later on. Funny, I thowt, but it were none o' my business.'

'What time would that be?'

'Just on eleven.'

'Late, wasn't it?'

'It were nowt to me. Jinny doesn't get enough exercise any road. Mrs Beaumont prefers to walk and Mr Gideon has his car. I sometimes drive Miss Una, when she's off delivering them books she writes and that's about it. I were glad of summat to do.'

'That Jessie,' Rawlinson said as they left the kitchen in search of Amelia Beaumont and her son and daughter. 'Little Prissy told me she helps Una Beaumont with that magazine.'

'Oh Lord, another of them! Votes for women and down with men! Makes you wonder what they'd do with us if they did get the blessed vote.'

Rawlinson drew in his breath but wisely refrained from comment.

Jessie did not live in, she had told them, but went home each night. The last time she had spoken to the master was early on the day he had met his death. She had arrived for work at Farr Clough just as Ainsley had been about to leave, much later than he usually did. Mrs Beaumont was with him, on her way to the shops. They exchanged a few words, remarked on the freshness of the morning, he had enquired after her father, who suffered from a lung disease caught from working in the wool dust, and now kept the newsagent's down Syke Beck Lane, when he was fit enough to open the place up.

This, Womersley surmised, was the shop for which Ainsley

Beaumont had held the deeds. So Jessie Thwaite had far less reason than most to wish her master ill. Not that he was inclined to look on her, any more than the rest of the servants, as one who might have killed her master.

'They don't know anything, this lot. We'd better talk to Mrs Beaumont, and her daughter, though I suspect they won't know anything, either.' Or if they did, they wouldn't say.

'Why do you have to do that, Mother?' Una demanded, irritated at seeing her mother stabbing tacking stitches into a sheet she was turning sides to middle. 'You don't have to.'

'Better the day, better the deed.'

'I don't mean because it's Sunday! Why do you have to do it at all?'

'They're good linen and there's still a lot of life left in them.'

Una, who had too often slept on sheets with an uncomfortable seam down the middle to agree with this, turned away impatiently, while Amelia's needle went on plucking through the sheets quicker than ever. Why did she insist on these unnecessary economies, on driving herself to fill every minute of her time from dawn to dusk with running this house? Grandpa had never expected it of her, but Una supposed he had known Amelia better than to suggest he should employ a housekeeper.

On her desk were the shopping lists she had been jotting down for the coming week: treacle, flour, sugar and a host of other things from the Co-op, the greengrocer, the butcher. All of which her mother would doubtless walk down into Wainthorpe to order, wearing a good coat, respectably gloved and hatted, to choose everything personally in order to make sure they understood Mrs Beaumont of Farr Clough would accept nothing but the best, and leaving all but the lighter things to be sent up, or fetched by John Willie or the boy. Una watched the flashing needle, trying to quell her exasperation. Sewing like that, when the familiar pucker between her brows indicated the onset of another of those headaches of hers, which worried Una now more than ever, after hearing about Grandpa . . . but his headaches had been of a different order altogether.

She sighed as she noticed, poking from under the billowing sheet her mother was sewing, a forbidden chocolate wrapper, most of her sympathy in danger of evaporating. A craving for sweet things was Amelia Beaumont's only discernible weakness; she hated anyone to know how difficult she found it to obey Dr Widdop's advice not to eat chocolate. Una was searching for something to say about it which would not upset the applecart when there was a knock on the door.

'I can see you're busy,' Womersley said, entering the small, over-furnished parlour where Mrs Beaumont was stitching at billowing yards of linen, her daughter sitting on a low stool near her. 'So we'll try not to keep you long. It's only a matter of knowing where you both were on the morning Mr Beaumont died.'

'That's soon told,' Amelia Beaumont replied immediately. 'Though I don't know what help you think it'll be. Una was here at home and I went down to Wainthorpe, and that's it.'

'What time would that be when you left?'

'Early, a few minutes after eight. I like to get my shopping done in good time.'

'You walked down with Mr Beaumont, I understand. Didn't he usually leave much earlier than that?'

'He generally did, but not that day.' Since her tight-lipped silence earlier, she had evidently decided to be more forthcoming. 'He didn't look so well and I asked him if anything was wrong, but he said it was only a bit of a headache and it would pass. I'm sorry to say I thought he'd had too much to drink the night before, though that wasn't like him – he had too much respect for himself for that sort of carry on.'

'Where had he been the night before, that made you think that?'

'At the Liberal Club, I expect. That's where he usually went if he was out of an evening.'

'And the following morning, where did you leave him?'

'We parted halfway down Syke Beck Lane, where that little path leads to the mill, past the dam. Walter Thwaite was just opening up and Ainsley went to have a word with him. I left them talking, while I went on down the road to the shops.'

'So you didn't use the short cut yourself, then, past the dam?'

'I've said, not this time. It was muddy and I had my good shoes on.'

Una put in scornfully, 'I take it all this is because you're wanting to know if either of us had anything to do with killing Grandpa?' She had relinquished the low stool in favour of a stance with her elbow propped against the mantelpiece that gave her more advantage. 'I suggest you'd do better to concentrate on finding someone who had reason to kill him. You're surely not suspecting my *mother*? Isn't it more likely to be someone who was looking for money?'

'That's a possibility we haven't overlooked.' Amelia Beaumont, Womersley reflected, would certainly be quite capable of tipping someone of Ainsley's weight over the wall of the dam, had she been so inclined, and not for the first time he thought she would make a formidable enemy, but he said mildly, 'We're trying to establish a pattern of his movements, that's all, Miss Beaumont. And you? Did you see him before he left?'

'No. But that wasn't unusual. He always breakfasted early.'

'But not that day.'

'Well, I don't know about that. I went straight into the kitchen when I came down and took a cup of tea into my workroom. It's all I ever have at breakfast. Then I went out, for most of the morning.'

'Where were you?' Rawlinson asked.

'A meeting with friends. No doubt you'll want their names.'

'Yes, Miss Beaumont. It'll do later. Did you see your brother at any time?'

'No. I expect he grabbed some breakfast earlier and rushed off, at the last minute as usual.'

'Is it right,' Amelia Beaumont asked suddenly, taking off her spectacles and narrowing her eyes, 'that Ainsley had a tumour in his brain?'

'I'm afraid that's what the doctors have said.' She nodded. 'How did you get on with your father-in-law?' he asked.

'With Ainsley? Well enough.' She resumed stitching the sheet draped across her lap. Not a woman to wear her heart on her sleeve. Whatever sorrow she felt at the loss of her father-in-law, she was keeping it to herself.

Womersley stood up. 'Thank you for your time.' He was not sorry to leave these two difficult and antagonistic women. They made him feel as though his collar was too tight. 'But before we go, I'd like to see Mr Beaumont's bedroom.'

'His *bedroom*?' Una's tone asked what could they possibly

want there, but she said nothing more and led them up the stairs. 'There's Grandpa's bedroom. You may go in.'

'Thank you, Miss Beaumont.'

That was all it was, an impersonal bedroom that might have belonged to any man. On the bedside table another small cardboard pillbox of those little pills the doctor said he ate like sweets. A pair of tortoiseshell-backed hairbrushes sat on a tallboy, over which a small wood-framed mirror hung; in the wardrobe were two or three pairs of well polished boots, a few good suits, pockets containing nothing, except for a crumpled piece of paper Rawlinson found in the breast pocket of a waistcoat. 'An IOU. Made out by Nathan Widdop, though it's only for one pound, seven and six.'

'That's more than a week's wages, for most, lad.'

'So it is. But the doctor pays his debts, it seems – if that's what the line scored through it means. Probably kept for this.'

He showed the back of the IOU. In Ainsley's own hand-writing was written the name of a doctor, with a telephone number and a London address. Was it possible he had kept this because he might not, after all, have been as averse to seeking a second opinion as the good doctor might have thought? Womersley put the scrap of paper in his pocketbook, making a mental note to have another word with Widdop.

There did not appear to be anything else of significance in the bedroom. Downstairs again they found Gideon in the study, staring out of the window. He turned and waved them to take a seat, but he remained standing.

'Please sit down, Mr Beaumont.'

He hesitated, then threw himself into a chair, legs stuck out, his arms folded across his chest.

'Miss Harcourt – Miss Laura Harcourt – is she staying with you?' Womersley asked.

'Yes, she has been working here, on the library, but she's gone up to London. She's intending to be back, from the note she left, but I couldn't say when. I see you have read the will.'

'Who is Miss Harcourt?'

'If you've seen the letters in that folder I gave you, you'll know as much as we all do. None of us had ever so much as heard her name until she arrived here to work for Grandpa.'

'Then you must have speculated on the reason for such a generous bequest.'

Gideon reddened, stuck his hands into his pockets and gave Womersley a level glance. He said roughly, 'Well, it looks pretty obvious, doesn't it? Though I must say, she herself professed to know even less about why she was left that money. If that's true, then I suppose that's what she has gone to London to find out; to see the solicitor who drafted that will – she hasn't seen those letters. I only discovered them after she'd gone.'

'I dare say we can wait until she returns. Meanwhile . . . what time did you arrive at the mill the day your grandfather died?'

'I'm not always there when the workpeople clock on, like Grandpa was, though he thought I ought to be. But I'm usually down there not much after, and as a matter of fact, I *was* there by half past six that day. Anybody will tell you.'

'But your grandfather didn't go down at his usual time. He was late that day and walked down into Wainthorpe with your mother on her way to the shops.'

'With my mother? I didn't know that, though I did wonder where he was. I hadn't seen him at home and I thought he'd already left. I wanted to speak to him before I went to Leeds to keep a business appointment. It was unusual for him to be late, to say the least, you could set the clock by him. Oh Lord, why did he have to be late that particular day?'

'He told your mother he wasn't feeling well.'

Gideon stuck his hands further into his pockets. 'He never told us he was ill, you know. He carried on with his life as if there was nothing wrong.'

'A brave man.'

'Or too pig-headed to seek advice!' There was a pause. 'God, I didn't mean it like that, it's just . . .'

'I know, Mr Beaumont. Your mother thought he had been at the Liberal Club the night before, and that was certainly where your man Sugden took him, but he picked him up at the mill. Odd time to be there, late at night, wasn't it?'

'Not for Grandpa! He used to pop in any old time, if he bethought himself. I expect he'd been playing cards at the club. That's what he did in his spare time, cards were a bit of a passion with him.'

'He drew a considerable amount of money from his personal bank account recently, five hundred pounds to be exact. To pay a gambling debt, do you think?'

'Grandpa? Not him, he was no gambler – only token amounts, anyway. He was a bit strait-laced about it – he didn't regard a few bob as gambling, he just thought it made people more serious about how they played . . . *five hundred pounds?*'

'Who did he play with? Any regular partners?'

'Whiteley Hirst more often than not, Dr Widdop, and another old friend from Wainthorpe. Sometimes my mother played whist with them. They'd all played together for years, even though Grandpa used to complain that Nathan Widdop was tight-fisted and occasionally "forgot" his debts, never had any cash on him . . . you know. He used to make him write out an IOU, however small the amount,' he added with the trace of a grin. 'I say, are you sure about the money he drew out?'

'You can check with the bank, sir.'

'Then I suppose he did. But why on earth—?'

'We'd be interested to know that ourselves, sir. Meanwhile, it would be helpful if you could recall what your grandfather did in the days immediately prior to his death?'

'I don't know that he did anything out of the ordinary. Apart from going up to London to change his will,' he added bitterly.

'Presumably you didn't know about the new will he'd made?'

'Why should I?'

'Well, it was in his desk drawer—'

'Look here, I was not in the habit of going through my grandfather's desk.' He had flushed darkly. 'Nor would anyone else in this house do such a thing.'

Womersley held up a pacifying hand. He thought it very likely true.

'I don't know what you're insinuating by all this but you've talked to Whiteley Hirst and you must know by now that my grandpa and I had our differences. But we understood one another. I loved him, in spite of what you might think, I—' He stopped, uselessly. 'Well, talk of the devil. Here is Miss Harcourt now,' he said, turning to look out of the window as the sound of a car engine was heard. 'With Tom Illingworth.'

It had not occurred to Laura until she and Tom left the train at Huddersfield to wonder how they were to get to Wainthorpe. The tram once more, she would have assumed, had she thought about it.

'Wait here, if you please,' he said as they emerged on to the Corinthian columned forecourt. 'I won't be long.'

He disappeared for about ten minutes and just as she was beginning to wonder where he was and feeling abandoned, a motorcar drew up noisily beside her with Tom in the driver's seat. She stared at this rather battered looking marvel, with two front seats, a bench seat behind, and open sides. He jumped out to help her in, pleased at her look of astonishment as he settled her in the front passenger seat, perched high above the road.

'Whose car is this?'

'Mine, for the moment. I have it on approval for a few days, from a man Gideon knows. Cross your fingers that it keeps going, though it hasn't stopped so far. I shall probably keep it. Do you have a scarf with you?'

'No.'

'Then take this and tie it round your hat. Otherwise you're very likely to lose it.'

He had thought of everything. A scarf which she suspected belonged to his mother, a travelling rug, a foot muff, even a dust-coat, in which she found herself covered from chin to toe once she had buttoned it up. He cranked the starting handle and after only a few doubtful coughs the engine caught and he leaped in beside her, fiddled with some levers and they were off. A few bumps at first, but gradually the car began to run better and Laura was soon enjoying the exhilarating speed at which they were travelling – twenty miles an hour, he said, and she could believe it. In fact the experience was quite pleasurable, if you closed your nose to the smell of burning oil, and the noise; if you sat tight on the buttoned leather seats, which were in fact comfortable and well-sprung – and just as well they were, since the ride was by no means entirely smooth.

'Jolly, isn't it?' Tom reached his hand outside to slap the side of the car as though it were a horse. He had to raise his voice to make himself heard above the engine. He seemed entirely to have recovered his good humour.

When they reached Wainthorpe she said, 'Will you stop at Cross Ings, please? I'd like to see your mother, Tom.'

He threw her a quick glance. 'Are you sure?' But when she replied with certainty that she was, he said nothing further and eventually drew the car into the silent, weekend mill yard.

They found Sarah, not in the best parlour where they'd had tea, but in the big, comfortable room that served as the main living room and kitchen, a room with a square scrubbed table in the middle and a range where the fire burned brightly.

Everything was tidy and Sunday-quiet, not even the hum of the mill from behind the wall. Sarah was sitting in a rocking chair, reading, wearing a cream shantung blouse, fastened by a small gold bar brooch at the high neck, and a belted dark blue skirt that showed off her still slim waist.

'Look who I've brought to see you. I promised I'd bring her back, didn't I? And Mother, I've told her. She knows now.'

Sarah took hold of Laura's arms and looked gravely into her face before enveloping her in a warm hug then settling her into a chair by the fire.

'Mrs Illingworth, when Tom brought me here the other day,' Laura said shyly, 'I couldn't think why I felt so much at home. Now I know why, of course. This used to be my home.'

'You were too little to remember it. You weren't yet two when you left us.'

'All the same . . . Tom has told me why I was sent away – because of . . . of Mrs Beaumont.'

Sarah's eyes rested on her flushed face. After a moment, she said, 'Don't make too much of that. I've known Amelia Beaumont all my life, we went to school together, and she was always self-willed, but there's no real harm in her.'

'Then why did she do such a thing?'

'Well.' Sarah hesitated. 'It's a long story.'

'We'd better have a cup of tea, then,' Tom said.

'You'll want something more than a cup of tea – you won't have had any dinner, I suppose?'

'I'm not hungry, really, Mrs Illingworth.'

'Are you sure? Well, if you say so . . .'

Laura would have liked nothing more than to seize on this chance to talk of her mother, but she had to learn how Amelia had managed to take her away – and why. Sarah moved the kettle from the hob on to the coals, brought the violet-patterned cups and saucers from the sideboard in the best room, while Tom fetched milk from the cellar, and from the corner cupboard a tin containing parkin, the spicy ginger cake Sarah had baked when Laura had first had tea here.

'Well, you see, it was when my husband, Tom's father, was

the office manager, here at Cross Ings. It was on a day when Ainsley had to stay at home, up at Farr Clough, on account of he'd slipped on the floor of the carding room and broken his ankle. Easy done, with all that grease everywhere.'

As he couldn't get down to the mill, Ainsley had sent for his bookkeeper. Tom was at school and Sarah and the child went up the hill with him. It was late summer, the bilberries were out up on the moor and Sarah had taken a basket to gather some for a pie. They had walked up Syke Beck Lane, Henry Illingworth carrying little Laura, and by the time they got to the top, where the bilberries grew in profusion among the heather, she had fallen asleep in his arms. She didn't waken when Sarah laid her on the grass on her shawl and when Henry left, took her basket to gather the berries, keeping an eye on the still sleeping child a few yards away, straightening up from the back-breaking work every few minutes. She soon had enough fruit, and decided to call it a day. As she started towards where she had left the little girl, she saw the shawl still lay spread on the grass, but the child had gone.

'My heart stopped, I'll tell you! It hadn't been but a minute since I'd last looked, and I thought at first you'd wakened up and toddled off by yourself. I was terrified you might have fallen into the beck and got carried away. I seemed to search for a lifetime, but it was all over in five minutes, you know. I looked up and there was my husband with you in his arms.'

They had met, he and Amelia, on the path from Farr Clough, Henry on his way back to where he had left his wife and Laura, and Amelia coming towards him with the child in her arms. Laura was kicking and crying, frightened at being held so tightly by a stranger, and Henry had snatched her back, demanding an explanation. But Amelia had fled, sobbing.

Laura was shocked. 'Why would she do something like that? Do you think she meant to harm me?'

Sarah shook her head. 'I've thought and better thought about it but no, it wasn't that. It was more likely – likely she wanted to keep her eye on you as you grew up, stop your grandfather getting too fond of you. Ainsley had always had a very soft spot for your mother.' She hesitated, then added quietly, 'Happen to turn him against you, if she could.'

'She wouldn't have done that, surely, to a child?' Laura exclaimed.

'There's not much Amelia wouldn't do, especially for her children, never forget that! But I've told you, I've known her all my life, and whatever she is, I don't believe her capable of hurting a child. Mind you, I pity anybody that gets the wrong side of her. She was always high strung, liked her own way, you know, and I don't reckon she's changed much. She could be frightening, even then.'

'But what did she hope to gain by doing something so – well, pointless, snatching a baby like that?'

'I don't suppose she saw it as pointless – maybe she thought she could make Ainsley believe your place was with your real family, not with me. But he wasn't as daft as all that, he knew what Amelia was like, that she could have made life miserable for you at Farr Clough. He was right to send you away, where she couldn't touch you.'

'And I was lucky, the people he sent me to were as good to me as you had been.'

'I only did my best,' Sarah said quietly, bestowing on her a warm, loving look. 'But oh, how I missed you when you went! God is good, to send you back, Laura.'

Fifteen

'You're nervous of meeting them all.' Tom paused with his hand on the door of the motor he had brought to a halt in front of Farr Clough. He had come round to hand her out, but Laura sat where she was, hesitating.

'Is it so obvious? Well, yes, to be truthful, I believe I would rather face Sim with his teeth bared at the moment,' she admitted with a shaky laugh. With all that had happened over the last few days her confidence had taken a battering and she was no longer as blithely sure of herself as she usually was. 'In fact . . . Maybe you would just stay with me, just until I've told them?'

He helped her down from the car. 'Do you need to ask? You should know that I will. I will stay with you – always, Laura, if you will let me.' He spoke urgently, gripping her arm, and she was conscious of his size and strength, some new purpose in him. '*Will* you let me?'

Shock and the suddenness of it made her heart thump painfully.

'It's too soon, I know. This isn't how I meant it to be, none of it. We should take time to get to know each other better . . . though I for one—'

She pulled her arm free. 'Please, Tom, no. I – I don't know. No, don't ask me . . .'

A painful moment of silence ensued. The silence grew.

'You're right, of course,' he said stiffly, at last. 'I should not have spoken. There are things you must know before . . . things I should have told you—'

He swore under his breath as the door was flung open and Gideon came out.

Their eyes held for a moment or two longer, but Gideon was waiting and in the end they had to move towards the house. Too full of what he had to say to have noticed anything, Gideon told them the police were here again, and abruptly relayed the shocking news they had brought with them about his grandfather.

'You mean – are we to understand he was attacked . . . killed?' Tom repeated.

'There doesn't seem to be much doubt about it. They're waiting in Grandpa's study, the police. They've been cross-examining everyone here, and now they want to see both of you. I warn you, they've been through all his papers, and they know everything, Laura.'

'What? Why do they want to see me?'

'I think, Laura, 'Tom said, 'that other business will have to wait for the time being.'

Gideon threw them a mystified look, but then he shrugged and went with them into Ainsley's study where the police were waiting, introduced them and informed the chief inspector that he had told the newcomers about the recent developments. 'You don't want me any more?'

'Not for the moment, sir.' The door closed behind him and Womersley said, 'Please make yourselves comfortable, Miss Harcourt, Mr Illingworth.'

He was sitting behind the desk in Ainsley's chair, a ponderous man of similar build to Ainsley. Comparisons stopped there, yet for one horrified moment Laura had the impression that it actually was her grandfather himself sitting there, as he had on the day she had arrived at Farr Clough, the clock ticking companionably behind him.

'This is a miserable business for you to return to,' he continued, 'but I just have a few questions about the day Mr Beaumont died, which won't take long. No doubt you've had a tiring day.'

That, Laura felt, was the least of it. The previous sleepless night, and everything that had happened today to turn her life upside down, culminating in what had just passed between her and Tom, the undercurrent of feeling still running between them, was beginning to make her feel light-headed. But he was an avuncular presence, this policeman, with a strong local accent, stolid but unthreatening. His sergeant, a fidgety, sharp-eyed, well-dressed young man with scrubby fair hair, who was perched on the edge of the desk, notebook at the ready to take down everything she said, no doubt, unnerved her more. 'We've been in London.'

'So I understand. I take it you went to see the solicitors who drew up Mr Ainsley Beaumont's new will?' Womersley's voice had taken on a different tone and Laura looked at him sharply. 'I must tell you that we have seen the will, and read the correspondence between Mr William Carfax and your benefactor.' He tapped the file in front of him on the desk. 'It seems we must congratulate you, Miss Harcourt. You are a very fortunate young lady.'

Laura stiffened. 'My benefactor, as you call him, was my grandfather.'

'Your grandfather?' There was a significant pause. Womersley and Rawlinson exchanged looks. 'Is that so? Then your father was—'

'My father was his son, Theo.'

'I see.' He looked at her consideringly. 'The letters Mr Beaumont exchanged with Mr Carfax did not tell us that.'

'Letters? I don't know anything about any letters. And as a matter of interest, nor did I know he was my grandfather – until today. In fact, he was a stranger to me. I had never met him until I came to work here on the library. For some reason he chose to keep me in ignorance of who I was.' She might one day be able to think of Ainsley more kindly, but at the moment the hurt of all those neglected years was still too much on the surface.

'Yet he left you a considerable amount of money. Which you also knew nothing about, of course.'

Colour flew to Laura's cheeks and Tom intervened indignantly. 'Look here, I'm not sure I like the tone of what you are saying. If you are hinting that Mr Beaumont was killed because of the money he left to Miss Harcourt, I can vouch for it that she knew nothing about it until the will was read – any more than anyone else did, if it comes to that. She had no idea she was in any way related to him, until I told her the truth. And the reason I knew that was because my mother cared for Laura as a baby, after her mother died, until she was taken to live with her new guardians.'

'All right, all right, Mr Illingworth. It's just that if we can get to know as much as we can about where everybody was at the time Mr Beaumont was killed, it helps to establish a pattern, don't you see? I'm sorry your mother died, as well as your father, Miss Harcourt. Would you oblige me with her name?'

'I don't see that has anything to do with what you're here for,' Laura replied, flushing even more, her chin lifted, 'but her name was Lucie Picard. She lived here and looked after the twins when they were babies. And as for what I was doing the day that Mr . . . the day my grandfather died, everyone here will vouch for it that I was working in the library . . . which is something, by the way, I shall not be continuing with. I intend leaving Farr Clough as soon as I can.'

'I understand you might want to do that, but I'm afraid it wouldn't be convenient just yet. We shall need you to stay here for a bit. We might want a few words with you again.'

She couldn't for the life of her see why, but he didn't speak as if there was any alternative. Then she thought, well, Gideon had asked her to finish what she had started. Irksome as the job had come to seem, she might, in actual fact, gain a certain grim satisfaction in forcing herself to do it. And then again, there was a more pressing matter to her. Tom.

'Would you like to see that correspondence?' the sergeant asked suddenly, looking at her more sympathetically than hitherto. Womersley clicked his tongue as if he didn't approve of the suggestion, but didn't demur when she replied that she certainly would, and the sergeant passed over a folder. She leafed through it, wondering how much more it was going to tell her than she had already learnt. 'I . . . can't read all this now.' Not here, not under the eyes of strangers. 'There's too much of it.'

'Take it with you, read it when you have the opportunity,' Womersley said after a moment. 'Now, Mr Illingworth, let's have a few details from you.'

Rawlinson took note of the fact that he was a railway engineer who had worked for several years in South Africa and was a veteran of the Boer War, which seemed to interest Womersley as much as did Ainsley Beaumont's provision for him in his will. But Tom, who never talked much about South Africa, cut short his inclination to chat.

'That "provision" for me, as you call it, was money he lent me to put me through my training. I paid it back, though he tried to insist I keep it. He had obviously determined to have the last word by leaving it to me in his will, but I've already said I won't take it. The loan was a business arrangement which I honoured, and I didn't want any favours.'

Rawlinson raised his eyes to the ceiling as if such high minded sentiments were beyond him.

'Mr Hirst,' said Womersley, 'tells us that he wanted you to take up a position at the mill, but you refused that, too.'

'Since my uncle has told you that, he has no doubt told you I was pretty angry with him over it.' His brows came together. 'I felt he was trying to run my life as he tried to run everyone else's. But it doesn't mean to say I killed him. In spite of everything, I actually liked the old man a great deal. And . . . I was on my way home when you say he was killed.'

'From where?'

'London,' he replied shortly.

'Thank you.' After a few more questions, Womersley said, 'I don't think we need keep either of you any longer, for the moment.'

At the door, Tom said, 'If somebody had such a grudge against Mr Beaumont that they needed to kill him, surely they would have found some better way than waiting until they could pick up a handy stone to hit him with? Wouldn't you be better looking for a down-and-out, a tramp, someone like that? God knows, there are enough of them around.'

'Thank you, Mr Illingworth. It hasn't escaped our notice.'

'And that's a statement of the obvious,' Womersley said testily. 'If you plan to murder somebody, a rock isn't usually the first weapon of choice. On the other hand, if it's unplanned, and the rock just happens to be there . . . You've already checked with the model lodging house?'

'First thing we always do, isn't it?' Rawlinson asked, touchy as usual on this particular subject.

Womersley considered him over the top of his spectacles. 'Aye, and with good reason, lad,' he said more gently. The model lodging house was where tramps, itinerants, the homeless or the desperately poor, those of no fixed abode, could be given a bed in a dormitory for the night. Even families could find temporary lodging there. The houses were subject to supervision by the police, and as such were always the first places to be visited when searching for suspicious characters.

'Well, it's been checked and there doesn't seem to be any likely candidate there. All accounted for. They've pulled in an old down-and-out they call Mucky Harry. He swears he had nothing to do with it but they're keeping him in the lock-up for now. Unless something else turns up, they'll have to let him go sooner or later, meanwhile he's happy enough with three meals a day and a bed.'

'No strangers seen in or around the town?'

'Sergeant Binns and his lot are still making enquiries. It won't do any good, though, will it?'

On the face of it, the very nature of the crime suggested a crude, random attack by some loiterer like this Mucky Harry character attacking Beaumont in the hope of what he could get. Maybe such a person had been interrupted, maybe somebody had come along and he'd panicked, got rid of the corpse into the water before there had been time to relieve him of his valuables? It would suit everyone if this turned out to be the case. Even Womersley, Rawlinson suspected. But he said, after a moment or two, 'This wasn't done by some passing stranger.'

'Oh, sure of that, are you?'

'No, but . . .' Rawlinson wasn't sure, in fact. Except for intuition and what the doctor, Pike, had implied – that there was no lack of people who had quarrelled with the victim. But there again, as Whiteley Hirst had suggested, daily spats seemed to be meat and drink to all of them, of no more consequence than a flea bite, and unlikely to have provoked murder. Though there was that torn inside pocket to consider – which might account for that missing five hundred pounds.

Rawlinson added, 'There's other possibilities – like somebody he knew with a grudge simply taking advantage of an unexpected opportunity that presents itself? Coming face to face with him unexpectedly on the path, a row blown up, tempers lost? The old man growing tired of it and walking away, the nearest handy weapon picked up by the killer?'

Womersley walked to the window, where he stood with his hands stuffed into his trouser pockets. 'All right,' he said without turning round, 'but assuming it was planned, who stands to gain by his death?'

Obviously, his heirs. Beneficiaries to a will were naturally prime suspects. All those falling within this category seemed to be genuinely grieving for the old man, but how far did that amount to play-acting? How certain was it that none of them knew what had been in the will? Were any of them in need of money? Money which would have come to them soon anyway – though apparently no one except his doctors had known he had such a short time to live.

'His heirs, yes. Which includes,' Womersley said, turning round, 'not only young Gideon, who stands to gain most, and his sister, but Laura Harcourt as well, don't forget. And Illingworth, come to that, and it doesn't take much to see those two are pretty thick. We'd best check she *was* in the library all the time she said she was – and check on Una Beaumont and that meeting of hers – and what time Illingworth actually did arrive back in Wainthorpe that morning. He was quick to give us the impression he didn't want that money Ainsley Beaumont left him, but we'll take that with a pinch of salt. If not for himself, he might be looking out for his mother. That house she lives in on the side of the mill, the one they want to pull down to build offices – now she's the owner, holding out for a good price could be very profitable.'

'What about Amelia Beaumont? She could have been lying when she said she had parted from Ainsley at the junction of the path. And she looks strong enough, in all conscience,' Rawlinson said, echoing Womersley's own previous thought. 'I wouldn't like to meet her in a ginnel on a dark night!'

Womersley passed his hand across his face. These were all long shots. But even long shots had to be followed up. Such as Whiteley Hirst, who had been left a generous bequest – though was that motive enough? People had been killed for much less. It would depend on whether he had known anything about it, and also on how desperate for money he was.

Rawlinson said slowly, 'We've been asking who stands to gain by this death . . . but put it another way – who stands to *lose* if he'd continued to live? Anybody who might fear to lose their good name, income, their freedom, even.'

Womersley stared. 'Aye,' he said heavily. Searching for someone this might apply to would spread the net wider, far beyond his family. Ainsley Beaumont had been in the wool trade all his life. He had a web of connections all over the Neller valley. There were well known rivalries among these hard-headed, well-to-do woolmen, and who could tell what enmities might have arisen? Not all the businessmen in the valley were scrupulous. They knew means of evading taxes, the law. He saw the enquiry stretching before him, the net needing to be spread ever wider. He did not like to think what his superintendent was likely to say to it.

'Jack,' he said, 'this might well be my last case – last murder case, at any rate. I wouldn't like it to turn into a policeman's nightmare.' Both of them knew this was possible, that this might end up as a seemingly motiveless crime committed by a person or persons unknown. And in that case, someone who was unlikely to be brought to justice. 'But I'm damned if I'm going to let it. That sticks in my craw, damned if it doesn't.'

'Shall we go and see the twins now?' Tom asked, as he and Laura left the study.

She shook her head. 'They've had one nasty shock – they don't need another, on top of it. Later, when they've adjusted.'

'Then, if and when you need me, let me know,' he said, oddly formal.

Laura slipped a coat around her shoulders and went outside with him, standing beside the car while he bent to the starting handle. The engine didn't fire immediately and suddenly he let the handle go and turned towards her. She could not help but feel he was regretting having said what he had before they had gone into the house and she shrank a little inside herself. The wind slapped her skirts around her ankles and whipped the hair loose around her face. Early dusk was falling, the sky was a cold empty green with only a slip of a new moon showing. Beneath it, the dark boggy moors beyond the edges of the garden stretched to infinity. Behind them, the loom of the house reared up, solid and dark. His face had a shuttered look and once more, it came to her how little she knew of him, really.

Abruptly, he said, 'This is a terrible thing that's happened. You're right, it alters everything.'

For a heartbeat, there was nothing but the sound of the wind and the restless stirring of the rooks as they settled on their nests in the ruined wing. Then he bent and placed a kiss lightly on her cheek, started the car and in a few minutes was gone.

Cursing himself for his blundering stupidity, Tom drove the car at reckless speed down Moortop Road into Wainthorpe, and then more circumspectly through the town and in through the entrance to Cross Ings.

He sat in the car to compose himself before going in to

face his mother – if he did not, she would know something was wrong, as mothers always did, or his mother at least – but his mind wouldn't be composed. It turned over and over what he had just allowed to happen. Had he learnt nothing from past events? Considering himself a mature individual who would not repeat past mistakes, and then acting like some callow youth? Those events in his past which he bitterly regretted but could never be erased? Frightening her before he could explain.

He had had such good intentions, God help him.

He stepped out of the car and went into the house, where his mother had the lamps lit and his tea was waiting. One look at his face, and she didn't after all ask him what the matter was.

Sixteen

Laura stood in the garden listening until the last sound of the motorcar's engine had faded, her coat pulled tight around her shoulders. The wind was sharp, but she didn't feel cold. Despite the unsatisfactory last few words with Tom, a feeling persisted that was warm and real, but at the same time elusive, and not to be damaged or lost by trying to capture it. Amongst all this sadness, was it wrong to feel the way she did?

She jumped as a figure suddenly appeared round the corner, the lanky Sergeant Rawlinson, a lit cigarette in his hand. He was equally surprised. 'Miss Harcourt! I heard the motorcar go and didn't realize anyone was still around. Did I give you a scare? I'm sorry.'

'No, no. I was just . . . taking a breath of air. I thought you'd left.'

'Mr Womersley's gone, but I stayed behind for a few minutes, to have a smoke – and to poke around a bit.'

'Well, I'll leave you to enjoy your cigarette and your poking.'

'No, please, give me a moment, if you can spare it. I'd like a word or two with you.'

Laura nodded, looked around and perched herself on a roughly fashioned stone seat, a large slab of rock set on two other rocks, placed in front of the square pool. Curious as to what the sergeant might want, she waited.

He put his cigarette out and sat at the other end of the seat. Abruptly, he said, 'It must have been shocking to find out about your parents as you have done.'

'Sad, rather than shocking,' she replied quietly. 'But – forgive me if I wonder what bearing that has on your enquiries? Why are you asking?'

He sat with his arms folded across his chest, holding himself tightly in. 'Maybe it's not my place to talk about it. On the other hand, maybe I understand better than most. See . . .' He stopped and then rushed on, 'I never knew my parents, either. It would give me a nasty turn to have them thrust on me now.'

'That's not how I feel. I was looked after and loved by Mrs Illingworth before being handed over to my aunt and uncle. I've been fortunate there, too, but I'm glad I know now about my real parents.'

'I was abandoned,' he said tersely. 'In a church porch. Found by the vicar. He'd no idea what to do with a baby so he went to the only person he could think of for advice. She was the village schoolmistress, Matilda Dacres, never been married, never wanted a child of her own, but she was a good Christian woman and agreed to keep me until they could find out what to do with me. I was still with her when she died, when I was eighteen.'

'She must have loved you, then.'

He shrugged. 'She did her best, I suppose. She saw that I was well fed and clothed and made sure I was educated properly.' He paused. 'Yes. She never said so, but I reckon she did, in her own way.' He slipped a hand inside his jacket pocket, took out his wallet and extracted a photo. 'That's her, Tilly. She insisted I call her that, her childhood name.'

Miss Dacres had been a woman with a determined chin, a firm mouth and a high-boned collar, but Laura thought she had kind eyes. 'She looks nice.'

'She could be a tartar! But I missed her like billy-o when she died.' He put the photo carefully away.

'Did you never want to find who your real mother was?'

'No!' he said roughly. 'She didn't want me when I was a baby, why should she want me when I was grown up? In any case, everybody knew who my parents were – a pair of travellers, good-for-nowts who'd been hanging around the place for several months. Sleeping rough, or at one of the common lodging houses if they could find fourpence for a bed. My mother and the man she was with disappeared after leaving me, and there wouldn't have been much chance of ever finding them.'

'I'm sorry, indeed I am.' Laura was, and for the mother, too. She had learnt a good deal in the last year at the Settlement about the heartache of women who abandoned their babies. 'But why are you telling me this?'

'Dunno, really. Mr Womersley would probably kick me to kingdom come if he knew.' He stirred restlessly. 'I was thinking about that fire, see.' He nodded towards the black bulk of the ruined wing. 'And then I saw you and – well, don't rightly know why I said what I did. I apologize if I've upset you.'

'Oh, please, you haven't.' He was a bony, edgy young man, impetuous and unwise in some things for all she knew, but this blurted out confession to her of his own circumstances had established some odd kind of rapport between them. The wariness about him she had felt in the study vanished. 'It was kind of you.'

'Kind? I don't know about that. It's just that we're up against a bit of a block in this investigation and I can't help feeling that something in Mr Beaumont's past, this fire here, maybe, might have a bearing on it. I might be wrong,' he finished lamely.

Oh yes, the fire.

Was it a coincidence that Ben Kindersley's manuscript, and the conflagration in which her father had perished, were both from the same time, twenty years ago, just before she had been born? There was so much she didn't yet know about these newly found parents of hers. She needed time, to come to grips with how she thought and felt about it all, to read that file of letters between Ainsley and William Carfax. She did not see how any of it could have any bearing on the death of her grandfather, or whether it would help to tell the police about that manuscript, but in one respect she felt bound to agree with the sergeant.

'You're right, there's some mystery surrounding the fire. Nobody talks of it, nobody mentions it. Nobody ever mentions my father, Theo.'

'It was a long time ago. People have short memories.' Or don't remember what they want to forget, he might have added. 'Would it be too much to ask that if you should learn anything, you might let me know?' he asked, as they parted.

She promised she would, and when he had left, she vowed to herself that she would search again through the few remaining shelves in the library she had not yet worked upon, in case there was something more that Ben Kindersley had left, something that might give an ending to that infuriatingly incomplete

story, though it seemed unlikely that there would be anything
more. She would, however, remove and keep the ribbon-tied
roll from where she had returned it to its original place. She
felt she had a right to do that. It was her mother's story, part
of her own story, what had brought her here.

Seventeen

Jack Rawlinson had legged it down Syke Beck Lane into Wainthorpe after leaving Laura Harcourt. It was an odd impulse that took him down there, but there was no one waiting for him at home in his lodgings, and he was hungry. He might just find something to eat, even on a Sunday evening. A pint of Tetley's wouldn't come amiss, either. A chat with the locals, maybe with a chance of picking up something useful.

It was tea time and the streets were relatively empty, a good time to have a wander around first and see what this one-horse town had to offer. Too much to hope there'd be any girls about – nice girls like Laura Harcourt, anyway.

He wondered how she really felt about what had come to light about her birth. Brought up as a young lady – and then to find you were the illegitimate daughter of a nursery maid. She seemed to be open enough about what little she knew, but he still felt he had told her more than she had told him. It was odd about Theo, her father. The fact that he'd fathered an illegitimate child, however shameful, hardly accounted for his name never being spoken. Dammit, the man was a hero. He had given his life to save his babies from a terrible death. How could a tragedy like that provide a motive for his father's murder twenty years later? Maybe it hadn't. Womersley was probably right: he had too much imagination.

He passed the police station with its blue lamp, the imposing edifice of the Liberal Club and two or three chapels, lights on ready for evening service. Already having the geography of this part of the town in his mind, he cut off a corner by taking the path through the municipal park on the hillside to that part of the town as yet unfamiliar to him.

This, then, was what they called 'Bottom End', where the streets and alleys were uncobbled and most of the houses were old and stone-slated, crammed into dirt yards and squares approached by steps down from the road. The town's pervading smell of raw wool was overlaid by something worse – there was a tannery somewhere nearby. It was noisier, too. Despite the Sabbath, and the hour, children played outside underneath the gas lamps, boys shinning up the posts and some, for devilment, chasing the screaming girls from their skipping. Outside an open door, two beefy women were having a fierce and noisy argument.

Eventually, he found an ancient looking pub called the Tyas Arms. Hunger getting the better of him, he pushed open the door. It didn't look up to much, but he was thirsty and he could see pies on the counter.

The landlord was surly but at least served a fair pint, and the pork pie was excellent, the crust crisp with no thick layer of uncooked pastry inside, the meat juicy and peppery. No one took much notice of him after the first few suspicious glances. The place wasn't exactly humming with trade. A few younger men created a bit of noise round the dartboard, but the older element, men in flat caps and collarless shirts, smoked and paid attention to their beer, conversed in monosyllables or kept themselves to themselves. He should have known better than to hope to glean a few juicy bits of gossip. A pound to a dried pea they would have guessed what he, a stranger in Wainthorpe, was doing here. Nobody was going to open up to the police. It wasn't that sort of place. He sat for a while, drank up and left. He might as well have gone straight home.

Having decided the way back through the park was the quickest route to his tram stop, he was approaching the steps that led up to its little iron gate when suddenly both his arms were grabbed from behind and he was thrown to the ground. He saw nothing before his face hit the flags, but he smelled beer and strong cigarette smoke, the taint of wool grease on working clothes; he was conscious of ripe body odour and the rank smell of poverty. Then he tasted blood and spat out a tooth. By which time his assailant had gone, along with his wallet.

He was trying to scramble to his feet, and feeling distinctly woozy, when his arm was taken again; this time it was a woman, a fat, middle-aged woman in a crossover pinny. 'Eh, lad, are you all right?'

'You see who it was?' Rawlinson mumbled, as distinctly as he could with his mouth still full of blood.

'Nay, he were off afore I could make out what were happening. I were just pulling t'draw-ons upstairs when I heard. You'd best see t'doctor, lad.'

Rawlinson put his hand to his cheekbone which he could actually feel swelling up beneath his hand. The tooth (not a front one, thank the Lord!) had not come out whole but broken off, leaving a jagged edge. It hurt his tongue. 'I'll be all right, thanks, missis.'

'That you won't. I'm off to fetch Dr Widdop. I reckon I know where he'll be.'

She nipped back into the house and came back, her head wrapped in a shawl. 'You stop here and don't move. Shan't be but a minute.'

He was still too dizzy to do anything else but remain where he was, slumped on the pavement with his back against the wall. He closed his eyes and minutes later opened them to hear Dr Widdop saying, 'Now then, now then, let's have a look at you. Good God, it's Sergeant Rawlinson, isn't it? What's happened?'

'It's nothing, Doctor. Hope I haven't brought you away from something important.'

He thought he heard the woman laugh, but it was only a cough, and Widdop said, 'No, not at all. Can we get this young feller inside, Mrs Brocklehurst?' He looked slightly flustered and the buttons of his waistcoat were done up awry.

'You'll live,' he remarked after the injuries had been examined and he had cleaned up the blood with warm water supplied by the helpful Mrs Brocklehurst. There seemed to be an awful lot of it, most of it coming from the cut above his brow that the doctor was dabbing. 'Nasty, but not enough to need stitches. Scalp wounds like that bleed a lot – and you've a thick skull, young man!' He administered iodine and a plaster, then examined Rawlinson's cheekbone. 'No bones broken – but you're going to have one heck of a shiner, I'm afraid.'

After thanking the kindly woman they left together. Widdop was concerned. 'May I offer you a bed for the night, Sergeant?' Rawlinson shook his head. 'No? How are you going to get home, then? By tram?' He cast a professional eye over the injured man. 'Very well, if you must. I think you'll be all right, but I'll walk with you to the stop. Sorry I can't give you a lift in my car. I usually walk when I come down this end of the town. The streets are too narrow to turn, and it's not worth the trouble finding somewhere to leave it. Got your fare?'

The thief had not rifled Rawlinson's trouser pockets and he

found he had enough small change to get him home. 'That was a nice woman,' he said as they walked along.

'Oh, I daresay she was glad to do what she could. She's a widow, bit of a gossip but she's all right.'

Rawlinson still wondered how she had known where to get hold of Widdop. He'd had his doctor's bag with him, but it didn't look as though he had been brought from an important case. He grinned to himself, remembering Mrs Brocklehurst's laugh.

By now his head had cleared somewhat and he was beginning to feel more of a fool than anything else. The encounter hadn't done a lot of good to a suit he was proud of and his shirt gave the impression he'd had a suicidal encounter with his razor, but they were the least of his worries. When this got out it would do his reputation no good. He reached his lodgings without mishap and took the pills Widdop had given him, and his advice to go straight to bed, but he spent a restless night, tossing and turning and thinking about the theft of his wallet. The thief had been lucky – or more likely had his eye on Rawlinson while he'd paid for his pie and pint with a pound and pushed the ten-shilling note of the change into his wallet. He cursed the loss of that, ten bob was ten bob, and he was slowly trying to put a bit by so that one day he might move out of digs and have a little place of his own – but he was more concerned to have lost the other things: the precious photograph of Tilly, his diary – and how, *how* was he going to explain the loss of his warrant card, plus – oh God! – his police pocketbook, all of which he kept tucked inside his wallet?

The next morning, after leaving a message for Womersley, he paid an emergency visit to the dentist to have the broken tooth attended to, and made a call on Mrs Brocklehurst to leave a bunch of flowers, much to her delight and embarrassment, and finally presented himself at the Wainthorpe police station.

'Don't say anything,' he warned as he entered, bracing himself for the jokes – and for the rollicking which was to come. The black eye Widdop had predicted had certainly materialized. He looked like a gargoyle fallen off a church roof and it was probably destined to get worse, but much more than that he felt a right muff for having lost what a policeman should guard with his life – his warrant card and his notebook.

'Good afternoon,' Womersley remarked. Rawlinson let the sarcasm slide over him, and Womersley wisely resisted any further comment, other than a raised eyebrow at the sight of his sergeant's picturesque face, watching with interest as Binns held out his hand towards the young man. In it was Rawlinson's wallet.

'What—?'

The photograph, the card and the notebook were still inside, although the ten-shilling note had gone.

'Found chucked over a garden wall. The money was the only thing he was after. Either he didn't look at owt else – or more likely couldn't read what it was, any road.'

He still had to run the gauntlet of laughs and ribald calls about his spectacular black eye thrown out by the overalled women and girl machine minders as, early next morning, he and Womersley walked through from the ferociously noisy carding room and into the relatively less clamorous combing department at Cross Ings Mill. Trying to ignore the women's jeers and keep his dignity, he nearly made things worse by almost measuring his length on a floor that was inches thick in grease. You could have scraped it up with a spoon, the smell of sheep was overpowering. He only righted himself in time by grabbing on to a skep full of huge bobbins of wool, which unfortunately was on wheels and began a slow slide away from him. But Womersley, pan-faced, was there to save him from disaster with a strong hand. Trying to ignore the laughter, his ears glowing, he followed in the inspector's wake.

By contrast, the warehouse on the second storey, busy as it was when they arrived, was a haven of quiet. Heavy bales of raw wool were being loaded through the hoist door from a wagon which stood in the yard below. Swinging through the air and into the big opening, they were grabbed by men ready to unhook and manhandle them on to trolleys, before wheeling them to the giant weigh-scales and then stacking them in their designated places.

George Quarmby was easily spotted. He was the one with the brown smock, the flat cap and the battery of pencils in his top pocket, noting into a small, thick, greasy book the weights as they were called out in hundredweights, quarters and pounds. He still looked dour, his black brows drawn together, but less furious than he had appeared when he had stormed out of

Whiteley Hirst's office on Saturday morning. When he spotted the two policemen, he gave a short nod. 'With you in a minute or two.' Almost as he spoke, the mill engine was shut off. It was time for breakfast.

In the sudden quiet a lad arrived, staggering under the weight of a trayful of steaming pint pots of tea; men began to look around for a place to perch and Quarmby licked his pencil and wrote the last figures in his book. By this time Arnold, the lad from the office, he of the ginger hair, had also appeared and was standing aimlessly by, waiting for the books. Quarmby said sharply as he handed them over, 'We're running a bit late, but tell Edwin Porteous I want 'em back here by nine sharp, think on! Go on, frame thissen!'

The boy escaped, presumably for the figures to be transferred into office ledgers, and Quarmby beckoned Womersley and Rawlinson to follow him into his tiny, glassed-in cubicle, containing a high stool and a shelf, a big clock on the wall behind, and nothing else. Quarmby perched on the stool and unwrapped a bacon sandwich from a red-spotted handkerchief, shook some sugar from a small tin into his tea and stirred it with the pencil from behind his ear. 'All right. Twenty-five minutes afore we start up again. What is it you're after?'

'A few questions about the day Mr Beaumont died, that's all, Mr Quarmby.'

'Oh, and why me?'

'Why not? We'll be talking to a lot more before we've done.' Likely everybody in the mill, even the town, Womersley thought gloomily, seeing the unhappy task stretching before them.

'Seeing as how he's been murdered, you mean?'

'Who told you that?' Rawlinson asked.

'No need to look so capped. Word gets round. But don't come looking at me.'

'You were having a bit of an argument with Mr Hirst when we saw you last,' Womersley reminded him.

'It's my job to have arguments with the bosses. It weren't the first and I doubt it'll be the last.' It looked as though he'd lost his taste for his sandwich. He threw them a sardonic look and folded up what was left of it into the red handkerchief.

'You're strong in the Trades Union, shop steward, they tell me, Mr Quarmby.'

'Do they? They'll have been telling you I'm a Labour coun-
cillor an' all, I don't doubt.'

'Very commendable.'

Quarmby gave him a sardonic look. 'I've had seven bairns
with bellies to fill on subsistence wages. They're all grown up
now, but I haven't forgotten what it were like. Bad old days,
and not over yet by a long chalk. Them as owns the mills
reckon they have their own troubles, but it's all relative.' He
drained the pint pot in one long swallow. 'Look, as far as it
goes, Ainsley Beaumont weren't so bad. But they're all tarred
with t'same brush, t'bosses. They're not in it for love, they're
in it for what they can get out on it . . . more brass and
t'biggest mill in t'Neller valley. Young 'un up yonder,' he added,
jerking his head in the direction of Farr Clough, high above
the mill, 'he'll be just as bad, now he's got some clout.'

Womersley took most of this with a large pinch of salt.
Though it was an undeniable fact that there were millowners
in the Neller valley – as elsewhere – who were regular tyrants,
it would be ridiculous to believe that every one of them ground
the faces of the poor – Womersley hadn't forgotten the plans
for the row of houses in Ainsley Beaumont's desk, the deeds
to the small tobacconist which provided Walter Thwaite with
employment and income. He knew that most of the owners
genuinely believed they treated their workers fairly, while they
themselves acted within their own lights and worked hard,
finding work to keep the mill going, often risking considerable
amounts of their own money. They paid statutory wages, and
did not lay workers off unnecessarily, but they one and all
abhorred strikes and those who instigated them. They were
wary, and with good cause, of the Trades Unions and men like
Quarmby, with a chip the size of a tree trunk on his shoulder.

'What time do you start work, Mr Quarmby?'

'Half six, same as everybody else.'

'Where do you live?'

'Hanson's Fold, Bottom End, but I don't come in anent the
dam, so I didn't see owt, if that's what you mean. You can
look at my time sheet if you don't believe me, but any road,
young Gideon'll tell you what time I came in. He got here
same time as I did. His granddad were as keen on him keeping
time as the rest on us. Lad only just made it afore th'engine
started.'

'It was Mr Beaumont's habit to stand in the yard as everybody arrived, wasn't it?'

'Aye, to notice latecomers and see t'gate locked. After that you don't get in till after breakfast and lose a couple of hours. Once late and he had you in his sights.'

'But not that morning?'

'I don't reckon so.'

Womersley did not dismiss the idea that if Quarmby had believed anything warranted killing his employer, he would not have hesitated. On the other hand, although he swore he had not come to work via the path beside the dam that day, a lie cost nothing. A dour little man, small as a bantam cock, with bitter brown eyes, he was wiry and muscular, despite his small size. He was a warehouseman, accustomed all his life to manhandling heavy wool bales. He would have the strength to heave a man bigger than he over a wall and into the water, easily. But Womersley was inclined to believe what the man said about his relations with the management. He might have unresolved grudges, but killing his boss would have gained him nothing.

Quarmby was looking at them from under his beetling brows as if deciding whether to say more. At last he said, 'Any road, I owed Ainsley Beaumont summat, never mind what differences we had. One of my lasses, my youngest, our Alice, were taken bad here, about six months since. Collapsed in front of her machine. He happened to be there and if it hadn't been for him getting her into the office right sharp – he carried her in hisself, and used his telephone to get the doctor – I reckon she wouldn't be here now.' His hand, where it rested on the scarred shelf, was bunched into a tight fist.

'Go on, Mr Quarmby.'

'He even helped one of the women tend her, and it were all over bar t'shouting by the time Dr Widdop got there. Doctors! You'd like to think they'd be used to a drop of blood, but he weren't. It right sickened him.'

He wasn't sickened over mine, Rawlinson thought, and it was more than a drop.

'Well, right enough, but even doctors can be upset.' Womersley recalled the nervous rash on Widdop's hands. 'Was it an accident with one of the machines?'

The engine started again. Quarmby slid from his stool and

picked up his empty pint pot. 'No,' he said. 'She were pregnant. She were sixteen, and the lad responsible had tekken his hook and buggered off, so it were just as well she lost the bairn, weren't it?'

'Well, Jack, what do you make of that?' They were standing in the mill yard, at the point where the path that ran alongside the dam joined the canal towpath.

Rawlinson had no time to answer. 'Inspector!'

They turned to see Porteous, the clerk from the office, puffing towards them. For a fat man, he moved fast. Even so, he was not one made for exertion and by the time he reached them he was panting hard. 'They're saying Mr Beaumont was murdered. Attacked. Is that true?' he said when he could manage it.

'It looks as though he was attacked, yes.'

Porteous nodded sagely. Womersley waited. 'Mr Porteous, is there something you want to tell us?'

Breathing more easily now, he said, 'Aye, there is something you might like to know. That morning, the morning he was killed, I nipped out for a smoke. All right, I shouldn't have done, but we're not allowed to smoke anywhere in the mill, it's too dangerous with all that grease – careless match or fag-end and it'd go up like Bonfire Night. As a matter of fact, we're not supposed to smoke anywhere on the premises, but Mr Hirst had gone across to the bank, so I, well . . . I just nipped out to snatch a minute or two, like.'

'And?'

'I walked down here, towards the canal, where we are now, and I saw him.'

'Who?'

'The boss.'

'Mr Hirst?'

'No, no, the master, Mr Beaumont.'

He had their attention now. 'Half past ten? He was dead by then,' Rawlinson said.

Porteous shook his head. 'You're wrong there. He was still very much alive, on the far side, over yonder, in the park.' He pointed across the river. 'With somebody else.'

'Are you sure of this? At half past ten?'

'Near enough.' Porteous began to pat his pockets, looking

as though he was about to produce an illicit cigarette now. He restrained himself and added that yes, he was absolutely sure, even at that distance, that it was Mr Beaumont he had seen.

A man of keen sight, Edwin Porteous. Womersley and Rawlinson had both turned towards the municipal park, where it sloped upwards from the valley, the same park Rawlinson had walked through the previous night. The distance was not all that far, but Womersley doubted whether you would be able to distinguish anyone's features clearly enough to swear who it was from here. But Porteous was adamant that it was Ainsley Beaumont he had seen.

'And the person with him?'

He was more evasive on that point. It had been a man, that was all he could say, a big man though, somewhere about the build of . . . Mr Hirst, say.

Womersley looked at him. 'Are you saying it *was* Mr Hirst?'

'Oh no, I couldn't be sure of that. Anyway, he was at the bank, wasn't he? He didn't get back until well after eleven.'

'Well, thank you, Mr Porteous.'

Porteous's big doughy face was full of spite as he turned to go. 'I'm right, you know.'

Womersley watched him waddle away. He did not take to Edwin Porteous. He did not like the heavy-handed hints about Whiteley Hirst. If the man had been so sure it was Ainsley Beaumont he'd seen, why hadn't he been as certain about the person he was with? But if his statement was true, about Ainsley at least, then it meant that the master of Cross Ings had not, after all, died shortly after leaving Walter Thwaite's shop. So where *had* he been between then and the time when Porteous claimed to have seen him? The park was not an inviting place to hang around in on a bleak and workaday morning. Unless you had an appointment with someone that you didn't wish to make too public.

'If this is right, we shall have to start looking at things in reverse. We've been concentrating on who could have followed him from the Syke Beck Lane end – or met him coming the other way. Now we have to think t'other way round. Seems more likely now that it's him that would have come in at the far end, the Moortop Road end.'

'And the person he was talking to in the park followed him.'

Womersley considered. 'Get yourself to the bank, Jack, and

see if you can get them to confirm what time Hirst reached and left there. When you've finished, go and have a word with Binns. We're going to need his constables to make some concentrated enquiries at the bottom end of the town to see if we can stir up anybody's memories – about Beaumont, or any stranger that might fit the bill. And while you're at it, it might be as well to try and get hold of Dr Pike again, to see if it's possible he'd only been dead a couple of hours.'

'Owt else?' Rawlinson asked.

'That'll do for now. I'm going to have a word with Walter Thwaite.'

He retraced his tracks, heading for the newsagent's shop. Presently, the dam came in sight. It was a raw, dark morning with a sneaky wind that ruffled the leaden surface of the murky water. It looked viscous and evil. As he approached he saw a woman standing beside the dam wall, staring out over the expanse of water; a small woman, hunched into a heavy coat. She had turned to walk away but when she saw him she stopped. He raised his hat, gave her good morning and was about to pass when she spoke to him. 'Excuse me, but aren't you one of the policemen?'

She was Sarah Illingworth, who lived in the house attached to the mill, a few yards away. 'Won't you come inside for a cup of tea?'

He hesitated only momentarily. Despite his turned up coat collar and the knitted muffler Kate had insisted he wore that day, he felt chilled, and he was never averse to tea. Talking to Walter Thwaite could come later. 'I will, thanks. I've been wanting a word with you, Mrs Illingworth.'

He followed her into the house and the bright, warm kitchen, where she invited him to take off his coat, made a strong brew of tea and poured it into sensibly large-sized white mugs. Pushing the sugar towards him, she said, 'Are you sure, then, that it was murder?'

'Pretty certain. Why do you ask?'

For a while she said nothing, looking into the heart of the leaping fire and nursing her tea with hands that were work-worn, strong and capable, but well-shaped. It was very peaceful, the humming of machinery an almost mesmeric background. She had not put on the light, despite the darkness of the morning, but the flames from the fire made a little oasis of brightness around them. He liked the look of Mrs Illingworth. A quiet woman, with soft dark eyes that just now were sad. 'It might be – well, nearly wicked, you know – to say such a thing, but in some ways it's a relief to hear you say that. Not that I'm glad he died the way he did, of course – how could I be? You know, he was in a right funny mood last time I saw him, and when they said it was suicide, I tell you I was shocked, of course. But I wasn't exactly surprised.'

'When *did* you last see him?'

'The morning he died.'

'Oh? What time would that have been?'

She widened her eyes at the urgency in his voice. 'Around half past eight, I think. Yes, it was, breakfast time, the engine had just switched off. He just popped in – he used to do that a lot, you know. We were friends from a long way back and he liked to stop and have a chat.' She smiled slightly. 'He even used to ask me for a bit of advice now and then! I thought he looked really poorly and I made him sit down and have some tea. Then he said he had something to tell me.' She coloured a little. 'He said he was very glad I'd had a happy life and then he said no matter what, I'd be all right after he'd gone, and so would Tom – my son. It was the last thing I expected to hear, but before I could answer him, he was taking some pills out of his pocket. He emptied the box and swallowed the lot. He said he had a headache and . . . I'm sorry for it now, but that made me speak to him right sharp. I looked him in the eye and told him what I'd been thinking for a long time – that anybody with a bit of gumption could see it was more than any headache and that it was high time he got himself seen to, he'd been looking like death warmed up for weeks.'

'And what did he say to that?'

Her eyes filled with tears but she blinked them away. 'He didn't deny it. He just laughed it off and tried to make a joke out of it, and said he wasn't ready to go just yet. And anyway he had things to do before he died.'

Almost the same words he had used to Widdop, Womersley recalled. Things to do. Reparation to his granddaughter, Laura Harcourt, but what else? Womersley thought of that money he had drawn out. A debt to pay, or *had* it been blackmail money as Rawlinson had suggested?

'And then,' Mrs Illingworth went on, gazing into the fire, 'a few hours later, he was dead, poor Ainsley. I hear tell he had a tumour, and I wouldn't have blamed him if . . . All the same, I'm glad he didn't do it himself,' she finished sadly.

'One of the things he did before he died, Mrs Illingworth, was to make provision in his will for his granddaughter, Laura Harcourt.'

Her eyes took on a watchful quality. 'Yes, I know. That was like him. Whatever else, he was always fair.'

Womersley wasn't altogether sure whether it had been fair to Laura to keep her in the dark all her life about her true parentage, but that aspect of it hardly concerned him.

'You looked after her when she was a baby, I believe?'

'Her poor mother died soon after she was born, not much more than a child herself, and Laura stayed with us for eighteen months.'

The hot tea was doing its usual job of temporarily easing the ever-present burn in his chest, the warmth of the room made him feel relaxed and comfortable, and Womersley didn't feel like moving, but he could not legitimately stay much longer. 'How long did Mr Beaumont stay with you?'

'Over an hour, I suppose, altogether. I told him not to move until he felt better, but he kept looking at the clock and in the end he said he'd have to go, he had to meet somebody at ten o'clock. And he did look a bit better by then,' she added defensively.

'He didn't say who it was he was meeting?'

'No, a business meeting, I suppose it was.'

He thanked Mrs Illingworth for the tea, shrugged on his coat and made his way towards the shop on Syke Beck Lane.

Eighteen

Ainsley Beaumont hadn't enlightened Mrs Illingworth as to who he was due to meet, but Womersley thought there was just a chance he might have mentioned it to the shopkeeper, Walter Thwaite. In view of the fact that he had owned the deeds to the shop, it was possible they were on friendly terms. All these people were of the same generation, they had grown up living their lives in this same tight community and, after all, Beaumont could not have known he was going to meet a possible murderer – the meeting might have had an innocuous purpose – although a rendezvous in the park, of all places, suggested some attempt at secrecy, or at least a wish not to make it too public.

The newsagent's shop was a temporary-looking building, not much more than a wood hut built on a brick base. Postcards and notices in the window advertised, amongst other things, the town brass band's first outdoor concert next month (weather permitting), Nellie Shaw's home-made cream buns and Fartown's next fixture. As he entered, a paraffin heater assailed Womersley with a powerful odour, compounded by the smells of strong tobacco, newsprint from the papers lined up on the counter and bundles of firewood and malodorous firelighters stacked on the floor. Behind the counter were colourful boiled sweets in bottles ranged along shelves, bags of sherbet and liquorice bootlaces.

Also behind the counter was Walter Thwaite himself. Hearing the shop bell, he rose from the stool he was sitting on, replaced his reading glasses with another pair from his waistcoat pocket and carefully marked his place in the book he was reading before putting it aside. Womersley saw it was a New Testament and recalled that Thwaite was, or had been, a local preacher on the Wesleyan Methodist circuit. A spruce little man, he was wearing a sleeved waistcoat and his shirt collar was stiff and white, his tie neat, his white hair brushed.

'How long have you been running the shop here, Mr Thwaite?' Womersley asked after a few words on the purpose of his visit.

'Since I had to give up working, on account of my chest.'

'Nice little business . . . must've been a godsend to you.'

'I'll not say it hasn't.' Thwaite was a mild mannered, quietly spoken sort of chap, but his light eyes behind his glasses were sharp. 'I reckon you'll have discovered by now who it belongs to?' Womersley nodded. 'I thought so. Aye well, Ainsley Beaumont had it built and set me up, and I paid him rent for it. That's what he called in for that day, his rent. He usually came when it was quiet so nobody would get nosey. He didn't want it known he was the landlord, and I'd like to ask you to keep it like that, if you can.'

'When somebody's murdered, nobody has secrets, Mr Thwaite.'

'I know that well enough, but that business was between me and him, even our Jessie thinks I was set up by our chapel fund and I'd like it to stay that way. She'll find out soon enough when I'm gone.'

'As far as I'm concerned, there's no reason why anybody else should be told – as things stand at the moment, that is. I can't guarantee more than that.'

Thwaite seemed satisfied. 'What can I do for you, then?'

'Just checking. I believe it was Constable Bradley who came to ask you about the time Mr Beaumont came in, and when he left?'

'Aye, young Cyril. As I told him, Ainsley stopped in for a paper, and I paid him his rent. I'd just mashed a pot of tea and he had a drop with me. We talked about this and that for about ten minutes and then he left.' Thwaite paused for a rattling cough that racked his thin frame and when Womersley waved him to sit down again, he seemed glad to do so. 'I've known him since we were lads, you know,' he went on when he could, leaning his elbows on the counter, revealing the protective celluloid cuffs he wore over the ones on his shirt. 'My father worked for his father, and I worked for Ainsley. Never any side to him, though. I'd like to think we were friends. It's a sorry do, this.'

'Were you one of those who played cards with him?' Womersley asked before the expression on Thwaite's face told him he had made a mistake. He'd forgotten the chap was a strait-laced Bible puncher, a working man who'd no doubt educated himself – enough at any rate to become a lay-preacher. Thwaite surprised Womersley with a wheezy laugh, however.

'Give over, Inspector! The likes of me aspiring to have friends in high places?' Sobering, he added, 'Any road, I don't hold with card-playing. Innocent enough if you don't gamble, but all too often that's what it leads to.'

'The doctor was one of his regular partners. And Whiteley Hirst.'

'I don't doubt that,' Thwaite said dryly. He seemed about to say more, but at that moment, the shop door was pushed open by a little girl of about ten in a clean, starched pinafore and polished clogs. She had a lame leg, and the clogs must have been heavy, but she skipped forward nimbly enough and held out the parcel she carried. 'Brought your medicine, Mr Thwaite.'

'Thank you, Annie. Here's the doctor's cigarettes.' The parcel was exchanged for another from under the counter. 'Mind you don't squash 'em in your pocket or he'll be looking to dock your wages! They're special cigarettes, cost a lot of money.'

'I'll be careful, Mr Thwaite,' she promised. 'And five Woodbines for me dad, please.' She handed over a penny in exchange for one of the flimsy green and orange paper packets that seemed to constitute the greater part of the shop's stock of cigarettes.

'And don't squash *them*, either. Why aren't you at school?'

'Our Billy's had German measles. He's getting better but I have to look after him and get the little 'uns their dinner 'cos me Mam can't have no more time off.'

'Well, watch how you go, love, and here you are.' He reached behind him for a jar of bull's eyes, opened it and let her choose.

She thanked him with a wide, bright smile, popped the sweet into her mouth and limped out, her cheek bulging. Thwaite watched her go. 'There's a grand little lass. Doctor gives her a tanner to bring my medicine, so's I don't have to go down for it. Very thoughtful.'

'Bit of a saint round here in fact, Dr Widdop, isn't he?'

'I wouldn't go so far as that! He has his faults, same as everybody else, but Wainthorpe would be a poorer place without him, that's for sure.' Womersley waited to hear what they were but Widdop's shortcomings weren't to be revealed that day. 'Well, like I was saying, it's a slack time around half past eight, folks already at work. I reckon I would have noticed anybody unusual going along that path.'

Trade could never be all that brisk and time must pass slowly.

The notices on the window were strategically placed so that from behind his counter, he had a good view of the outside world. A real miss-nowt corner. He wondered how much Thwaite actually made from the shop. It could hardly be the proverbial little gold mine.

'Right, then, that was half past eightish. What about later in the morning, up to a couple of hours later? No strangers?'

'Later on?' Thwaite repeated, making a business of realigning the run of *Wainthorpe Couriers* on the counter. 'One or two women, and kids off school, and only them as I would have expected to see, like.'

'And the other way, coming back up the path, Mr Thwaite?'

'Nobody,' he said, bending to pick something up off the floor. As he straightened up, he was seized with another fit of coughing, leaving him bent over the counter without breath to speak. He was the poorest liar Womersley had met in a long time. No doubt his religion forbade it. But as he sat up, his breathing still laboured, there was a stubborn set to his mouth. He wouldn't – perhaps couldn't – say any more.

'I won't trouble you further, Mr Thwaite, But before I go, weigh me a quarter of mint imperials, will you?'

Laura, despite having cravenly asked Tom Illingworth for support before facing Una and Gideon, had suddenly taken the bull by the horns, and without giving herself time to reconsider, told them of what was, to her, their amazing new-found relationship. There had been none of the painful scene she had expected. In fact, she was almost certain they had been prepared for something of the sort. After the contents of the will had been revealed, they had evidently half-guessed that something of that nature must have been the reason behind the legacy. More surprisingly, neither of them seemed unduly put out. The truth was clearly more acceptable than what they had probably suspected, that she had been an illegitimate child of their grandfather. They had not been old enough to remember their father – much less the nursery maid who had been Laura's mother. Ainsley had been the only father they had ever known, they had loved him, and it was evidently a relief that his integrity remained intact.

After this, Laura did not think it wise to mention what had caused their grandfather to send her away from Wainthorpe as

a child; it was enough for them to know that she had been
Theo's child; there was no point in underlining the bitterness
Amelia must have felt at her husband's betrayal, and perhaps it
would never be necessary for them to know of that incident
in her past.

But how were they going to take to the fact that she was
their half-sister? Would they regard her as a cuckoo in the nest,
as her mother had been in that family? She felt that her continued
presence here could do nothing to improve the situation, and
she said, 'I shall be leaving Farr Clough just as soon as the
police tell me I can do so. And by the way, I shall not be
keeping that money for myself. It will go to the Settlement
house where I worked in the East End.'

Gideon shrugged and said he supposed Grandpa had done
what he saw as right, and the money was obviously Laura's to
do with as she wished, but he looked at her more warmly. As
far as Una was concerned, it was apparent that Laura could
have said nothing better. She smiled for the first time since
Laura's return. 'You couldn't do better with it than that,' she
said.

Preparations were going ahead for the funeral, ready for when
the police could 'release' the body, as they said. Amelia was
shocked that the master of Cross Ings was not to have a big,
impressive farewell. A big send off – plumed black horses,
carriages, a funeral procession a hundred yards long, Bethesdsa
chapel packed, and a ham tea to follow was the least a man
of such importance as Ainsley Beaumont was entitled to. It
was what everybody would be expecting. They'd cry shame
on this disregard of tradition. But Gideon was adamant. He
stuck to his decision that in the circumstances it must be a
private affair, for family, close friends and old business acquaintances. Una supported him, and neither were to be moved.
Their mother was much affronted.

And then she astonished Laura by coming into the library
for the first time ever since she had begun work there and
stood looking at the now tidy shelves for some time before
she said, though still very tight-lipped, 'You've done a good
job, I must say.'

Laura could not be sure, but she thought Amelia actually
smiled. A mere shadow of the smile she had occasionally seen

bestowed upon one or other of her children – but never having been at the receiving end before it unnerved Laura.

Nor did Amelia's capacity for engendering amazement stop there. Tentatively, she put out a hand and actually touched Laura's sleeve, though she quickly withdrew it and stood with her hands clasped tightly in front of her, as if afraid she might do it again. She said abruptly, 'You're a bonny lass, just like . . .' Then her lips closed firmly. 'Don't let it go to your head, that's all.'

Was she referring to Lucie – to Laura's mother? Of course she was, she could have meant nothing else.

All the same, Laura was so taken aback, quite unable to account for this about-face of Mrs Beaumont's towards her – unless it was that she was finally convinced Laura had indeed come here in all innocence – that she could think of no way to further the conversation; and in any case, she was certain Amelia had gone as far in conciliation as she was likely to go.

They stood there, equally embarrassed.

It was Amelia who suddenly put an end to it. 'Forgive me, Laura, I am not myself. I haven't been myself for a long time now.' She gave her one last look from those dark, unfathomable eyes, and then she was gone.

It was the first time she had ever used Laura's Christian name.

'I'm afraid Mr Hirst's putting the wages up. He can't be disturbed,' Porteous told Womersley and Rawlinson when they arrived with a request to see the manager.

Rawlinson paid no attention, but banged on the connecting door between the two offices. 'It's the police, Mr Hirst,' he shouted, 'We've something important to say to you.'

After a moment, the sound of a key was heard turning in the lock, the door opened a crack and Hirst's lugubrious face showed itself. 'I'm busy.'

'We shan't keep you long.'

For a moment, it seemed as though he might be about to shut the door again but as Rawlinson's foot moved towards it, he sighed. 'All right come in, then, but I can't spare more than a few minutes.' He kept the door open just wide enough for them to get through, and when they were inside, locked it behind them.

'You have to be careful,' he said, gesturing to the table, where banknotes and piles of coins were neatly set out, ranging from half-crowns and florins, through to coppers and silver coins of lesser denominations. A trifle more conciliatory, he offered a handshake to each of them, passing on the metallic taint of money.

On a wheeled trolley by the table were stacked a pile of large tin wage trays, very like the tins Tilly had used when she made buns, except in scale, Rawlinson thought. They would be heavy when Hirst had transferred to each numbered tin the due amount of money, calculated from the time sheet on the table before him, ready to be doled out into waiting hands. An old custom, as like as not, but he found himself repelled. These were the meagre wages for long hours of hard work at the machines. This way of giving it seemed uncomfortably akin to doling out charity.

Hirst sat down heavily. He looked greyer, older, slightly weary, the sad bloodhound look of his face intensified. 'What do you want, then?'

'To go back to the morning Mr Beaumont died,' Womersley began. 'I believe you went across to the bank.'

'Yes, I walked over to pay in some cheques. Why do you ask?'

'How long were you absent from the office?'

'Nearly three quarters of an hour. Longer than I should have been, but they happened to be very busy.'

'Did you come home via the park?'

'The *park*? Melsom Park? Of course I didn't. It's at the other end of the town.'

'We've been told that you were seen there – with Mr Beaumont.'

Hirst had not allowed himself to be idle while they were talking, counting more money from the blue paper money bags into neat piles, his long fingers stacking them. Now he put down a five shilling stack and stared. 'Who said that?'

'Never mind.'

'No need,' he replied after a moment. 'I know who this came from. It was Porteous, wasn't it?' Womersley said nothing. 'Well, of course it's a lie.'

'What has he got to gain by lying about a thing like that?'

'Purely to create aggravation for me.' He finally put aside the money. 'A year or two back, Edwin Porteous was suspected of dipping his fingers in the till – not a large sum, just some petty cash that was kept in the front office. Nothing could be proved, but there happened to be an office lad who'd left a bit sudden just about the same time, so Ainsley gave Porteous the benefit of the doubt and let him stay on, which I wouldn't have done, and I said as much. Before that, he'd always gone to the bank with me for the wages – as a safety measure, in case anybody got ideas about helping theirselves to the money on the way back, you understand, but after that one of the woolsorters was assigned to go with me, and still does. Now I put the wages up myself, without assistance from Porteous. He's never forgiven me.'

Womersley had no doubt all this was true enough, and suspected this latest wasn't the only aggravation Hirst received from the clerk. He was prepared to believe Porteous – as far as it went. Maybe he *had* spotted Ainsley in the park with someone. And although he couldn't seriously have expected that pointing the finger at Whiteley Hirst would be believed, he might have hoped it would give him some uncomfortable moments. There was evidently no love lost between them, though he was surprised Porteous hadn't given more thought to the stupidity of upsetting Hirst, who had no reason to see he was kept on now that Ainsley Beaumont had gone. That there were people like that, prepared to tell outrageous lies simply to create mischief, Womersley didn't doubt. It wasn't the first time he'd come across this sort of thing: someone with a grudge, not really expecting their accusations to be taken seriously; it was simply done out of spite, to cause an annoyance or embarrassment – or to cast aspersions in a 'no smoke without fire' sort of way, which could be damaging enough in itself. Everyone would remember that Whiteley Hirst and Ainsley Beaumont had been forever at it, sniping at each other, arguing. The fact that they always made it up without evident resentment didn't alter that. This time it might have gone too far.

Baseless as they may turn out to be, these were points that, as police, they couldn't disregard. Checks had already been made – at the bank and with the time office, which Hirst had to pass on his way back to Cross Ings. The times he had given tallied with what he'd said, but it still left some leeway. How long would it take to creep up behind a deaf man and kill him, then double back?

'Mr Beaumont has left you a substantial amount of money in his will, I understand,' Womersley said suddenly.

Hirst reddened. 'Aye, well, that's no surprise. He told me he'd see me right, after he'd gone. We go back a long way. I've been here, man and boy, for near as long as he had, after all, and I'd like to think he appreciated what I'd done.'

Rawlinson, perched on the edge of what had been Ainsley Beaumont's desk, had his fountain pen out and his notebook open, but he was fidgeting about in his restless way with the inkwell, the pen tray and the paperweight. Womersley frowned.

'Have you any idea why Mr Beaumont should have been in the park that morning, Mr Hirst?'

'If he was.' He almost laughed, as if the idea was totally bizarre.

Rawlinson made a sudden exclamation of annoyance and the others looked at him. 'Sorry, don't mind me. I made a blot – rotten fountain pen.'

Hirst impatiently indicated the blotting paper on the desk and said to Womersley, 'I thought you said Ainsley was killed about breakfast time?'

'Given what we had to go on then, yes, I did. We might have to readjust that.'

'What would you say if I told you Porteous used to be an amateur boxer?' Hirst asked deliberately, not above using a hint of malice himself.

'Was he, by Jove? Hard to imagine him that fit, now.'

'Fit enough to hit a man over the head with a stone – and to tip him over the wall into the dam.'

But Porteous had no reason to be anything but grateful to his employer, if what Hirst had just said was true. Any problems the clerk had were with Whiteley Hirst, hence the rather pointless attempts to pay him back with petty annoyances.

Hirst was beginning to look restless, evidently keen to get back to his money-counting, and for the moment, Womersley had nothing more to ask. He stood up, ending the interview. 'Thank you for your time, Mr Hirst. We'll be in touch.'

Outside, he said severely, 'And what was all that about your pen, Sergeant, when you were supposed to be taking notes? It's beginning to get on my nerves, all that twizzling about. Or was there something in there you weren't saying?'

Rawlinson looked crestfallen. 'I didn't think it was so

obvious.' Then he grinned and dived into his pocket, bringing out the pink blotting paper he'd used and neglected to return to the desk top. A six inch square piece which had been folded over once, and while one side had been well used, the other had only two or three words blotted on to it. 'Lead me to a mirror. Might be nothing, but Beaumont was working late the night before he died, wasn't he? And nobody's thrown away the blotting paper on his desk.'

'Sometimes I wonder about you, lad,' Womersley said, shaking his head. 'This isn't one of your Sherlock Holmes tales, you know.'

Rawlinson looked stubborn. 'We'll see.'

And back at the police station, with the aid of a mirror Mrs Binns in the adjoining police house produced, they did. Just a name, looking as if it might have been the superscription on an envelope. A name Sergeant Binns immediately recognized.

Nineteen

It was Tom who offered the facility of his new car to those who were attending the suffrage meeting in Halifax. Second-hand though it might be, he was able to claim with justification that it was more reliable than Gideon's, and even Gideon couldn't argue with that. Though Emmie Broomhead had been his only reason for offering to act as driver in the first place, Gideon decided he would go with them anyway, declaring the women would need protection, should any of the violence occur which only too often broke out at such meetings – and besides, he added with a grin, Tom might need a mechanic.

Jessie Thwaite had been persuaded to go along, taking Emmie's place in the rear seat with the other two girls, though it would be a squash, all wrapped around in heavy coats as they needed to be. Jessie was hesitant about leaving her father alone, but he insisted.

'Get off with you, and don't bother about me. I'll enjoy a quiet evening on my own.'

He came out with her, muffled in a scarf and overcoat, to have a look at the car.

Tom told him it would go at thirty miles an hour, if pushed. 'Well, I don't know, Tom Illingworth,' he said, looking bemused. 'This is a sight different from flying down Syke Beck Lane on that bicycle of yours like you did when you were a lad. We'd have been born with wings if we'd been meant to go that fast!'

Tom laughed as he reached a hand outside to release the brake. 'Safe as houses. Don't worry about Jessie, Mr Thwaite.

He stood at the door to see them off, a frail figure dwarfed by his big overcoat. Jessie scolded him and told him to go indoors, but he stayed where he was, smiling and waving them off until they turned the corner.

The prospect of jaunting over the moors at speed, however serious the end purpose, lifted their spirits. They became rather jolly, Gideon urging Tom to pass the trams lurching up and down the steep gradients, never mind the twenty mile speed limit. Daft, that was. Motorists should be allowed to drive at a speed they considered safe.

The girls huddled together for warmth, laughing and holding on to their hats. Laura was glad they were a crowd. She had been in a curious state between agitation and elation ever since her last meeting with Tom, and had only managed to deal with her emotions so far by not thinking about them.

The dingy room in a church hall near the Cloth Hall in Halifax was already packed when they arrived. It probably would have been anyway, said Una, but one of Mrs Pankhurst's daughters, Sylvia, was to be present and any of the women of that now-famous family was a big draw. The stage was backed with banners, worked in the WSPU colours of purple, green and white, and the platform was crowded with women in their best hats, as if to give the lie to the notion that the only women to be interested in women's rights were those who cared not a button for their appearance. A buzz of energy pervaded the hall, so that the cold, and the draughts, and the hard seats, were somehow not so noticeable. They began by singing *Jerusalem,* two hundred Yorkshire voices, mostly women's, raising the rafters.

Not all of them were women, though. It was encouraging to see a fair sprinkling of males – unless, as Una remarked in an acid aside, these should turn out to be hecklers, throwers of bags of flour, or planted policemen. It was good to see some working men. On the whole they were not the most ardent supporters of the Cause. George Quarmby, the Union man from Cross Ings, along with his wife, a small, stringy woman as dour-looking as he was, had nodded to Gideon as they claimed seats further along the same row; there were a few other men, better dressed, who looked more like teachers and professional men, and a couple with pencils and notebooks at the ready who could only be journalists.

The meeting began with some tedious business about the proposed Women's Exhibition to be held in Knightsbridge in May, a big occasion which would hopefully raise both awareness and funds for the WSPU. Miss Pankhurst – who was, their vivacious chairwoman reminded them, with a bow and a smile directed at the daughter of their eminent leader, a trained artist – had graciously designed banners for the occasion. Much applause. Volunteers and supplies were now urgently

required, she went on, to man – or should she say *woman*? –
the various stalls intended to sell regional produce. Several
women at once volunteered their services. To fill the West
Riding representatives' stall, Yorkshire parkin and curd tarts
were immediately suggested. Some fine woollen shawls, locally
woven. Purple and green cushions, embroidered with the
Yorkshire White Rose emblem, and hand-painted china decor-
ated likewise. A milliner was inspired to offer half a dozen
hats. Perhaps, suggested someone, getting carried away, they
could have a bazaar of their own, as well, to raise funds for
the local branches.

Laura listened and wondered if this was what suffrage was
really all about; there was something incompatible with the
gentle art of setting up and running bazaars and the escalating
violence within the movement, while more and more women
were getting themselves into prison, hunger striking, damaging,
defacing and setting fire to property. Broken glass, according
to Mrs Pankhurst, was the most valuable argument in present
day politics. Endeavouring to raise funds by selling trinkets and
tea sets and baking parkin seemed to have little to do with all
that, and would surely only arouse derision and more opposition
in the men who were against them, another proof that women
were incapable of thinking in any way beyond hearth and home?
Laura sensed she was far from being alone in this; there were
stirrings in the audience and between Jessie and Una long-
suffering looks passed.

It was a relief when Sylvia Pankhurst rose to enthusiastic
applause, but she was not to speak long this evening, it appeared.
She was here to introduce and recommend the next speaker,
a very popular choice. W.B. Empson was a man noted locally
for his stirring oratory and his wholehearted support of the
women's movement, outspoken on radical issues and well
known to many of them, through his books, newspaper articles
and speeches. He was not on the platform to begin with, but
appeared when he was called on to speak; a tall, middle-aged
man, he walked on to the stage with some panache, twirling
a walking stick. Like a music hall turn, thought Laura. Any
amusement faded, however, as Empson began to speak to an
audience which became hushed and quiet the moment he
began his introductory words.

He was younger than Laura had first thought him, perhaps

no more than in his mid-forties, a handsome man, though his face was lined and the fall of hair over his brow was more silver than dark. His scholarly stoop suggested a middle-aged academic, but his voice when he spoke was that of a young man. He was a powerful orator, and an actor more than a little, and he spoke in a ringing voice, using that silver-banded stick theatrically, like a stage-prop, leaning forward, his hands cupped over its handle. Then waving it, brandishing it like a sword, stabbing it on the floor to emphasize his points. What a humbug! But when he got into his stride, he seemed to forget his mannerisms – and so did Laura. His arguments had cogency, there was truth in the pictures he painted. He passionately believed in universal suffrage, for both men and women, he supported Trades Unions and fair wages for all, and above all, Lloyd George's promises for redistribution of wealth in his People's Budget. His eyes flashed. His face was noble. He drew himself up to his considerable height and spoke with grave concern and common sense, captivating his audience, male and female, speaking with such honesty, sincerity and depth of feeling that some of the women round about them were in tears. Laura found herself almost moved to join them, and even Gideon, who had sat throughout with his arms folded, joined in the applause at the end with hearty approval. And Una? His speech had ignited a flame in her. There was silence when he had finished and then a roar of applause, and she was on her feet with the rest, her face incandescent.

When the applause died down, Empson bowed but did not take the seat which had been left vacant for him, and walked off the stage. The performance – Laura could not think of it as anything else – had perhaps taken it out of him.

'There, what did you think of that?' She turned to Tom, sitting on her other side.

'The speech? Marvellous. The rest of them? Blinkered, perhaps,' he returned, smiling. 'Right about their ideals, perhaps, but mistaken in the way they're going about it. Nothing's calculated to rouse opposition more than violence. Are you of their persuasion? I can see you might be.'

'Certainly not! As a matter of fact, I agree with you about the violence.' Yet more and more did Laura agree with their aims and ideals. The constant reiteration of them at Farr Clough was infectious.

Tom, however, was not inclined to pursue the conversation and went to find them the cup of tea that had been promised. They appeared to be back on their former footing. Perhaps he had only been angry with himself for being so precipitate, and not offended that she had so quickly appeared to reject his overtures out of hand. More likely, he regretted an impulsive moment, she thought as she joined Una among the women gathered at the back of the hall.

Empson's speech had been worth the effort of turning out on a cold night, they agreed. 'I wonder if I could persuade him to write something for *Unity*? But I can't ask him now,' Una said. 'He's being mobbed and there are people I want to see. I shall have to find out his address and then I'll write to ask him.'

'I'll get it for you.'

The speaker sat at a table with his books and pamphlets displayed, and Laura waited her turn, reluctant to push herself forward. However, when he happened to look up and see her standing at the back of the crowd something prompted him to ask, 'Is there anything I can do for you?'

He beckoned to her and the sea of women gave way. She passed on Una's hope that he might write something for her magazine.

'*Unity*? Oh yes, I've seen it, and admired it. Una Beaumont, isn't it, who produces it? Is she here?' Laura waved to where Una stood with her friends, a tall and graceful figure, unusually animated, her eyes shining and her blonde looks enhanced rather than diminished by the black she was wearing. He considered her thoughtfully for several moments. 'She is in mourning? And you, too?' he asked, turning back to Laura

'Yes. A . . . relative has died.'

'My condolences to you both. Well, when you're ready, I shall be honoured to help. Let me give you my address.'

'I'm afraid she won't be able to pay you,' Laura warned. He waved a hand. None of these little magazines could pay. 'But *Unity* has a good circulation,' she added.

'That would clearly be an advantage.'

He had a slow smile of great charm. But he was much less flamboyant than he had appeared on the stage. He scribbled something in a notebook, tore the sheet out, folded it and handed it to her. She slipped it into her bag. 'And you are, Miss . . . ?'

'My name's Harcourt, Laura Harcourt.'

He shook her hand. 'I look forward to hearing from Miss Beaumont, and have the privilege of meeting her – and you, too, again, Miss Harcourt, I hope.'

Tom drew the car up outside Jessie's house. Immediately, Jessie noticed that the light was still on. 'He hasn't gone to bed yet!'

She flew up the short path to the house. Una and Laura looked at each other and followed. They found Jessie kneeling beside her father's chair, her arms around him and her head buried against his shoulder. Walter Thwaite had died sitting in his armchair, a rug over his knees, his hands on his Bible. He looked as though he had quietly gone to sleep. Jessie raised her head, her face blank with shock. 'I should never have gone. Left him with nobody to sit with him.'

'Jessie, how could you have known?' Una said gently. 'He was happy for you to go this evening, and I'm sure he died quite peacefully. Look, let me make you a cup of tea . . .'

But Laura had forestalled her and was already stirring the dying fire, lifting the kettle from the hob and putting it on to the coals, where it immediately began to sing. She went into the little scullery behind to look for the teapot and when she came back, she found Tom had followed them into the house. It took him only a moment to realize what had happened. 'We'll fetch Dr Widdop,' he said immediately.

'It's too late,' Jessie said, lifting her head. 'But I'd like to see Matthew Pike. Please ask Dr Pike to come.'

With all that had happened, it wasn't until she was undressing that Laura remembered the address the speaker had given her. She took the folded paper out of her bag so that she would not forget to give it to Una the next day. It wafted open as she tossed it on to the dressing table and, catching a glimpse of what was written on the inside, she opened it fully. For several minutes she stared at it, then refolded it and put it back on the dressing table.

Walter Thwaite's funeral had taken place, but until Ainsley Beaumont's body was allowed to be interred, those at Farr Clough were in a state of limbo, restless and unable to settle to anything. Gideon dashed at the crack of dawn to Cross Ings and returned late, as if the place would fall down without his continual presence, but even he could not stay down there all night. He seemed to have lost his taste at the moment for the friends he used to racket around with. Una, too, appeared not to know what to do with herself. There was a limit to the letters and articles even she could write, and she had been in a strange state of feverish excitement ever since the Halifax meeting. They sat around in the evenings in Una's workroom, the three of them, reading, talking, playing the occasional game of cribbage . . .

One evening, wondering how she was to get through the next hour or two without yawning her head off, Laura wandered over to the piano, opened the lid and began plonking out one of the latest jolly tunes, singing what words she could remember. Not much of a performance, but about as much as she was capable of, and it earned her a round of applause.

Gideon looked at his sister. 'Go on, Una, your turn now.'

Una hesitated, then took Laura's place. After a moment, she began to play. Laura didn't recognize the piece. She was not musical, as *Kelly from the Isle of Man* had amply testified. Scarlatti perhaps? At any rate, it was one of those quick, rippling pieces that need a high degree of skill to play. She went to sit by the fire, listened and watched Una's long white fingers flash over the keys. It was only a short piece, and as the last note finished, she sat with her head bent, her hands resting on the keyboard.

'There now, that wasn't so bad, after all, was it?' Gideon said.

'I'm out of practice.'

'Not so bad!' Laura exclaimed. 'Gideon, how many people can play like that?'

'I'm not all that good. But I was taught by one who played better than I ever could.'

'And now that you've started again,' Gideon said, 'you go on. It's the first step that counts.'

She looked at him oddly, without saying anything, for a long time. 'You're right. The first step. I can do it, of course I can. I've stayed here too long.'

'That's not what I meant.'

'But it's what I mean.'

There were undercurrents here that escaped Laura.

Una's face flushed, her eyes were bright, 'As soon as the

funeral's over, I shall go to London and work for the movement there. I spoke to Sylvia Pankhurst at the meeting and I
know I would be welcomed with open arms. Write to your
friend Eva and tell her she has another recruit, Laura.'

'That would not be a good idea, Una.' Gideon's face was
pale and set now.

Laura saw what he meant. Una, she was afraid, was the stuff
of which martyrs are made. Chaining herself to railings,
breaking windows, prison, hunger striking . . . And what was
all that about the piano?

'What about Mother?' Gideon said at last.

'She has no obligations to Grandpa now. And I've none to
her – she can marry Whiteley Hirst and be happy ever after.
It's what he has wanted for years, after all – and so has she,
though she won't admit it.'

Twenty

'Well, Jessie Thwaite, this is it,' said Jessie to herself as she perched, despite the cold evening, on the low wall at the end of the plot her father had liked to call his bit of garden. 'Time you made your mind up.'

Not much bigger than a tablecloth, really, the garden, but it had been somewhere Walter could grow a cabbage or two, a few potatoes, some rhubarb, when he'd been fit enough to look after it.

Below her, underneath the wall where she perched, was a big drop down on to a dirt footpath, eight feet of stone buttressing the street of houses. Alongside the path rushed a little brown beck. Beyond, the land sloped even further towards the town. She could see right across Wainthorpe and its mills and chimneys, up to the hills on the opposite side of the valley and the moors on top where her father used to take her to listen to the laverocks when she was a little girl.

The funeral over, she had just finished parcelling up in brown paper Walter's Sunday clothes: his best suit, shoes and shirt that he wore to chapel and when he was preaching; and his razor, his shaving pot and his badger-hair brush. He had possessed nothing else worth keeping, apart from his books. Every copper he had ever been able to save had been spent on the few second-hand copies he had treasured as if they were miser's gold, but Jessie had no personal use for them. She was not much of a reader, especially not of John Wesley's sermons. No doubt the minister would find someone who would be glad of everything. His Bible, Jessie kept for herself. She had no need of any other possessions to keep the memory of her father alive.

The worst task finally done, she had methodically scrubbed, swept and polished the already spotless little house from top to bottom, blackleaded the grate with Zebo and polished the windows, inside and out, until they gleamed. All that expended energy and she was still left with the problem of what to do about her future.

Jessie's mother had died when she was seven, and Walter

had brought her up single-handed. Nobody ever got the chance to pity the motherless little girl, however; somehow there were always decent clothes to wear and a hot meal on the table. Walter had taught himself to cook as well as any woman, and would come home from his work in the mill and bake their bread for the week from half a stone of flour, or set a stew in the oven to simmer all day. She always had a little cake for her birthday. But he didn't spoil her; he saw to it that Jessie, as she grew older, learned to do her share in the house. She grew tall, strong, and capable and when her father's health began to fail it was her turn to look after him. She had always known that Walter's little business, selling newspapers and tobacco, had not belonged to him, but it had been a shock to learn that it was not a chapel charity fund which had set him up in the wood hut as she had thought, though the money had come via the chapel. Once, years ago, Ainsley Beaumont had had a share in ownership of the shoddy mill where Walter had worked, and where he'd contracted the disease which had finally killed him, and now she had learnt that it was he who had provided the means to set Walter up, swearing all members of the administrating fund at the chapel to secrecy on pain of not receiving any more of his generous yearly contributions. Anger had bubbled up in her when she learnt who her father's benefactor had been – in effect the man in whose employ his health had been ruined. It made her realize why her father had never told her, but she considered his Christian charity and forgiveness had gone too far in allowing Ainsley to make this sop to his conscience – unless, of course, it was a case of heaping coals of fire . . . She sighed. No, her father had not been so devious, or vengeful, nor indeed had Ainsley Beaumont been a tyrant. But Jessie did not always find it easy to separate black from white.

What was she to do now? Working with Una, becoming involved with the Cause, had opened her eyes to other possibilities, another world. She wasn't educated enough to do anything fancy, but the practical idea of becoming a nurse, put there by the new doctor, Matthew Pike, had insinuated itself into her mind when she had realized how fast her father's health was failing, and had had to accept that she would soon be left on her own. Of course, Matthew Pike had only suggested this because . . . Well, never mind that.

Her life stretched in front of her, hers to do with as she wished, but somehow it didn't seem as appealing as she'd thought it would. A cold little breeze touched her and she hugged herself. Spring was coming fast to the valley. A haze of green misted the hawthorn hedges and by the path below a shaft of sunlight touched some hazel catkins, powdery gold against their black twigs. Come on, Jessie! Stop feeling sorry for yourself! And suddenly, with a laugh, she hitched up her skirts and scrambled over the wall, hung on and then let herself go. She still hadn't forgotten how to land lightly. By the tumbling little beck, she broke off a few of the hazel twigs, then walked on towards Syke Beck Lane and round to the front of the house. Even Jessie balked at clambering back up the wall. When Matthew Pike arrived, the living room was cosy with the fresh fire she'd lit; she'd set the catkins in a stone jug on the green plush table cloth and had a pot of tea ready.

If he had a pound for all the cups of tea he'd drunk since coming to Wainthorpe!

Matthew had had a hard day, and had something on his mind, but after a while he became more relaxed, rocking gently back and forth in the rocking chair, cradling his cup of tea, very much at home in this little house, with this young woman he'd come to know so well, and hoped to know even better. 'What are you going to do, have you given it any more thought?' he asked presently.

'It's too soon, just yet,' she answered evasively. 'I might just as well stay on at Farr Clough as I am for the time being. I'll have more spare time to help Una.'

'I've something to tell you,' he said abruptly, looking at her seriously, 'I think I'm about to take the plunge and leave Wainthorpe.'

Which was just what her heart did. Took a plunge. Plummeted like a stone. 'But . . . I thought you liked it here. Working with Dr Widdop.'

'He's a fine doctor, a fine man. The patients love him, but when they send for 'the doctor' it's him they want, Jess, not me. I'm not popular. I haven't got a fancy car that makes them think they're being looked after by somebody special, or clothes that make me look like a professional man, and God forgive me, I haven't got a bedside manner – or not the one they think is appropriate. Altogether, Wainthorpers don't think much of me.'

'Well, you don't always think much of them, either,' said Jessie bluntly.

'Not when they shut their minds to everything new, no.'

All this was partly true, she knew, but he was not doing himself justice. 'My father liked you. Better than Dr Widdop.'

'And God bless him for that, but your father was a saint.'

'Saints can sometimes judge other people very hard.'

'Walter? Hard? Why, what have you done, Jess?'

'Me? No . . . it's not me.' She topped up his tea. 'Matthew, just give folks time. It's only they're used to Widdop, and his old ideas. They've both served Wainthorpe pretty well for a long time now.'

'I know,' he said grimly. 'That's the whole point. The men don't like being told it's not a good idea to drink all their wages away, so he doesn't tell them, and the women – well, you know what I feel about that, Jess. We've talked about it often enough.'

Oh yes. From the moment he had arrived in Wainthorpe, he had been trying to introduce the delicate matter of birth control, but she knew he felt himself up against a brick wall. He said again what he'd said a dozen times, 'A desperate woman will try anything – hot baths, gin, or worse – to "bring themselves on". It's not looked down on, rather as a form of contraception. When will they learn prevention's better than cure?'

'And what about the men?'

'Oh, they're just as bad, or worse. They think it's all up to the women.'

'Well, Dr Widdop tries, too, you've told me.'

'In a way. He should press his point more. But he'll only go so far. The truth is, I suppose, he and I just don't see eye to eye. I doubt if we ever will. It's time to move on, Jess.'

She stood up to take the teapot from the hob. Her face was red as she turned back and he said suddenly, 'Come with me when I go, Jess. We make a good team, we have the same ideas, we think alike. We could, you know, start afresh, both of us, in a new place.'

She had recovered herself a little. 'And what about me being a nurse?'

'Oh, that! You could do better than that. You could train to be a dispenser, to read prescriptions, mix medicines, roll pills.'

He sat there, his hair like a collapsed haystack where he had run his hands through it. Besides a good brush and combing, it needed cutting, His tie was askew and one point of his collar turned up. He needed a woman to look after him. He was a clever man, and there were a lot of things he knew, but he didn't seem to have learnt that yet.

He said suddenly, 'Something's worrying you. What is it?'

'Not *worrying* – just a bit of a mystery. Matthew, somebody came to see Dad that night, the night he died. Had a cup of tea with him.'

'Sam Titmuss?'

'No, he couldn't come that night.' She blinked. 'That's why I left Dad on his own . . .'

'Jess, my love, he could have gone any time, you know that. He died peacefully.'

'I know, and I'm thankful for it but . . . it was the cups and saucers, see.'

'Cups and saucers?'

'They were in the wrong cupboard, Mam's best china, Indian tree pattern, in with the old everyday stuff. Somebody that didn't know that had used them, washed them up and put them back in the wrong cupboard.'

'Somebody from the chapel, perhaps? Does it matter?'

'No, but it's funny, nobody's said anything about being here. I can't help wondering if . . . if they'd been here when he died—'

'This is not a road to go down, and I won't have you choosing to,' he said, standing up so suddenly he sent the chair swinging wildly on its rockers. He took her by the shoulders and looked into her face. She was nearly as tall as he. 'It's nothing, and you have better things to think about – such as the answer to my question. Have you forgotten already that I asked you to come away with me?'

'Oh, and haven't you forgotten something? I'm a respectable woman, Matthew Pike.'

He saw her eyes come alive with laughter again, felt her warmth and generosity. 'Of course I haven't forgotten. I didn't think I needed to say I love you. Why else would I ask you to marry me, you silly woman?'

Twenty-One

Cross Ings Mill was shut down for the day when eventually the master's funeral came, and despite the decision Gideon stubbornly refused to alter – that his grandfather's interment should be a quiet, private affair – many of Wainthorpe's shops were closed as well, in recognition of the passing of one of its most notable townsmen. Amelia, magnificently dignified in new black, compelled to accept what she considered to be a very second-rate send-off, was slightly mollified by this, and by the number of people who turned out to witness in silent respect the passing of the short funeral cortège.

The service was short, dignified and moving, but Laura was shocked to see, in the background behind those who stood at the graveside for the committal, the two policemen who were investigating the murder. What were they doing here? Did they come out of respect, or what? They could only be a painful reminder to everyone of the circumstances of Ainsley Beaumont's death.

And then, when the coffin had been lowered into the ground, the last prayers said, and the crowd was dispersing, she saw with a further shock someone else she recognized. 'Is something wrong?' asked Tom, following her fixed stare across the wreaths and flowers.

'That man—'

'Do you want to speak to him?'

'I think I must.'

'Well, then.' Taking her arm, he strode rapidly after the man who was heading towards the gates. Laura called his name.

He halted and turned, and when he saw who it was courte-ously raised his hat. 'Miss Harcourt!'

'I am surprised to see you here, Mr Empson.'

'When I saw you – and Miss Beaumont – in mourning at the meeting, I made enquiries and decided I must come to pay my respects.'

'We should talk,' Laura said abruptly, 'But not here. You haven't met Mr Illingworth – Mr Empson.'

They shook hands. 'I was at the meeting when you spoke, Mr Empson. A fine speech.'

'Thank you.'

The rest of the mourners were walking away from the grave. Most of those who had followed the coffin had left and now the family, the hand-shaking and receiving of condolences over, was ready to depart for Farr Clough. The two policemen were speaking to the editor of the local paper.

'By all means let us talk, if you so wish. But perhaps now is not the best time,' Empson said.

'We must.'

'A moment, if you please.' Tom walked back quickly and spoke to Gideon, then to his mother. When he returned, he said, 'They will go on without us. I know somewhere we can talk, if you wish to. Not the best place, perhaps, but I can't think of anywhere else.'

A little way from the cemetery, down in the town, was a very old, stone-slated building tucked into an awkward angle between two steep streets. *The Tea Shoppe*, though dark and very small, was a popular Wainthorpe rendezvous, with its flower embroidered cloths, delicate china and pastries oozing with cream; a haunt of those ladies who had time and money to spare for taking tea and cakes in the afternoon. Fortunately, so late in the day, only one of the half a dozen tables was taken.

'Mrs Ormerod, Mrs Booth,' Tom acknowledged the occupants as they passed.

The two ladies watched with avid curiosity as they took their seats – Laura, who was already the subject of much speculation in the town, and Tom, the local wanderer returned, his presence equally intriguing, and particularly Empson, the stranger. Gentlemen did not often come into this place, whose main function was to provide a trading post for the exchange of information and tittle-tattle. The newcomers, however, were irritatingly shown to a table in the farthest corner, just out of earshot, and only after tea had been brought and poured did they begin to talk, and then in low voices which did not carry.

'We know who you are, Mr Empson,' Laura said directly. 'I have told Mr Illingworth how you gave yourself away by your handwriting when you wrote down your address for me. I'd already found a manuscript you had written in the library at Farr Clough.'

She was not likely to forget the shock she had felt on seeing that particular handwriting once more, the immediate recognition. She had seen it before, and recently. There had been no mistaking the idiosyncratic curls and the Greek 'e's, the left-handed, backward slope of the letters, and no need to compare it with that on the roll of papers she had found in the library. He might just as well have signed his name as Benjamin Kindersley.

He did not conform to the picture she had in her mind. He was twenty years older, of course, than the young Ben Kindersley who, as described by himself, had been a big, muscular young farmer's son; this man was certainly tall, and there was no reason to think he was not still strong, but any breadth of shoulder was obscured by the slight stoop of someone who had spent much of his life bent over a desk, reading or writing.

'So you found that old manuscript? I showed it to no one because I was afraid it might offend by being too . . . honest. I left it behind, though not intentionally, when I quitted Farr Clough in something of a hurry.'

'You *are* Ben Kindersley, then?'

'Not a fact known to many, now. I have worked professionally as William Empson for so long, and become so changed, that I've almost forgotten Ben Kindersley myself. And for my part, Miss Harcourt, I know who you are, and may I say that I am more than happy to meet you at last? Delighted, in fact. I have followed your progress for many years.'

'Mine?'

'We kept in touch, Mr Beaumont and I, after I left Farr Clough. He had been the best of friends to me when I needed him, and continued to be so.'

'I read your account of how he found you in the blizzard and took you to his home, you and . . . and Lucie Picard. My mother.'

'Ah. So he decided to tell you himself, after all?'

'No. It was left to Mr Illingworth here to do that.'

He looked at Tom with interest, then back to Laura. 'He meant to tell you, I know. And would have done, had he still been alive.'

Laura stirred her tea. 'Why did you leave Farr Clough?'

A shadow crossed his face. 'You may well ask. There was the fire, as you must know, and after that, it was no place for me. The family had lost a son, a husband and father. And Lucie . . .' He hesitated. 'You must not blame her for what she did, Miss Harcourt. She was very young and her head was easily turned, and I believe she had given no thought as to what the consequences of her actions might be, until the terrible outcome.'

Tom said, as the silence lengthened, 'Are you telling us that she was responsible for that fire?'

Empson shook his head, as if to clear it. 'No, no, no! But she would not speak of it, would say nothing to anyone, even me. In the end, Dr Widdop advised me to go away and leave her alone for the time being, come back when she had recovered from the shock. Ainsley promised he would see that she was taken care of meanwhile – a promise he kept faithfully.' His tea had grown cold, undrinkable, with a skin of milk on the top, and he pushed it away. 'I was hurt and angry at her rejection of me, and God help me, it didn't take much to let myself be persuaded to leave. Ainsley lent me the trap, since I could still not walk too well, and John Willie Sugden drove me away.'

'To Manchester?'

'No. I went home, back to the farm, made my peace with my father as best I could. I waited to hear from Ainsley and at last he wrote to tell me of the child Lucie was expecting. I was young, too, and judged harshly. I stayed away. And then, later, there was another letter, when she died, leaving a daughter.' He brushed a hand across his face. 'Lucie's child! You may imagine how I felt, knowing I had no claim on you, Miss Harcourt – Laura. I took comfort in knowing you were being well cared for . . . by your mother, I believe, Mr Illingworth?' Tom nodded.

'I stayed at High Brow and worked there with my father until he died, and until two of my sisters were married and settled. By then I had had articles published, and my work was beginning to be known. I sold the farm and left with my eldest sister, Prue. She is still with me, she keeps me and my house near Hebden Bridge in order. Neither of us has ever married.'

'What *did* happen, Mr Empson, that night of the fire?'

Empson looked from one to the other, then shook his head, but Laura said, 'You know, I know you do. Please, Mr Empson. No one else speaks of it. My father died that night – don't you think I have a right to know?'

After a moment, he said slowly, 'I cannot.'

The shop bell jangled and the two police officers, Rawlinson and Womersley, entered and crossed to their table. Tom half rose from his chair but the gangly sergeant pressed him down with a hand on his shoulder.

'Sorry to interrupt, Miss Harcourt, Mr Illingworth.' Womersley's big presence loomed large. 'Mr Empson, sir, I believe? My name is Womersley, Detective Inspector, and this is Detective Sergeant Rawlinson.'

'Yes, I am William Empson. How did you know me?'

'We came across your name, never mind where.' He hesitated. 'Well, as a matter of fact our local man here, Sergeant Binns, recognized it, on account of articles you write for *The Wainthorpe Courier*. The editor pointed you out at the funeral.'

'Then what can I do for you?'

'We should like a few words, sir. At the police station?'

'May I ask what this is about?'

'We are investigating the death of Mr Ainsley Beaumont, and I've reason to think you might be able to help us with our enquiries.'

'I don't understand.'

'We believe you may have been the last person to see him alive.'

Laura threw a glance of consternation at Empson, but after a moment, he said calmly, 'I suppose that's entirely possible. But can we not talk here? I have a feeling what you want to hear concerns us all.'

Womersley considered. 'All right, I don't see why not,' he said unexpectedly. He glanced across the room, then jerked his head at Rawlinson.

The sergeant immediately took aside the elderly waitress who was coming for their order. She began to argue but after a moment she gave in and shrugged. 'All right. It's not long to closing time any road.' While Rawlinson went to the door and turned the shop sign from 'Open' to 'Closed', she went to her other customers' table, 'I'm sorry, Mrs Ormerod, we're closing now.'

The two women, who had finished their tea, but had picked up the menu and were on the point of reordering so as not to miss anything, eventually left after some highly indignant protest, vowing to each other it would be a long time before they showed their faces in *here* again. 'Don't worry,' Tom remarked dryly as they watched them depart. 'They'll be back, they'll have plenty to pass on.'

'Bring us some tea, please, will you?' Womersley smiled at the waitress, as he and Rawlinson pulled up chairs. 'Just tea, no sweet stuff. Make it strong, lass.' He leaned back. The chair creaked in protest. 'Right then, let's start with what you were doing in Wainthorpe on the morning Mr Beaumont died. And the purpose of your visit.'

'I came to meet Mr Beaumont, at his request. We had not met for many years, though we had corresponded regularly. It seemed rather strange that he should choose the park as our rendezvous, but I could think of reasons why he did not want me either at Cross Ings Mill or at Farr Clough. We talked for perhaps half an hour. When we had finished conducting our business we parted and went in opposite directions. I went home, and I presumed he was going back to the mill. And that is essentially all there is to the matter.'

'Not quite,' Womersley said dryly. 'What was the nature of the business between you?'

Eventually Empson said, looking at Laura, 'He wished to extract a rather unnecessary promise from me – that I would never enter into discussion about . . . about certain events.'

'And made sure you would not. With five hundred pounds, to be exact?'

Empson was not, Womersley thought, a man easily disconcerted, but he reddened to the roots of his greying hair. 'He *attempted* to, in a way, but he misjudged me,' he said stiffly. 'I had promised and I do not go back on my promises. I do not take bribes, either, even for good causes – which is what he suggested I should do with the money, give it to any cause I thought fit. Naturally, I refused – and he apologized. "I should have known," he said. "But take it anyway, and use it where you think it's best needed. I've no need of it now." I should, Inspector, be exceedingly interested to know how you knew about the money.'

'So you didn't take it?'

'Well, yes, in the end, I was persuaded. The five hundred pounds has already been paid over to the Children's Mission in Halifax. You can easily check.'

'Thank you, we will. So, after you left Mr Beaumont, you say you went straight home?'

'I took the tram. It would have been ten thirty-five. I heard the Town Hall clock strike the half hour as I approached the terminus and the tram left a few minutes later. I shall be remembered. There was some consternation when I proffered a twenty pound note which the conductor could not change, for my fare – I'm afraid I had neglected to provide myself with enough small change to get me there and back. In the end, when I promised to refund the fare to the company, the conductor was good natured enough to let me ride without a ticket, hoping his inspector wouldn't board the tram. The incident amused him, I think.'

'Hmm.' Unlike the conductor, Womersley found these sort of people irritating, on too high a plane to bother about such practicalities as offering a twenty pound note, which most folks had never even seen, for a tram fare. But he saw no reason to disbelieve the story, which could easily be verified. He brought Empson back to more immediate matters. '"Certain events", you said. Mr Beaumont wanted your promise not to talk about – what?'

'You may rest assured, it has nothing to do with his death.'

'Well, you know, the fact that he wanted a promise from you makes me think it has. You might have to reconsider your promise.'

Empson's mouth set in a straight line. But at length, he sighed. 'Very well. He told me that he'd decided to make an end of it—'

'Good God!' Tom interrupted. 'Do you mean – he *meant* to take his life then? It could have been suicide after all?'

Womersley said shortly. 'It could not, Mr Illingworth.'

'No, indeed,' Empson said. 'That was not what he meant. He intended, he said, to put an end to all the repercussions that fire had left behind. His exact words were, "It's gone on long enough, I don't mean for it to go on after I've gone." It was then he told me – which I could not doubt, for I'd already seen it in his face – that he was terminally ill.'

'What had gone on long enough?' Womersley asked.

'I don't know.'

Maybe this was the truth, maybe not. He could not tell from Empson's face. He seemed to be a man who would tell the truth on principle, but in a tight corner, anyone might lie convincingly. Yet Womersley began to hope for a motivation at last. 'You say you don't know what it was, sir, but I dare say you can hazard a guess?'

Empson hesitated, and looked at Laura. 'Have I your permission to speak of personal matters, Miss Harcourt? Your mother . . . the fire?'

'I think it's more than time they were spoken of. In any case, it's no secret now who my parents were. All of us here know.'

Womersley glanced towards the waitress, who had been making several impatient sorties from the back room. They were going to be turned out any minute. 'Give us a bit longer, love?' To Empson, he said, 'Come on, then, we'd better have the whole story.'

'If you insist. Though there's not a great deal to tell, after all.' He steepled his hands. 'It happened over twenty years ago, when Lucie Picard and I were guests at Farr Clough.' Briefly, he stated the circumstances of their arrival, and how Lucie had come to be employed to look after the twins. 'We were there right until the time of the fire.' His eyes closed for a moment. 'That terrible night has stayed with me ever since, as I'm sure it has with all those others who were present.'

'And they were?' Womersley prompted.

'Ainsley and his daughter-in-law, Amelia Beaumont, the doctor, and Whiteley Hirst. They met regularly to play cards. Sometimes I was asked to take the place of one of them, which did not always please Amelia, especially when I was lucky, as happened that night. She was annoyed and showed it by being particularly irritating, amusing herself by interrupting and peeping over our shoulders to see the cards. I was partnering Whiteley Hirst against Dr Widdop and Mr Beaumont, and we were all rather glad when she left the study to bring some refreshments from the other wing, the part of the house she and her husband, Theo, occupied.'

'Where was he?'

'Oh, he never joined us.' He paused so long he seemed to have forgotten they were all there.

'Well, Mr Empson?' Womersley said impatiently.

Empson said flatly, 'The fire started, and destroyed all in its path. A brave man perished. What else is there to say?'

'How did it start?'

'What does it matter? How it ended was what mattered, with Lucie and the children's lives saved.'

But then, as if the memories wouldn't be contained, the words tumbled out. 'It was a wild night, a wind with scatters of rain on it tearing across the moor as it does up there, and howling down the chimneys. We were absorbed in our play and none of us noticed how long Amelia had been gone, half an hour, maybe much longer. Then the door crashed open and one of the servants rushed in, shouting that the wing was on fire, and they couldn't find Mrs Theo anywhere. We rushed outside and found pandemonium, shouting and panicking, flames sky-high, Sugden working like a Trojan on the hoses. But the wind was fanning the flames and it was clear the fire had too great a hold, and anyone in there would have no chance. Then, like a miracle, Theo appeared in the doorway, carrying Lucie. Somebody took her – the doctor, I think – and Theo rushed straight back into that inferno – for that's what it was by then. At the same moment one of the maids appeared with Amelia – God knows where she'd been, her hair was wild, and when she saw Theo going back into the house she shrieked like a lunatic and tried to follow . . .'

When his voice was steady enough he went on, 'The next thing we knew, Theo appeared at an upstairs window with the babies in his arms. He dropped each one safely out of the window for us to catch. Then . . . then he disappeared.'

For a long time no one said anything.

'How *did* it all start?' Laura whispered.

'Who knows? It was thought the curtains caught alight, from an overturned lamp. At any rate, it went up like a tinder box. The whole house might have gone, God knows, if the rain hadn't started to come down in earnest.'

'What do you think Mr Beaumont meant by repercussions?' Womersley said at last. 'I think you must know.'

Empson gave no answer until he had thought it over. 'Do as we've all done, Inspector. Let sleeping dogs lie. It was a terrible tragedy – but twenty years have gone some way to heal those old wounds. Why open them again and cause more misery?'

Because, Womersley thought, there came a time when sleeping dogs had slept long enough and had to be awakened and let loose.

Twenty-Two

Toiling up that dispiriting hill yet again to Farr Clough the following afternoon, with Rawlinson three steps ahead, Womersley told himself that evidence must be out there somewhere, if only they could find it. Within reach *had* to be the answer to the question of just what it was that had created a situation that still cast its shadow over the present – if only he could grasp it. Ainsley Beaumont had told Empson he had determined to put a stop to something which had gone on long enough. As long as twenty years? Had what actually happened at the time of the fire been enough to warrant the old man's murder? Had the fire even been started deliberately, for purposes as yet unclear?

He would talk to them all, the survivors of that terrible night, beginning with Amelia Beaumont. A delicate business that would be, not least because she was the one who must have suffered most, losing her husband, even though she knew he had been faithless to her and had fathered another child on the young woman who looked after his own children. If she had known what was going on between them before the fire, emotions must have been running high – and from what he'd seen of her, Womersley was prepared to bet the bitterness of it was still with her.

'I have told you all I know,' Empson had said, but Womersley was not so sure. There had been a certain reserve, a hesitation about that statement. But he'd made no demur when Laura Harcourt had offered to hand over to Womersley that manuscript he had written as a young man, though both had insisted he would find nothing more than had already been told. Maybe not, but Womersley wanted to see it, anyway.

Amelia Beaumont was not in, they were told on arrival at Farr Clough, but she was expected back within the hour. At Womersley's request, Jessie Thwaite let them into the study to wait. He had heard that her father had suddenly died, and although it had been obvious he was a very sick man when they had spoken, he was sorry. He had liked the man. At the same time, he cursed that moment of sympathy which had stopped him from pressing Thwaite more about who or what he'd seen on the morning Beaumont was killed.

'I expect you'd like some tea,' she said.

'Thank you, we would, lass.'

'Don't know about tea, hot water bottles wouldn't come amiss,' Rawlinson observed when she'd closed the door behind her. 'Keep your overcoat on, sir, I should, unless you want to freeze to death.'

Previously the study had been a comfortable and restful sort of place. You could feel the difference now. Already it had a melancholy, abandoned air, not helped by the absence of any fire. The ashes had been cleared but no new fire laid, just a fan of pleated paper placed in the grate. Womersley wasn't given to fancies, but the room was not only cold, it was soulless, no heart in it, as though something, and not only its master, had stopped breathing.

It was Laura Harcourt who brought in their tea, and a roll of ribbon-tied papers. 'Here's Ben Kindersley's story – Mr Empson's, I should maybe say. I'll leave it with you, but he would like it returned when you've finished with it.' She hesitated with her hand on the doorknob. 'Is there any chance I can go back to London now?'

He thought she looked strained, her pretty hair carelessly gathered up, her eyes shadowed. 'Yes, but leave an address where we can get in touch with you.'

'Thank you.'

Womersley unrolled and read the manuscript. She was right. There was nothing in it to throw light on the present situation, except for the revealing sentence at the end which showed Kindersley had been aware that something was going on between Lucie and Theo Beaumont.

He passed it over to Rawlinson and held his teacup in both hands for warmth. A room without a fire was like a clock without a tick. Well, of course! That's what it was! Not only the lack of a fire that made the room so unwelcoming, but also the absence of that slow, regular tick-tock in the background. The long case clock had stopped, and likely not of itself: they must have neglected to wind it. In all probability that was a job the master had seen to – and Womersley, who liked clocks and had formed a particular admiration for this one, clucked and went over to set things right. He couldn't see that anyone would object to him performing this domestic duty. It did a clock no good to be left unwound and run down.

Opening its door, he bent to retrieve the weights at the extent of their long chains, now almost touching something that had been placed below them, a box of some sort. He lifted it out and put it to one side while he wound the clock, supporting each heavy weight in his hand as he pulled its chain, adjusted the time and set the pendulum swinging. Only when the clock had resumed its regular tick did he nod, satisfied. Ridiculously, the room seemed warmer.

Now he turned his attention to the box. It wasn't large, just a dull, metal cash box that he might have missed but for the glint of the brass handle on the lid. It was locked. So the old man might not have been so very certain about his family's lack of inquisitiveness into his private affairs as they had thought. A cash box left around might have excited some curiosity. Funny place to hide it, though – but effective.

'Where did you put the key you found in that folder, Jack?'

The little brass key had become mixed up with all the other unidentified ones in the desk drawer and Rawlinson offered up three likely looking candidates before they found the right one. Inside, however, there was nothing more exciting than a cheap penny notebook with shiny, soft red covers and, secured to it by a rubber band, an envelope, personally addressed to Ainsley Beaumont at Farr Clough, marked strictly confidential, originally sealed with wax and registered.

The envelope had been opened, the seal broken, and the letter inside was headed with the name of the Beckinsale private detective agency, with an address in Leeds, just off the Headrow. A report was clipped to the letter, also a bill, which was hefty. Mr Everard C. Beckinsale, who signed his name in flowing script, wrote a somewhat rambling letter, consisting mostly of assurances that the 'subject' had no suspicions that enquiries had been made about him and his affairs. Womersley skimmed through the report with a quick stab of excitement, and tossed it over to the sergeant.

'Well,' he said when Rawlinson, too, had finished reading. 'Well. What d'you think of that?'

'Whiteley Hirst! Who would have thought it?' Rawlinson grinned but he was clearly as flabbergasted as Womersley.

If the facts of Mr Beckinsale's report were verifiable, as no doubt they would be, then Whiteley Hirst was in deep trouble. To the tune of seven hundred and fifty pounds, plus interest, owing to a moneylender who was threatening to take proceedings to recover his dues. 'I have not yet been able to ascertain,' wrote Mr Beckinsale, 'why the subject needed to borrow this money, but in the event that you wish me to continue further with the enquiries, I look forward to hearing from you.'

Womersley sat back and sucked on a mint. 'Hirst,' he said thoughtfully. 'He has a lot of authority down there at Cross Ings, more than you'd expect from his position. Beaumont evidently trusted him – so what the heck prompted him to have him investigated?'

Rawlinson shrugged. 'Who knows? But if he owed that amount of money, Beaumont's death couldn't have come at a better time for him. He knew there was something for him in the will, admitted as much, didn't he?'

What had Hirst been up to? Obviously, Ainsley Beaumont had had reason not to trust him. Yet he had left money to him in his will. Womersley shook his head. 'It doesn't make a lot of sense.'

His first excitement subsided. He reached out for the little red exercise book, and saw when he opened it that it wasn't going to offer any clarification, either. Only the first page had been used, where a list of names had been written, each with a date beside it. Women's names. It was meaningless – unless Beaumont had found out that Hirst had been a secret woman-izer, and the money had been borrowed to support this? Someone putting pressure on him over it, for instance? Maybe one of the women themselves?

His eyes rested on the last name on the list.

For a while, it didn't register, then with a rush of adrenaline, all the vague suspicions present at the back of his mind, the unrelated facts and the half-remembered conversations began to come together. It was as if a candle had been lit, illuminating the dark corners of a room, as if the clock had started ticking again. Charlie Womersley was not normally an intuitive man, but this time he knew with absolute conviction that this was why Ainsley Beaumont had been killed, this notebook was what the killer had been looking for when he had attacked the old man, ripping the inside pocket of his jacket in his haste. All for nothing, since the notebook had been here all the time, locked in the cash box.

His death still amounted to murder.

Womersley should have been exultant, but he felt strangely saddened, without any satisfaction that the case was coming to a close, a job well done, the perpetrator responsible being brought to justice. This was different. There had been many years of friendship, however it had been expressed, between the victim and his killer. Murder born of desperation was a sorry affair, yet just about comprehensible, but for a man to murder his friend was, in Womersley's book, loathsome beyond the pale.

'So, we *were* on the wrong tack with a random killing,' Rawlinson said, wanting to justify himself.

For a long time, Womersley didn't answer. 'It looks as though we've been on the wrong tack about a lot of things, Jack,' he said heavily at last.

'Such as what, for instance?'

Hitched on to the edge of the desk, tapping his foot, Rawlinson waited for an explanation, but Womersley sat lost in thought, until at last he stood up, batting his cold hands together. He felt very tired. 'All right,' he said, 'I'll tell you when we get going. We'd best get ourselves moving, get down into Wainthorpe and see our friend Hirst.'

'He'll have some talking to do.'

'He will that.'

'What about Mrs Beaumont, then?'

'It's getting too late to wait for her. I want a word with Jessie Thwaite, though, before we leave. And before we talk to Hirst, there'll be a few things to tie up. For one thing, we'll need to call in at the police station where there's a telephone. I want to make one or two calls, to the Super for one. And then – a visit to Dr Widdop, I fancy. If anybody can fill us in on the details, it's him.'

*   *   *

Nathan Widdop sat before a roaring fire in his comfortable study, stroking a fat black cat on his knee, a lighted lamp and a glass of single malt at his side. Grizelda's rhythmic purr indicated pure pleasure, something of a rarity from her these days. She was getting old and bad-tempered. Older, as we all are, thought Widdop. He was fifty-nine, and not by any means ready to be sent out to pasture; all the same, he tired more easily these days, his joints were stiffer, he looked forward increasingly to the rare quiet evening at home with a glass of whisky. The time for retirement might be coming sooner than he had anticipated and he didn't welcome it, now there was no Margaret – the nurse he'd met and married thirty years ago – to share it with him.

His hand moving over the rippling fur, he noticed the rash on the back had completely gone. Matthew Pike had suggested Grizelda might be the cause of it, that it might be due to a cat-induced allergy, but Widdop knew better. He had always kept a cat, she was the last of a long line. The rash was simple urticaria; he was unfortunately one of those who suffered a more than normal reaction to insect bites, stings or nervous stress. Pike was an acute young man, but he wasn't always right.

His new assistant was turning out to be a disappointment, perhaps worse. A threat, perhaps, to the status quo. A bright young fellow, a hard worker, he had at first been a welcome addition to the practice, but lately he had hinted he might be having thoughts of moving on. Just qualified, hard up, the young fellow couldn't be unaware that he had landed on his feet here, so why was he thinking of leaving?

He was young and enthusiastic and didn't always agree with Widdop's ideas, in particular, the subject of family planning. Despite what he thought, however, Pike wasn't the only one who tried to change his patients' attitude to that. Widdop had been urging it on his patients for years, though without conspicuous success. But one couldn't force it on them, as Pike tried to do, not seeing – or refusing to admit – that to many, including some doctors, it was distasteful, unthinkable, irreligious or downright sinful. To others – well, the women were mostly all for it, but it required some degree of cooperation from the men, and mostly they just shut their ears and said that was women's business.

He stirred restlessly, dislodging Grizelda from her comfortable position; affronted, she leapt off his knee and retired to the other side of the fireplace, where she sat watching him through slitted eyes. He took a sip of whisky.

He had lost yet another patient today, following soon after Walter Thwaite, and he felt sad, but not overwhelmed. He hadn't been able to prevent either, but he rarely felt guilt over a death. If you were a doctor, that way lay madness. Nor did he allow himself to grieve when a patient died. His duty was to the living, to alleviate suffering in whatever way he could. The Thurlough lad had been young, tubercular, with no future, and Walter Thwaite – what sort of life had it been for him, coughing his lungs up?

The sound of the doorbell pealed through the house but he didn't stir. If it was an emergency, Pike was there. In a moment, however, Ada Crawshaw was announcing the arrival of the police. She could send them away if he didn't want to see them.

Widdop sighed. He was philosophical about having his leisure hours disturbed but that inspector and his sharp-eyed, restless sergeant were not welcome tonight. One had one's duty, however.

'No, it's all right. Show them in.'

The two men seemed to fill the room with their bulky presence, bringing a whiff of frosty air in with them. 'Take their overcoats, Ada.'

'Thank you, it is warm in here.'

'Please sit down, gentlemen. Drink?'

'No, I don't think we will, thank you.'

'Well then, what can I do for you, Inspector?'

Widdop did himself well, thought Womersley. This room, unlike his shabby consulting room, was comfortable, even luxurious, with a thick turkey carpet and deep armchairs, large, glass-fronted bookcases in the fireplace alcoves. Nice pictures on the walls and a cut glass decanter and whisky glass on the table beside him. Widdop looking at ease and relaxed in leather slippers and a velvet smoking jacket. He pushed to the back of his mind the thought of Kate and his own warm fireside on this cold night.

'For a start, Doctor, I was hoping you could tell us something about Whiteley Hirst.'

'Whiteley?' Surprise flickered in those wise, worldly eyes. 'Well, I dare say I can. I've known him for many years.' He stretched his legs out towards the fire and sat back, prepared for a bit of gossip once more. 'What is it you want to know?'

By reason of his profession, Widdop must be privy to many secrets, and used to keeping his own counsel, and Womersley said, 'This is confidential, you understand, but I won't beat about the bush. It's come to our knowledge that Mr Hirst has recently become in difficulties – in debt to moneylenders for a large sum of money.'

'Has he, by Jove? Horses, I expect. It's not much of a secret that he likes a flutter. But who are we to judge? Every man should be allowed some indulgence.' He raised his glass and took a sip of the whisky. Firelight winked on the cut glass, lent planes of shadow to his face. He was a man, if rumour and his outward circumstances were true, who had money enough to live a life of ease and leisure, yet he had chosen this hard-working existence. Underneath his bluff bonhomie must lie a private, sensitive man the world was not allowed to see. A man of ideals. A man who had decided on his own path and walked it alone. He sighed as he said, 'I wasn't aware it had such a hold on him, however, and I'm surprised.'

'You've played card games with him for years, did his gambling streak never show?'

'We've never played for money.'

Womersley produced the scrap of paper found in Beaumont's waistcoat pocket and held it out. Widdop read it and laughed. 'Real money, I meant. This was about the upper limit.'

'Turn it over, Doctor.'

When Widdop read the London doctor's name written on the back, he was silent for some time, then he said, 'So he did take my advice, after all, or at least he was thinking about it.'

Womersley didn't answer this as he took the scrap of paper back. He returned to the subject of the card playing. 'Mr Hirst was always content, then, to play for such low stakes?'

'He didn't have much choice. It was Ainsley who set the limits.'

'We've been given to understand he was playing with you on the night of that fire at Farr Clough. Do you remember anything happening during the game that had any bearing on what happened?'

The doctor considered before saying quietly, 'Whiteley Hirst has many good qualities. What do you know about the fire?'

'We've been told you and others were there, playing cards, Mrs Beaumont went out to bring refreshments, the fire started while she was out, and her husband lost his life saving his children.'

'That's true, but Theo wasn't the only hero that night. Amelia foolishly tried to follow him when he went back inside to rescue the children – she was hysterical – but Whiteley Hirst ran in after her and dragged her out. He saved her life and was lucky to get out himself, with only that scar on his forehead – which you've doubtless noticed – to remind him. A piece of burning timber or some such set his hair alight – and burnt his hands, too.'

He reached out one of his own long, well-cared-for hands on which a gold signet ring gleamed, an onyx cuff-link, and poured another inch of whisky into his glass.

'I see your rash has gone, Doctor,' Rawlinson remarked.

'That? Oh, yes. It comes and goes.'

'Going back to that IOU,' Womersley said, 'That doctor's name I showed you, on the back. I have to tell you that I spoke to him myself, over the telephone, not an hour back.' He was not yet at ease with the telephone as a means of communication, its crackling lines and distorted speech seemed to him hardly worth the struggle, but he had persevered. 'Dr Leeming is not a brain surgeon, never has been. He's retired, in fact – from practice, that is. But he is still a member of the General Medical Council.'

'What did Ainsley want with him, then?'

'They never spoke. Dr Leeming has never heard of Mr Beaumont. I had to apologize for disturbing him with my call.'

The shade of anxiety that had crossed Widdop's face left it. He eased his bulk back into his chair. 'So?'

Womersley said quietly, 'Do you know who Alice Quarmby is?'

'Quarmby? I know several Quarmbys, the name's not uncommon in Wainthorpe. Alice – let me think. Alice. Yes, of course, the young woman who was . . . taken ill at Cross Ings. What about her?

'And Annie Wood, Lucy Pickersgill, Amy Helliwell, a dozen others whose names I can't quite recall, what do you know about them?'

Another silence fell, and lengthened, then Widdop said, 'Perhaps you'd be so good as to explain what you are talking about?'

'They were the reason Mr Beaumont had Dr Leeming's address – he was threatening to report you for unprofessional conduct.'

Widdop raised incredulous eyebrows. 'He would have had no cause to do that, I assure you. Any . . . associations . . . I might have are never with any of my patients.' His eyes met Rawlinson's. They both knew he was remembering that night when Rawlinson had been attacked, and Mrs Brocklehurst had known where to find him, but Rawlinson kept silent.

'I'm not talking about that kind of association, Doctor.' Womersley produced the little red notebook and placed it on his knee. Widdop's eyes fastened on it. He swallowed.

After a while he said, 'Before we go any further, it's important that you understand something – I like women. I respect them – and I know what I'm doing. No woman has ever suffered any adverse effects because of me.'

'Maybe only by the grace of God. Did you think of that when you doctored Alice Quarmby?'

'I think . . . no, I *know*,' Widdop said, dropping his neutrality and speaking with a sudden contained savagery, 'that what I do is better than self-induced abortions, or the attentions of some backstreet crone with her gin and knitting needles.'

'That's as maybe.'

'I *know*, Inspector . . .'

More than once in his career, Widdop had not fought for babies to survive who were born malformed or damaged in any way. It was a kindness to already overburdened parents, who didn't have the resources to shoulder that sort of respon-sibility. But more than that were the babies unwanted before they were born, the women who had come to him in trouble, begging him to do something. Women with too many mouths to feed already, hopelessly struggling to raise a large family in poverty; women who were at risk of not surviving yet another birth; those who were in trouble for a different reason, young girls, maybe, abused by God knew who. He had his own ethics – he had never given help to those whose trouble came from extramarital affairs, and very rarely to those who had simply anticipated marriage. He chose well, and looked after them to see that they didn't come to any harm. He couldn't help knowing that among the working women of the town, he was regarded as someone next to God.

Until Alice Quarmby, last year. He had impressed on her, after he had helped her, the necessity of taking a few days off from her work at Cross Ings, where she had to lift big bobbins of wool half her own height and weight on to still-working machines. But she had ignored his advice, terrified of what her father would do if he found out, and collapsed dramatically at the feet of Ainsley Beaumont, the master, just as he happened to be passing her machine. He'd had her carried into the office, the only possible place, and sent for Widdop. By the grace of God, Widdop had arrived there in time. But it had been a near thing, and it had shaken him. More than that, he was left not knowing what the girl had said before he arrived. Of those whom he had helped before, none had ever died, and the others had kept their mouths shut. Would Alice Quarmby do the same?

Time passed and nothing happened, until Ainsley had decided to interfere.

'Well, Dr Widdop.' Womersley tapped the notebook. 'Isn't this what you were looking for when you murdered Ainsley Beaumont?'

Widdop gazed down into the glass he'd been holding in his hand, then put it back on the table, untouched; the cat jumped up on his knee again, and he waited as it circled until it found itself a comfortable position. 'Can you imagine what it might be like,' he said at last, 'for your life and all you've ever stood for to suddenly be turned upside down?'

He had spent twelve exhausting hours at a cramped little house in the lower end of the town. A new life had been brought into the world, and at least the child had been a healthy, if undersized, specimen – which was more than could be said for the mother; he was her seventh surviving baby and would be her last. Almost certainly, she would not survive another pregnancy. Widdop had been almost as exhausted as she was. As he'd told Rawlinson, he rarely took his car to that end of the town – finding somewhere suitable to park that elegant but cumbersome piece of machinery was more bother than it was worth, and he'd been glad to stretch his legs. Automatically taking the shortest way home, he'd walked alongside the dam, looking forward to a good breakfast and then to snatching a few hours' sleep.

And there, totally unexpectedly at that time in the morning, he had come across Ainsley, who had accosted him once more with the subject of Alice Quarmby.

'The lass nearly lost her life,' he had accused when he had first come to Widdop with it, one morning in his surgery, after Widdop thought it had been forgotten. 'What do you know about that business, Nathan? Come on, it's no use you blustering. She's not the first, is she? I've kept my eyes and ears open . . . and I have it all down in black and white.' He'd patted his pocket, which Widdop had taken literally to mean the evidence was kept there, only to realize later that was not always the case. 'And I mean to use it. Call yourself a doctor? You're a scourge to the community.'

Widdop's motives had never been so clear cut as Ainsley, a man who saw things always in black and white, right or wrong, believed. So implacable, so sure he was right. What did he know of the despair that takes hold of women at such times? Women who threw themselves into the river, put their heads in the gas oven? The woman who had thrown herself off Linbridge viaduct into the heavy traffic on the road below?

'No, I don't think you will use your "evidence", Ainsley,' Widdop had heard himself say, 'and I'll tell you why.'

To Womersley, he said now, 'I was sure, you see, that I'd found the one way to hold him off for a while, at least until I'd had time to think what to do. I let him believe I was prepared to make public what I knew about that fire at Farr Clough, about Amelia's part in it.'

After a moment, Womersley said, 'Let's get this clear. Do I understand you to mean Mrs Beaumont was responsible for the fire?'

'Only by accident. But for twenty years she's been labouring under the delusion that people will think she killed her children by neglect. Ainsley knew that to make the truth general knowledge would have finished her. He pitied her for it and I was confident that, for her sake and for her children's, he would have done anything to keep it quiet. But he ought to have known from the first my threat was an idle one. Amelia Beaumont is my patient, and I do not breach patient confidentiality – in any case, I would never have done such a despicable thing, even had she not been my patient. But it took him some time to realize and accept that.'

The coals in the grate settled themselves and a flurry of sparks flew up the chimney.

'I can see you find all this hard to believe, Inspector . . . let me explain. That night, when Amelia went into their own part of the house to make the sandwiches, she ran upstairs first, intending to check on the children, and found Theo and that nursery maid together. Imagine the shock, to anyone, never mind someone as highly strung as Amelia! She rushed blindly downstairs, completely hysterical, crashing into a table and knocking it over, then straight out of the door, leaving it wide open. What she did in the next fifteen, maybe twenty minutes, she says she doesn't remember, but when they went looking for her, fearing she might be trapped inside the house, they found her wandering around outside in a frenzy, tearing her hair. By then the fire was raging. It hadn't taken long to get hold . . . the table she'd knocked over had a lamp on it, there were floor length curtains, and the wind had funnelled the flames. Technically, I suppose, it was her fault, but it isn't that which has troubled her ever since. Though she could hardly have imagined the house was going to catch fire behind her when she rushed out, she remains convinced, still, that if people learn what part she had in it, it will be said she started it deliberately, intending to kill her husband and the girl he was with, forgetting all about her children. And the truth is that she *hadn't* given a thought to them, what she'd seen had temporarily wiped everything else from her mind. She has lived with that guilt ever since.'

'My God,' Rawlinson said, 'people wouldn't, after twenty years?'

'Have you ever lived in a small town like Wainthorpe, Sergeant?'

'No. I was brought up in a village.'

'Then you should realize even more that people have long memories in such small communities. And there are, I'm sorry to say, those who would be glad to believe anything of Amelia Beaumont. Poor Amelia, so conscious of her humble origins. And so mortified, so shamed by her husband – a *Tyas* – having fathered an illegitimate child.'

'So how long did Mr Beaumont go on believing you'd carry out this threat of yours?'

'Until he'd had time to think it through, and called my bluff.'

Which had been on that fateful morning, when they had met by the dam. 'I knew he could ruin me if he so chose, but I'd had a hard night and was desperately tired, and in no mood for ethical arguments. He refused to admit I was simply doing what any doctor should do – trying to alleviate suffering. But I would not allow him to browbeat me into promising I would not do the same thing again, should the necessity arise. In the end, he simply turned away, the discussion, as far as he was concerned, was at an end. He would report me, and that was that.

'You know, I think it was the *contempt* with which he turned away from me that drove me to do what I did. Afterwards, I was ashamed. Not ashamed that I killed him – if I was to continue with my work, what else was I to do? And as I told you before, he had very little to look forward to.' He sighed and took an elegant sip of his whisky. 'I was ashamed because it was such an *amateurish* thing to do, for someone like me. After all, there are other methods I could have used to kill him – had the thought of it, or the wish, ever crossed my mind even for a moment, that is. But that way out had never occurred to me. I have never been a violent man, but at that point,' he said, 'simply, a sudden rage took hold of me. For one moment I would have liked to swing him round, punch him in the face, knock that righteousness out of him. But, ill as he was, his age . . . I could not have looked him in the eyes and struck him. And yet, seeing him walk away, a primitive urge took over . . . I saw a big stone standing proud of the dirt path . . .'

The doctor closed his eyes. 'He had been my friend for thirty years and it was the only thing that had ever stood between us.'

'And after all that, you didn't find this book. What made you tip him into the water?'

'By then, he was nothing but a body. I am no stranger to dead bodies but . . . I didn't want to have to look at him. Besides, putting him in the dam gave me time to get away before anyone else came along.'

Rawlinson said, 'Brushing your hand against the nettles on the path. Nettle rash, not worry or tension.'

A pause. 'As you say. Nettle rash. I should have been more careful. But don't dismiss the worry, or the tension.' The cat suddenly jumped off his knee and he fastidiously brushed his trousers down. 'I didn't think I had it in me, you know. But we are all capable of irrational, incomprehensible actions. Even if we believe we have justification, we do things we know to be wrong.'

As he came to a halt, he looked sadly round the room. 'I am very tired, Inspector. I've had enough. I shall have to go with you, I suppose?'

Womersley was surprised at the easy capitulation, because he thought Widdop a vain man, vain of his reputation. Perhaps he had always known that retribution waited, somewhere along the line. He had been walking a tightrope for so long, maybe he had subconsciously been preparing himself for it. 'Not yet, I'm afraid. There's the little matter of Walter Thwaite. Why did you visit him on the evening he died?'

Widdop sighed, and sat back. 'Oh, Walter, yes. The last time I had seen him I hadn't liked the look of him. But he was always reluctant to call me out, or to come and see me, even, so I thought I'd pop in and see him.'

'As a good doctor should. But I think the truth is that you went to see him because he'd seen you coming from the dam footpath after you'd killed Mr Beaumont.'

Widdop smiled very slightly. 'I can see what's on your mind, Inspector, but no, I didn't go there with the intention of slipping anything into his tea! It was a matter of assessment – what he was likely to do about what he'd seen, whether it was possible I could get away with it. I see now my chances of that were never very great – not after you discovered . . . that.'

He waved his hand towards the innocent looking object of his downfall, nothing more than a penny notebook, bearing a dozen or so names.

'When I came out on to Syke Beck Lane after . . . after it was over, Walter called out a good morning to me, but I didn't stop. I had no inclination to chat – and more than that, I had blood on my shirt. My housekeeper wouldn't remark on it, she's used to it, and I had just spent several bloody hours with a patient. But Walter had noticed it – and would certainly remember. When I went to see him, he made us both a cup of tea, and after a while, he told me there was something he wanted to say. He seemed very agitated, and then he suddenly began to have one of his breathless attacks. I did what I could, and tucked a rug around him, built up the fire. He reached out his hand for his Bible and I passed it to him. There was nothing else I or anyone else could do. I knew, and he knew, he was going. He died quite peacefully, just like that. How we would all like to go, I suspect. I cleared away the tea things and went.'

'Leaving his daughter to find him.'

'I could not afford to do otherwise, in the circumstances,' he said coldly. 'A neighbour saw me, I suppose?'

'No, but the best cups are always used when the doctor visits, aren't they? Before we came here, we spoke with Jessie Thwaite. You put them away in the wrong cupboard.'

He waved a hand. Then abruptly, he said, 'What's to become of Whiteley Hirst, then?'

Hirst had told them everything when they'd confronted him before coming here. He said when Ainsley Beaumont found out about the debt, an almighty thunderstorm of a row had blown up. After it was over, the air cleared, Ainsley declared he had no intention of letting Cross Ings and the name of Beaumont be dragged through the muck. He would pay off the debt himself. Hirst was, however, to pay him back, so much a week taken from his wages. Which had looked to Hirst as though he would be in debt to him until the millennium. He was chastened, and finding it hard to believe that Ainsley had still remembered him in his will.

It isn't vouchsafed to many of us to know when our end will come, Womersley mused. In that way Ainsley Beaumont had been fortunate. He had been able to spend his last weeks making amends, endeavouring to leave the world a better place than the one he had inhabited.

Which, if they were being charitable, perhaps Nathan Widdop, after all, had also tried to do.

Epilogue

Six months later

'It's very small,' said Philip, inspecting the upstairs room which was to be their sitting room.

Two armchairs, a bookcase, a rather dingy William Morris wallpaper.

'Never mind that, it'll do nicely,' announced his sister Eva, who never had doubts. 'If we paint it white it'll look so much bigger. Una agrees, and we're the ones who'll be living here, after all.'

'The piano takes up such a lot of room,' Una said doubtfully.

'But it's something we mustn't be without. Or rather you must not, Una, or so your brother insists.' Eva Carfax was a small, dark person who had taken to wearing a collar and tie and severely tailored costumes recently, and it gave her a schoolmarmish air which went with her decisive way of speaking. 'You're just being lawyerly and pointing out the faults, Philip. What do you think, Laura?'

Laura, sitting on the rather lumpy armchair, agreed with both opinions. The room was actually quite nice, if you disregarded the wallpaper. It *was* small, especially with four of them in it, but it had good proportions and it overlooked the park, and a magnificent beech tree stood in the garden beneath and reached up to just above the window sill. At this time in the afternoon, the autumn sunshine flooded in and the beech leaves were turning a glorious golden brown. In the fireplace stood the bunch of yellow and bronze chrysanthemums (and a handsome copper vase to put them in) that Philip had brought as a house-warming present, making a further splash of colour and giving off a sharp, bitter-sweet autumn smell which filled the whole room.

But there was no denying the piano did take up a lot of space. It was another present, from Gideon this time. He had told Laura decisively it was the only way Una would ever get over the loss of the talented musician who had taught her and with whom she had been in love; a man who'd died young, leaving her bereft and with a stubborn disinclination to touch the piano. 'But she'll never get over him properly if she doesn't play again.' Then he laughed. 'Besides, my sister is nicer when she's making music, nicer to herself and to other people. Encourage her, if you can, Laura. Music might even soften Miss Carfax up a bit, in time.'

'It would be good for her.' They smiled. 'Will your mother stay at Farr Clough?'

'She won't marry Whiteley Hirst, as Una believes. She'd rather have him as a faithful admirer – one she keeps an eye on, after . . . you know, the money and Grandpa and all that. No, I'll look after her and she'll look after me until I marry, and then . . . who knows? Meanwhile, she's all right.' He added, 'I think you should visit her, Laura. It would help her to forgive herself.'

'I will,' Laura had said after a moment. 'I will.'

And maybe I'll look around for a bachelor girl establishment like this, she thought now. But alone, a place of my own, where I can be myself.

Eva Carfax and Una had achieved their own independence after much opposition from Mr Carfax senior, and slightly less from Gideon. He had accepted Una's decision to live in London and be at the centre of things, if she mistakenly but so passionately wished it, but he was not sure about this Miss Carfax. From all he heard of her, he wrote to Laura – after the one time he had met her when he had accompanied Una on her journey to London – he was very much afraid she was going to draw Una into the militant contingent of the suffragette movement. Una wouldn't take much persuading – and Miss Carfax was very persuasive . . . bossy, sometimes, as even her dearest friend Laura must admit. She was the sort that swallowed one up.

Yes, Laura wrote back, but Eva was good as gold, really. One couldn't have a stauncher friend, and if Una was determined to carry her women's rights principles to their extreme, no one would stop her. Unless, perhaps, Eva's brother, Philip, who had become very taken with Una over the last few months. Chetwyn Square, where Una had been staying with Laura and her family until she found somewhere to live, had never seen so much of him, Lillian had declared. Not on account of Laura, which contrarily put Lillian's nose a little out of joint – it was one thing not to approve of Philip's attachment to Laura, quite another when one had to watch it transferred to another. But truthfully, she was relieved when the small flat had been acquired, and had been quite charming about offering advice as to curtains and its general decoration.

'I'll put the kettle on,' Eva decided. 'Our first cup of tea in our new home! Do thank your aunt for the walnut cake, Laura. All men like walnut cake.'

'I don't,' said Philip.

'There's always bread and butter. Tom Illingworth will do it justice.'

'Tom?' The book of curtain samples on Laura's lap became of consuming interest.

'He's coming for tea, if he can. Nice he's so often in London, now he's working for the LNER railway. Which one of these samples do you think is best, Laura?'

'Oh, this one,' Laura said, choosing at random.

Soon after this, she left, murmuring her excuses. She had been scheduled to attend a *thé-dansant* at Claridge's and had only just remembered it.

'Let me get you a cab,' Philip offered.

'No thank you, Philip, I'll walk.'

Outside, she decided there was now no possibility of getting home in time to change; her escort would already have called at Chetwyn Square and found her absent. No use bothering about the excuses she would have to find for her shocking ill manners, either. In any case, the golden afternoon was too delicious to spend indoors, and her thoughts were now not at all suitable for carrying on even the mildest flirtation with Freddie Fford-Oliphant.

The summer's heat lingered on, and she wandered into St James's Park in her light silk dress, a grey shot silk that sometimes looked lavender. Its skirt was a little too narrow for hurried walking, the heels of her black buckled shoes too high, and her lavender and black lace hat with its sweeping brim was pretty, but precarious in the breeze. And somehow, although she had thought it delightful when she chose it, knowing how fetching she looked in it, after the last hour in the flat with those two determinedly plainly dressed friends, the hat felt suddenly frivolous.

She paused on the bridge over the lake. Below, a small boy in a sailor suit was feeding a family of ducks, while his nurse clutched a handful of his blouse, imploring him not to be too adventurous so near the water. Laura watched, trying to overcome the mixed feelings which had risen like boiling milk at the mention that Tom was expected for tea. She made herself feel calm and tried to stop thinking about him.

Indeed, it had become her chief preoccupation in life at the moment to avoid thinking about Thomas Illingworth. She wondered if she'd ever become used to the sharp pain, somewhere near her breastbone, whenever his name was mentioned.

But, oh bother, she couldn't *stop* thinking about him.

The last few months she'd spent in trivial idleness, trying to do just that. She had thought about working again in Stepney, such a refuge for an unhappy heart, but before she had made a fool of herself by asking, Uncle George had pointed out that her position there might now be an embarrassment, after the money she had donated. And so the summer had worn away, Laura once more drifting in her aunt's wake. Not unaware of her unhappiness, her aunt and uncle had done their best, spoiling her with presents, clothes, weekends in the country, non-stop activities designed to wean her away from something they did not understand, and because she had wanted to be weaned, she had let them spoil her and tried to believe she was enjoying herself. Truthfully, she felt it was her very nature that was being spoiled by this shallow existence, meaningless compared with that of Una and Eva, filling their days, and all their spare time, with work for the WSPU and the many friends they had made in the movement; there was sisterhood and comradeship that Laura envied but could not bring herself to join in with wholeheartedly, much as she would have liked to.

She wrote often to Jessie, now married to Matthew Pike. They had moved over to Bradford, to another working-class practice whose patients would no doubt frustrate Matthew as much as the Wainthorpe patients had ever done. But at least they wouldn't be talking to him about 'the doctor' as they still referred to Widdop. The whole of Wainthorpe had reeled under the shock of Widdop's arrest and sentence, while the practice had been taken over by two doctors from a neighbouring partnership.

William Empson had written to thank Laura for the return

of his manuscript and asked if he might continue to write to her. It was the beginning of a correspondence which she found far more rewarding than the short conversation in the Wainthorpe tea room, one which was blossoming into friendship. She looked forward to his letters, which were amusing, sometimes philosophical, often about the pressing issues of the day, and which made her wonder if he was trying, gently, to awaken her enthusiasm for the subjects. If so, he was succeeding. But more than anything, it was the reminiscences about his youth, and the farm, his sisters and, of course, Lucie, which he loved to put down on paper and which made Laura so eager to read them. She began to feel that she knew and loved Lucie, her mother, as he had known and loved her.

Of course, Tom Illingworth had come to see her on his visits to London. Three times, to be exact – each visit less satisfactory than the previous one, though in what way Laura would have been hard pressed to say. For no reason she could name, except that there was an awkwardness that had not been present between them until that time at Farr Clough when she had rejected his advances. He was not still taking umbrage at that, surely? If he was, would he have come to see her, charming Lillian, and talking with George, who had found him a very 'sound' young man, high praise indeed?

But then, there had come a day when he hadn't arrived as he had said he would, and nor had he returned since . . .

Below the bridge, the little boy's supply of bread was giving out and the fleet of greedy ducks suddenly set up a raucous noise and began to swim away, their instinct for self-preservation guiding them unerringly towards a better source of free food in the shape of an old man with a large brown paper bag. The boy set up a roar of frustration and as Laura watched his struggles with his nurse, she felt a hand on her shoulder. Startled, she spun round, and could hardly believe it was Tom Illingworth himself who stood there, conjured up like some bad genie from a bottle. He was breathing heavily, as though he'd been running.

'Why, Tom!'

'Laura. The girls told me you had just left when I arrived at the flat and I guessed you'd take this way.'

'Yes, the park is lovely at this time of year.'

They stood looking at each other. 'How very elegant you look,' he said.

Then we're an elegant pair, she thought, struck anew by his appearance. So handsome he looked in his smart London suit, his high buttoned jacket, carrying a pair of lemon gloves. Not at all like the slightly dishevelled, windblown young man she had first met on the moor beyond Farr Clough. And how tanned and fit!

'How is your mother?'

'Very well. Settled in her new house. She likes being within walking distance of the town, and so near her sister. Your aunt and uncle are well?'

'Very well, thank you.'

'Look here,' he said abruptly, 'let's cut all the chat. I have something to say to you – apologies, explanations to be made.' She was very still, staring over the lake towards the domes and roofs of Whitehall, visible beyond the leafy arches of the trees. 'Please, will you listen to me, let me have my say? After that I will go away and you need never see me again, but hear me out first, hmm?'

She held her breath, sensing they were entering deep waters, but looked at him steadily and gave a slight nod.

What he had to say was in fact soon said, but she had been right. These were deep waters indeed, deeper than she could have imagined. He gave it to her in terse sentences, letting the bald facts speak for themselves . . . An unwise and unhappy marriage, too young, when he had lived in South Africa . . . now dissolved . . . things easier to arrange out there, but still, the time it had taken . . . he had just returned from a return visit to finalize things. And now it was over, a sore and painful episode in two lives.

He said, speaking rapidly, 'If only you knew how I regret it, all of it . . . I should never have married her. She saw better than I it would be no use, but she let herself be persuaded. I should have listened, waited.' He looked taut and vulnerable and extremely wound up. 'I regret it deeply, especially because of you. I had hoped you returned my . . . fondness, I let myself believe, but I was a fool . . . We need never see each other again. When I've finished the job I'm doing, soon, my next one may be anywhere in the world.'

Divorce, she thought, still staggering from a revelation of something she could never have dreamed up.

Divorce did not carry the same social stigma for a man as

it did for a woman. A woman should remain true to her marriage vows, whatever the circumstances, where a man might sow his wild oats and nothing be thought of it. 'If a woman divorces her husband,' she said, 'she doesn't easily find acceptance, even in this enlightened day and age. But it's easier the other way round, for a woman to marry a divorced man.'

He met those clear, candid eyes that saw so directly, and were clearer than ever.

'I wouldn't put you through that, Laura. In any case, your aunt and uncle would never let you marry a divorced man.'

'They can't stop me, I am over age. But you underestimate them. If my happiness depended on it, if that was what I was determined to do, they would never try to prevent it.'

The angry little boy ceased his roaring and was walking quite happily away holding his nurse's hand. A swan sailed into view, two squirrels ran up a tree, one after the other, the golden leaves of autumn fluttered in a shower on to the bridge.

'And does it?' Tom asked, breathing hard. 'Does your happiness depend upon it?'

'Yes,' she said simply. 'Yes, it does.'